I0546476

Other Books by Joel B Reed

The Jazz Phillips Mystery Series

Murder in the Choir*

Murder by the Board*

Murder in the Kirk*

Murder was a Blast*

Murder by the Queen*

Murder on the Run*

Jazz in the Cross-hair*

Jazz in the Golden Light*

Jazz Plays the Big Easy Blues*

Jazz Draws a Wild Card*

Jazz and the Black Widow*

The Cowboy McKee Intrigue Series

Angels Fight Dirty*

Black Seraph*

Children of Dust*

A Devil on DOS*

Even Angels Cry*

Other Novels

Paul Radford's Private War*

Paul Radford's Alaskan Exile*

Paul Radford's Return to Peru*

Raven Wolf (Journal of Martin Quinn)*

Ashes in the Outhouse*

Ashes of the Dead*

(*Available in print)

LAKOTA SPRING

A Native American Odyssey

by

Joel B. Reed

White Turtle Books
Canby, Minnesota

This is a work of fiction. While it is true to life, it is not factual. The events reported and the characters associated with these incidents are figments of the author's imagination. Any resemblance between any of these characters and any actual persons, living or dead, is purely coincidental. While proper place names refer to actual cities and towns, any businesses and governmental offices mentioned here are fictitious.

All quotations from The Book Of Common Prayer are in the public domain. All quotations from the Holy Bible are either from the Authorized Version of 1611 AD, which is in the public domain, or are paraphrased based on the author's understanding of Greek text.

Dedication

This story was inspired by a newspaper account of the life of the late Lance Corporal Gordon James Oliver of Okreek, South Dakota. It is offered as a tribute to his memory and as a tribute to the many American Indian warriors who have died in military service to a native land which has consistently treated them with such disdain.

The fathers have eaten sour grapes and
their children's teeth are set on edge.

Jewish proverb

Omega

1   I am shattered by the bell. The first shrill pierces the crystal air, shatters the magic of the high valleys I call Home. Desperately, I try to shut it out, to shield this place where all is well. What...? The question remains unformed as the second shrill explodes like shrapnel, rips me from this place I love, hurls me screaming earthward into the darkness this place calls dawn. I see the face of my brother, John, fade into the mountain mist as I fall, fade into a red mist rising bright as the setting sun. Jesus.... A prayer for deliverance escapes my lips as my hand flies to intercept this intruder, to hurl it back into the darkness. Then I am awake. I snatch up the telephone. What! I snarl savagely. What! I command the blunt instrument. I have no idea why I am so full of rage. I just am, like a bear roused too early from hibernation.

Then time is frozen. Ice forms around my heart. Rage becomes fire in ice, hard and brittle as diamond. I hear a voice I know telling me what I do not want to hear, saying I must come. Then there is silence. Frozen moments falling one onto another as an avalanche carries me away, buries me deep within it. The voice sounds again, asks if I am there. I open my mouth. The only answer that comes is a deep sob rising from the depths of my being. No! God, no! I see the face once more. He looks so sad, my friend. Then the voice speaks again. I hear my own voice answer numbly. I hear it tell the other I will come. Right away.

I find myself fully dressed, hurtling down the road. As from a great distance, I see the needle pass sixty-five. Why am I speeding? The question floats disembodied in the frozen air. I see the needle climb past seventy-five. There is no hurry, not now. I am doing ninety, faster than I ever imagined this small car could run. I am going to crash if I don't slow down. I feel the thought lazily filter down my frame, detached from all meaning, bumping down and down along my leg like a partially inflated balloon. Who the hell cares? The thought tumbles into my mind as I see the needle reach ninety-five.

Then it happens. There is nothing I can do to control it. Of its own accord, my foot lifts itself from the accelerator. The needle begins to drop. One sharp turn on the wheel.... I look at this thought as it rolls down my arms. I am somehow watching from outside the car, above and to the rear. This is insane. Yet I see my hands wrench to the left violently. I hear the tires scream, see the small car roll over and over along the deep ditch, end over end as it folds itself around my body like a steel glove. What is going on? The hands will not obey. They remain steady on the wheel as the needle continues to drop.

Suddenly I am at the turnoff. I see lights blazing at the house on a rise a mile away. The green glare of its safety light is pierced by the red and blue flash from the police car parked in the driveway. I recognize another vehicle, a new Suburban which does not fit in with the junked cars and trucks parked at random around the yard. I know most of those do not run. I remember when each of them did, even the oldest. I remember learning to drive, urging the steel mammoth along a dusty road, knuckles white on the wheel and my friend laughing at my fear. Again I see his face and the memory breaks my heart. I feel tears running down my cheeks. Why? Yet even as the question rises, I know the answer. I have known it a long time. While I don't like it, and there was nothing I could do, I know. With the knowing I feel deep anger rising like a volcano through the ice.

I park by the police cruiser. A white-faced deputy tries to stop me from going into the house. I see him trembling, but I insist. I am barely coherent. The sheriff hears me and comes out. His face is grim and drawn. He tells me I don't want to see what is in there. I hear myself insist again, my voice strident like a screeching hawk. The voice on the phone which woke me comes from the back of the house, urges the sheriff to let me in. The deputy lets me go at the sheriff's nod. I hear the sheriff tell me it's in the kitchen but I am moving already. As I leave the front room I hear him warn me once again it is very bad.

Then I am there. I do not make it through the kitchen door. What I see is like a horse kick to the belly. I brace myself on the door frame with both hands, gasping. I cannot speak. My guts feel like they are being ripped out by a giant claw, and a great heat descends over my head like scalding water as brilliant white light blinds me. Then there is nothing, only gathering darkness. The last thing I hear is a voice I know well, a voice sobbing over and over. Jesus, no! Jesus nooooo ....

Corn Creek Wake

2   April 1, 1973. It is a good day for dying. That is what the elder said to them as they were standing at the barricade, but I don't know. He is old now, at least forty, and his children all have children of their own. One of them is already a grandmother. He has lived his life. What is left for him? Mine is just beginning. I have not fathered a child. To my shame I have never known a woman, and to die without fathering a child..... I don't like that. It feels wrong. But what of people like my friend, Mike Kills-In-Water? He is only twelve now, a year younger than me. He has had a woman. At least, that is what he told me. It was with an older woman and he has no reason to lie. She is at least sixteen and has a child, so why should he lie? She has no man and her father is a drunk. It is said he gave her the child himself. Maybe Mike gave her another one. Does that make it a good day for him to die?

Or was the elder just teasing? Was he just trying to scare us? April Fool's! Yet I saw one of the men at the barricade load his rifle. I handed him the bullets, one by one. They were real and I know what they can do. I used a rifle just like it two years ago when I shot my first deer. I saw what it did to the deer, how it tore his insides apart. So this is no joke. It would do the same to me or to Mike. It would tear our guts apart. Is that a good way to die? (entry from John K's second journal)

I am not sure what the year is. I could find out visiting the graveyard, but that is seventy miles away over icy roads. Or I could look it up in the almanac, eight feet away on the other side of the room. Maybe I will, but right now I just want to keep writing. I've put this thing off too long as it is and I'm afraid even two minutes spent looking it up will break my concentration. I'll start searching and something else will catch my eye. So I'll chase that rabbit and when I look up, I'll find the whole afternoon gone. My grandfather used to call this Old Timers' syndrome.

Come to think of it, the year was 1963. It was the year John F. Kennedy was shot. So I am past four years old, just under five. Yet, the memory is fragile, like an image seen at dusk. When I look at it too

3

hard, too directly, it disappears. Then I look away, and it is there again. The details cannot be seen directly, only with the corner of the eye.

For the record, my name is Randall Dale Lyle and I was there almost from the beginning. I go by RD now, mostly so people can tell me apart from the rest of my family. They called me Randy back then, and I'd like to hope I still am. They called me that because my dad went by Randall after his own father died. Before that he was Junior because my grandfather was the first Randall Dale. The old man is who first called me Third Bird and continued calling me that until I asked him not to any more. It took a lot of fights on the playground to convince my classmates I was either Randy or Third, not Turd, and even at our last class reunion someone called me that. Once. I reminded him what I do and he damn near jumped through his ass backing off. He also apologized, like I knew he would. He has political aspirations and knows it just doesn't do to piss off the press, not when they know where the bodies are buried. And I know. I've lived here all my life and I know where they all lie buried. That's what I do for a living, find out who did what to whom.

This didn't start with me. Our family has always run to news hounds, even before the first Randall set up the Thunder County Clarion here in Winner. One of my great grandfathers was a Civil War correspondent for a New York paper and two of his brothers started one of the first papers in Kansas City. It went under and they ended up working for the competition, but that's the way it is with us. We'd work for the Devil if that's the only news job around. Considering some of the people who own the rags that paid us, I'd say we have.

Anyway, that's who I am although this story isn't about me. I was just one of the bit part players, even though John K was one of my best friends. No, make that my very best friend. This story is about him and his family, and my claim to fame is that I was there for almost every part. Even when both of us were gone away from here, we stayed in touch, and I think that is what I was for him, a touchstone. When things weren't clear he knew he could come to me for straight talk. I am a newsman, trained from the cradle up, and I don't hold with lies. I don't always know the truth, but I call it like I see it, and I think John K respected that. I was one white man he could depend on to tell him the truth. When it came down to my word or one of his Indian buddies, he always took mine, and I know that bothered him. It ate him alive having to go to a *wicasu* for straight talk, and I think that's why he didn't call me in the end. He called them, instead, and they had nothing to give him, not even the truth.

So what was the truth? The truth was I loved him and honored him like a brother, like they never did. The truth is I still do. That is why I am telling his story. It is not fun, although we had some funny times, too. Yet it is true, to the best of my understanding, and the least I can do is tell the world the truth about Sergeant John Kenneth Lyons, United States Marine Corps.

Semper fi, John K. That's the truth of who you always were. *Semper fidelis.* Always faithful.

As I said, I am somewhere between three and five when first we meet. I am also so scared I am about to pee in my pants. Aside from my dad and mother, there's no one I know here, and the people are different from anyone I have ever seen. Their clothes are old and worn, and their faces are old and wrinkled. I see men wearing grey hair in braids hanging down each shoulder and they are talking in a way I cannot understand. Every once in a while I catch a word or two I know, but their voices are so soft I can scarcely hear. When they speak it is like the rustling of a quiet breeze whispering its way through tall grass.

My dad seems to understand them, but this does not surprise me. He is like God, able to do anything. As I look at him, he is speaking to them in the strange way and I see my mother sitting by his side, nodding, too. Every once in a while she says something to one of the women sitting near her and it scares me to hear her speak and not understand her words. Then all the women look at me and tell her something in Indian and I cannot meet their gaze. I hide behind my father, clinging to his leg and burying my head under his arm. He holds me close and I can feel his strength. I am safe there, held close by his arm.

The women laugh and my mother rises and picks me up. She holds me close, asks me what is wrong. I can't find words to tell her and she smiles. Gently detaching me from my father, she takes me up and finds a seat among the women, holding me in her lap. She introduces me to them and I can understand what she is saying. The women tell me solemnly they are glad to meet me and I am amazed to learn they speak my tongue. I shake the hands they hold out, pulling my arm back quickly when I am done, like touching a frog the first time. The women smile when they see this and nod. They say something to my mother in Indian. My mother tells me they say I am a fine looking boy, but I somehow know they have said something else. They remind me of the tame ducks by our pond, standing with their beaks together, nodding and murmuring quietly. Then someone says something else and they begin to talk again, ignoring me. I am glad, glad I am invisible once more and glad to be in my mother's lap. I feel her strength, so different from my father's.

As I sit in my mother's lap, I look around the room. We are the only white people here. The rest are Lakota, people of all ages. Most of them seem very old, much older than my parents. Most of the men are wearing faded jeans and western cut shirts open at the neck. Some of them are wearing moccasins, but most of them have cowboy boots like my father is wearing, and almost all of them are smoking. I recognize the bright red spot on the packs they take out of their pockets and I know the slogan by heart. Lucky Strikes Mean Fine Tobacco.

But some of the older ones have red strings with yellow paper dots hanging out of their shirt pockets. I know these men roll their own, Bull Durham, and my fear gives way to fascination as I watch an elder with long grey braids carefully fold his paper and shake out the yellow flaked tobacco to fill it. I am amazed at how gently his ancient fingers roll the paper around the tobacco, carefully pressing the flap down after he has licked it. I see him carefully twist the ends to keep the tobacco from falling out, then flick a kitchen match with a thumb nail. The paper flares when he touches the flame to the paper and I forget myself. "Bull Durham!" I declare in a loud, deep voice.

Startled silence fills the room. Everyone is looking at me. Then the elder grins and everyone laughs. He has almost no teeth left. When he says something in Indian, they all laugh again and some of them clap. I see my father give my mother a wicked look and feel her shake her head. He is grinning and for the first time in my life I am aware of what my father is thinking. He is remembering other conversations with my mother about Bull Durham. Only Bull Shit is what my father calls them, I think because it always gets a rise out of my mother. "Junior!" she says whenever he does it. "Not in front of," she pauses, then spells it out. "B-i-g E-a-r-s!"

Somehow I know she means me, and I wonder why she doesn't want me to hear it. Grandpa says it all the time, and so does my father, mostly when he reads the Denver paper. The next thing Grandpa always says is, "Those bastids never get it right!" I want to ask him what a bastid is, but I am afraid to. The one time I did was at Sunday dinner and was told not to use that word. Later I heard Grandma giving him her opinion and I learned some other words. I always wanted to ask what cussin' means, but I'm sure it must be a Bad Word, too.

I hide my face in my mother's lap. A few moments later I hear the soft murmuring resume and now I feel less afraid. These people feel like my Grandpa and Grandma, safe even though they smell different. I wiggle around until my mother sets me on the floor, but I don't stray far from the safety of her skirts. This is still strange territory, very much different from where we live. The floors here are wooden and quite worn, and the walls are dingy. What keeps the house warm is a huge iron kitchen range, the kind fueled by wood, and the only light from outside filters through smoke stained windows. In the corners I see coal oil lamps like the ones we use camping, but these aren't lit right now.

I am fascinated with the wood stove. I know there is one like it in my Grandpa's hunting lodge, but I never seen it used. Nor have I ever seen one in a home and I watch as one of the men brings in a load of wood and shakes the grate with an iron handle he hangs back on the wall. Then he opens a small door, holding the handle with a dirty rag as he opens it. Inside I see glowing coals and he nods, satisfied by what he sees. Taking another iron handle from the rack on the wall, he opens the top of the stove, releasing a light puff of smoke, and begins to drop wood into the opening. When he is done, he replaces the top pieces and hangs the handle up again. Turning around, he sees me watching and grins. He says something in Lakota. "Fire," he says in English, and then says the first word again in Lakota, "*Peta*." I repeat the sound, PEH-ta, and he nods. "*Peta*." I have just learned my first word of Lakota.

Bold now, I begin to explore the house. I walk down a dark hallway, drawn to the light shining through the open door at the end. Halfway there I am met head on by a little boy who comes running out of the room. He is a little smaller than I am and comes to a stop when he sees me. The smile disappears from his face. Like strange cats, we eye one another silently, waiting to see what will happen. Neither of us blinks, neither moves. We are statues cast in stone at this sudden encounter. Somehow we understand the rules of this ancient rite. One cannot move until the other does and we wait in silence.

We are saved by a young woman coming out of the room. She grabs the other boy and he laughs. She tickles him and I understand she was chasing him. She looks like him and I decide she is his mother. Later I will find out she is his grandmother, although she is raising him. I will also learn the man at the stove is his grandfather, his mother's father.

7

This is common among the Lakota, grandparents raising the children, but I do not know this now. All I know is the woman is very pretty and looks younger than my mother. Yet for some reason, I do not feel shy or afraid. Maybe it is because when she smiles, she looks like my own mother.

"Who are you?' she asks me. Then she answers her own question. Adults seem to do this a lot. "You must be Junior's son." I nod and she introduces us. "This is Johnny." The other boy barely nods, moving his head two millimeters, maybe three. "What do they call you?" she asks me.

"Buster Brown," I hear my voice saying. I am as surprised as she is by my answer.

"Oh, be careful, Johnny," she tells the little boy, pretending to be afraid. "Don't ask him again or he'll knock you down." The smile disappears from his face and he watches me closely.

"No," I say, pointing to his shoes. "Buster Brown."

The pretty lady laughs uneasily. Johnny is wearing high top sneakers and she does not know what to say. "Buster Brown?" she asks. "You mean shoes?" I nod dumbly, not knowing what to say. Suddenly I am scared again, and I feel tears stinging my eyes. The young woman sees this. "Hey," she tells me. "It's all right. You can be Buster Brown if you want." She reaches out to me but I am to afraid to go to her or even take her hand.

We are rescued by my mother, come to see where I have wandered to. She calls my name, Randy, completing the introduction. I am not surprised she knows the other woman. My father and mother know everyone, even the Indians no one else knows. She greets Johnny's grandmother with a warm smile and asks about other people of her family.

Johnny and I are forgotten for the moment and we look at each other for a while. Then something happens. He smiles and looks down at my boots, then laughs. I look down and see a big smear of potato salad on my right toe. I look back down the hall and see white tracks leading to where I am standing. At the other end of them is a plate someone has set on the floor. Then I laugh and suddenly we are friends. He runs back down the hall toward the kitchen. I look at my mother, who nods and smiles, and I follow.

Johnny doesn't stop at the kitchen, or even in the room where my father is sitting. He runs past them and to the top of the stairs leading to the basement. He looks up and sees I am following, then runs down the stairs.

I find him waiting for me at the bottom of the stairs. He is not smiling and looks scared. I stop and look around. We are in a big room lighted by coal oil lamps. I see many people sitting around the walls of the room on wooden benches. They are not talking or smiling. Some of them look very sad. Others sit smoking quietly, their cigarettes making bright glows in the smoky darkness. There is a very old man sitting in one corner, quietly playing a drum and singing so softly I can barely hear.

The song the old man is singing captures me. I have never heard anything like it. Nor have I ever seen anyone like him. To my eyes he is older than the hills, much older than even my grandfather. The skin on his face is like soft leather, deeply lined as it hangs from the high, sharp cheekbones on either side of his large nose. His eyes are deeply sunk into his brow, yet even though they are closed I know they can see me. His white hair is braided and wrapped tightly with blue cloth where it crosses his shoulders, and at first I think he has no shirt. The color of his buckskin tunic is almost the same as his skin and a shell necklace hides the line between his shirt and his neck. On his feet are traditional beaded moccasins, decorated with colored quills rather than beads, and above them, faded denim jeans, almost white with age and almost hidden by the fringe of his tunic. This is gathered to his waist by a beaded girdle, and from this a long beaded pouch hangs almost to the floor. I know without having to be told this is someone very special.

When the old man finishes the song, he looks at me. His eyes are like deep, dark pools of midnight sky. Deep within them there is a faint blue light, far too faint to be the reflection from an oil lamp. The blue light grows as the eyes envelop me, surrounding me with a strange warmth I know well. They tell me I have nothing to fear, and when the old man extends a claw like hand, I go to him.

As I stand before the old man looking deep into his soul, I begin to see things in a way that feels familiar, yet strange. The blue light turns into a cobalt sky lighted by a warm yellow sun, warm on my back and arms. I am high above the earth, higher I than I can imagine, and I see tiny brown ants on the yellow land below me. Yet I know they are not ants, but buffalo, and as I watch I see smaller creatures surrounding them. Then the buffalo begin to run, chased by the tiny tan dots that are men, and I see a few of them fall. I know the people will eat well this winter. Nor have they hurt the herd.

As I soar, the seasons pass beneath my wings. I see great blizzards blow out of the north, then melt away to the greening of the earth and the brightness of wild flowers. I see the leaves turn in the cottonwoods by the ribbon that is called the Niobthatha, the Wide-spreading-water. Then the snow comes again and it is frozen and I see smoke rising from the lodges of the People in the winter camp. I see women gathering wood and men riding out onto the prairies.

The seasons pass and I see a great dark storm forming in the east. With it come strange men and their women, and they bring a strange sadness. There is sickness the People have never known, and with it comes a strange death of the spirit. The people walk like the living dead, defeated and senseless, slashing each other with their new iron knives. Yet above the dark cloud, the sky is still bright cobalt and the gentle yellow sun is warm along my back and arms. And as I see them fall down to the dust, I see the People's spirits rise from their bodies and take wing in the clear air.

I blink and I am once more looking into the face of the old man. He says a single word, *waste*, WASH-tay, and I know what he means. Somehow in looking into the deep pools of his eyes I have learned my second word, *waste*, and I know he is saying all things are good.

Then I feel a strong presence at my side and I look up. It is my father, come to find me, and he speaks to the old man in his own tongue. I am aware of great respect in the way my father talks, and of equal respect in the way the old man responds. When they are done, the old man looks at me and smiles. "*Waste*," he says, moving his hand from left to right, palm flat and facing down. I repeat what he says with the same gesture and he nods. I understand our conversation is done, and all is well between us. I don't know how I know, but I do.

My father takes my hand and turns back to the stairs, but something has caught my attention and I tug back. At the far end of the room there is a long table draped with a bright colored blanket. There are candles burning in front of what look like pictures, and I see a large white box sitting in the middle. It is a strange box and the lid is open. I want to know what is inside it.

I look up to my father, asking. He nods and follows my lead, and as we approach the table I see it holds many other things. There are beaded necklaces and some wild flowers, and right in front of the white box there is an eagle feather, its end bound tight in bright red cloth. There is also a turtle shell rattle and I reach out to pick it up. My father pulls me back, and when I look at him, he shakes his head. I can look but not touch.

I stand on tiptoe, trying to see into the white box, but the rim is too high. I feel my father's hands under my arms and his strength lifting me so I can see. Inside the box there is a boy my age. He looks like Johnny and he is asleep. Yet he looks strange, too, as if he is very sick. The color is gone from his face. His skin is green, almost grey, and he is lying very still. I wonder why he is sleeping there, why the old man is singing again as he plays his drum. I look at my father. His face looks very strange, very sad. I see tears in his eyes and I am scared. I have never seen my father cry.

I look back at the boy lying in the white box. He is wearing buckskin, like the old man, but there are many more beads on his shirt. Around his neck there is a necklace and a beaded medallion. The beads on the medallion are mostly white, with a blue outline running around the outer edge. The center is a blue circle of beads with curved arms tapering back almost to the outer edge. The curved arms remind me of how the water drains from the bathtub when I pull the plug, and I find my eyes drawn to the very center of the circle. I see a tiny black bead there, almost invisible against the dark blue that surrounds it.

My father waits patiently as I look. His feeling of sadness is almost like a blanket surrounding me in his arms. Yet I do not stop. I must see what is here.

My eyes move to the bright beaded sash at the boy's waist. It is very like the one the old man is wearing, only smaller, and the bottom of the boy's tunic is fringed like the one the old man wears, too. Yet his leggings are not denim, but made of skin the same color as the long shirt. They are fringed along the side and on the boy's feet I see moccasins beaded with all the colors of the rainbow.

I turn and look at my father. He nods and sets me down, but as he does my hand touches the eagle feather lying in front of the white box and knocks it to the floor. There is a sudden silence and someone gasps as I stoop to pick it up. I set it gently back in place, but when I turn, everyone is looking at me strangely. Suddenly I am very frightened and cannot even turn to my father to hide.

Then the old man nods and speaks softly. "*Waste,*" he says, making the same gesture with his hand as before. I feel the tension leave the room as quickly as it came, and people turn back to their conversations as if nothing had happened. Yet, I am still afraid, not knowing what I have done wrong. "*Waste,*" the old man says to me, and once again he makes the sweeping gesture. Then I understand. "*Waste,*" I say back to him, making the same sigh, and he smiles. It is done, and all is well.

My father and I move to the other end of the table. There is a bowl of cigarettes there and he takes two. I am surprised when he hands me one of them, but I take it and he smiles to reassure me. Somehow, I know not to ask him about it right now.

I am startled by a strange noise that raises the hairs on the back of my neck. I look and see three young women standing in front of the white box. One of them is bent over into the box and the other two are clinging to her, crying out in high quavering voices. I hold tight to my father's hand and follow close behind as he moves to the other side of the room and stands in respectful silence.

The high keening goes on for several minutes. It hurts my ears and my father holds me close, holding a hand over one ear as he presses the other into his leg. I can still hear the awful sound, but it does not hurt my ears, and while I have never seen anything like this, I am not scared standing by my father's side. I see that the old man has fallen silent, too, and I know something very important is going on.

After a few minutes, the young women on either side dry their tears and gently pull the other young woman back from the white box. I look and see the feather has not been disturbed from where I set it, and this seems strange. Then I look at the young woman in the middle. She looks like the boy in the white box and I think she is his sister. Later I will learn she is the boy's mother and I will wonder how this can be. She looks younger than my older sister who is just starting high school. How can she be his mother?

Then two older women join the three and draw the mother to a seat on the side of the room. The old man starts singing again, and I am surprised to see my mother is one of the older women comforting the mother. The other is Johnny's grandmother. Later on my mother will tell me she was a God-mother to the boy in the white box, and that the woman I met in the hall is, too. When she does, I do not know what she means except that we are somehow related, like family. Still later, I will discover Johnny and I are closer than most brothers in the white man's world. Now, I know he is simply my new friend.

I am surprised to find Johnny standing next to me. He has been there all along and his face looks strange in the low light. It is flat, without expression and I cannot read it as he looks at the white box and at the grieving woman. "Who is he?" I ask him. I feel my father's hand squeeze mine. When I look up, he shakes his head. I am surprised because he always gives me an answer, even if it is one I do not understand.

"My brother," Johnny whispers back. His face does not change. I want to ask why his brother is sleeping in the box, but I remember my father's warning. "Come on," Johnny says, turning to the stairs. When I look up, my father nods, releases my hand. He starts to say something, but stops. I know what he was going to tell me, to stay close by.

We get to the top of the stairs and Johnny goes into the kitchen. I smell cooking but it is not time to eat yet. He takes me into a room down the hall, across from the room where he ran out. The room we go in is tiny and there is barely room for us to stand. I see boxes of things stacked along the walls. There are blankets and dishes and even some toys in the boxes. "For the give-away," he says, seeing my look. He crawls up on the bed and motions me to join him. "This is my room," he says proudly. "This is where I sleep."

I nod and start to ask him what a give-away is, but I remember my father's warning. "I have my own room, too," I tell him. I see another box along the wall, one set apart from the give-away boxes. "Are those your toys?"

Johnny nods and goes to the box. He digs out a small foam ball. It is blue and white and shaped like an egg. "You want to play some football?"

I nod before I remember. "It's raining outside. We can't. We might get sick."

Johnny blinks, as if I have just told him red is blue. "I play in the rain," he tells me. "I don't get sick." Then he shrugs, takes a worn deck of cards out of the box. "You play Go Fish?" he asks me.

I nod. This is a game my mother and I play all the time, but when Johnny gives me my cards, they are strange and not at all like my cards. They are red and black and have spots on them, except some of them have pictures of people. "Wow!" I say, impressed. "These are big people cards."

Johnny nods. Somehow I know he thinks what I have said is strange. "My cards have pictures of fish on them," I tell him.

"I never saw any cards like that," he says. "You got any fours?"

The cards are so big I have trouble holding them. When I try to count the spots, they fall out of my hand and Johnny laughs. "Look at the numbers," he tells me. "Don't count the spots."

I try to fit the cards back into my hand, but they fall out again. Johnny laughs and shows me how to hold them. I clamp down tight with my thumb and it works, but after a while my hand starts to hurt and I have to lay them down. "Change hands," Johnny tells me and I try it. It is much easier to hold them in my left hand and pretty soon I am playing the game almost as good as I do at home. Neither of us knows how to keep score so we use a matchstick for each hand. When we get bored with the game and stop, my pile is almost as big as his.

It is still raining outside and not time to eat yet, so we look at comics and talk about our families. We tell each other about our grandfathers, the funny things they do, and we laugh a lot together, trying to outdo each other making faces like our grandfathers make to scare us. Then I tell him about my older sister, the silly things she does, and we laugh some more when he tells me things about his aunts. Somehow I don't think it strange they will be attending the same school next year. I don't understand this makes them the same age as my sister. My mother was the youngest and her sisters are much older.

Without thinking, I ask him about his brother. "When will he wake up?" I ask. I see he does not understand and I tell him, "Your brother. The one asleep downstairs in the white box." Yet as I say this, I know I have done something wrong. The smile disappears from Johnny's face and he gives me a strange look.

"That is Willie," he tells me. "Willie won't wake up, ever. He's dead."

Dead. The word drops like a small stone in the quiet pond of my soul. Dead? I don't understand and I am afraid to ask. I know what dead is. Dead is animals lying by the side of the road, hit by cars and trucks. Dead is run over again and again, smashed flat and dry as a dinner plate. Dead is the color of red and the neighbor's dog lying in a pool of blood. Dead is what will happen to me if I play in the street. How can Willie be dead? I tell my new friend all this, and that he must be wrong.

Johnny looks at me a long time. His next words shock me. "Go shake him," he says. "Stick a knife in him. See if he wakes up." Yet the voice coming out of his mouth is not Johnny's voice. It sounds like the voice of a grown man, full of rage, and I am scared. Who is this man I thought was a child?

I run out of the room, seeking my father. When I find him I cling to him, trembling. "What's the matter, son?" he asks, but I cannot answer. I disobeyed his warning and asked a forbidden question. "Did something happen, Johnny?" he asks my new friend gently. "Did you boys get into a fuss?"

"No," Johnny tells him. "He asked me when Willie will wake up and I told him Willie is dead." His voice is flat.

My father nods and extends an arm. After a moment, Johnny comes to him and he holds us both for a while. When we get restless, he sets us down. "Death is part of life, boys," he tells us, but neither of us are listening. Someone is bringing a fresh chocolate cake into the kitchen and both of us spot it. Yet somehow the next words of my father stick in my mind, even though I do not understand them now. Or maybe I hear them so often growing up they seem there from the beginning. "*Sic transit gloria mortis*," he says dryly, drawing a chuckle from my mother. Then he returns to the quiet conversation he is having with the elders in Lakota.

We are on our way home. The sun is down and I see stars out as we walk to the car. The rain quit in late afternoon and the air is cool and clear, and this is the part I like best. It is more than an hour's travel back home and I have the back seat all to myself, stretched out on a blanket. I watch the stars pass by in the window, and the few high clouds lit bright by a rising moon, though it is not yet over the horizon. I know I will fall asleep, and the sleeping while the car is moving is what I like. It is like being rocked in my father's arms on the gallery porch of my grandfather's house while the grown-ups sit and smoke and talk.

Lots of people have long porches like this, but my grandpa is the only one I ever heard call it a gallery. When I asked him why, he said it was because he liked to shoot at cars driving by, but I know he was fooling me. I know because my mother scolded him for telling me that. He told her I knew he was kidding, but I could tell she was still mad.

As I watch the stars pass in the windows I listen to the low murmur as my parents talk. They are speaking French now, which is what they use when they don't want me to know what they are saying. For a while they spelled words out, but I caught on and they speak French more. When I was small they only used it late at night after we all went to bed, and sometimes I would stay awake just to listen. I like the sound. It is like they are singing to each other, especially late at night. What I never understood was the strange noises which followed, noises that sound like the soft murmuring of hogs on my uncle's farm. When I asked them about it at dinner one night, I was sorry I did. It made my mother blush and my father laugh. He told me a time would come when I would understand without asking. He tells me that a lot. What I understand is that when he says that, the subject is closed.

Tonight they are talking in the singing way. My mother looks around and I pretend I am asleep. I see her slide across the seat to my dad, who is driving. She kisses him on the ear and he chuckles. She looks toward me again, but my eyes are half shut and she can't tell I am awake. A moment later the car lurches and my dad laughs. He forgets to speak French and tells her she's going to make him drive off the road. They both laugh and I wonder what she did. Then she turns on the radio and I hear soft music. The next thing I know is there is bright light in my face from the dome light as my father lifts me up and carries me in the house. I am so sleepy I drop of again on his shoulder, and I don't remember being undressed and put to bed. Yet I do remember them standing side by side at my bed, both kissing me gently before I close the door. The last thing I hear is their voices as they pass down the hall to their room, my father's voice speaking French and my mother's deep, throaty chuckle.

Two Thunder

3 March 15, 1981. Today is the Ides of March. It was a bad day for Julius Caesar, one that ruined his whole year. I wonder if he was really killed the way Shakespeare said or even if it was on the Ides of March. Or does it really matter? It's a good story, one I can see happening today. Change the names and the continents and set it a couple of thousand years in the future and you have the story of Red Cloud and Spotted Tail. I can almost hear Sinte Gleska saying, "*Et tu,* Red Cloud?" The difference is that down home on the reservation, Red Cloud got away with it.

Today is the Ides of March and a blizzard is blowing outside. Even though spring is supposed to be here in just a week, the temperature is right at zero, which means at least twenty below with wind chill. So I think Red Cloud would have waited at least a few days this year. Or maybe not. Assassination is a matter of opportunity as much as intent. This year the Ides of March seem better for sitting close to the fire and plotting strategy, not for jumping on a horse and riding off to kill a political rival. Even if you get the dire deed done, there are bound to be other people around to take offense, and a long, cold ride home. This is what Napoleon didn't consider about Russia, the long walk home.

I understand the seasons are much different in Rome. There it gets warm early in the year and March is a very mild month. They say the weather gets much milder then, even in England, and April in Paris is supposed to be incredibly beautiful This is probably why European poets rave on about the beauty of spring, why they write love songs about it. Where they grew up, spring is beautiful and a time of renewed hope.

Yet, whoever thinks spring is a beautiful time of year has never lived very long in South Dakota. Around here, spring is ugly. Even winter, with all its harsh realities is not as bad. Winter simply kills, very quickly and without mercy. Then it hides what it's done under a clean blanket of snow. So even the smell of death is sealed in frost, and only the sharp noses of wolves and coyotes can find what is hidden under the drifts.

On the reservation, it is when spring comes that all the ugliness is revealed. The snow melts, the earth turns to mud and the rivers run dirty in their courses, flooding out of their banks. Then, as the frost retreats, winter's corpses are revealed. The smell of death is spread across the land

So even while the days grow warm, spring is not a good time for the Lakota these days. Nor has it ever been. The food runs out in the spring. So does the carefully gathered fuel for the lodge fires. What game is left is thin and weak, and very hard to find. Cold and hunger are constant, and many of the elders who made it through the long winter return to the earth in the spring. So do many children. There is sickness then, a sickness that comes no other time of year, and it strikes down the weak, the oldest and the very young.

Yet, the worst thing is that even though the grass is growing green in sheltered places hope dies in the spring. Hope dies even as the promise is given. There is always one blizzard too many, one more funeral too soon, one government check which comes too late, one thing more too much to bear. So people slip away. They wander off into the storms and die. They take their own lives. They get drunk and kill each other, with knives or on the road in cars. So while the white poets sing of beauty and love in the springtime, on the reservation the death song is the stark reality of a Lakota spring.... (from John Lyons' early journals)

November, 1963. The next day we are on the way back to Johnny's for Willie's second day of wake. I've never been to an Indian funeral before this and I want to know more about it. My father answers my questions with great patience, but when I ask him something about last night, he gets a grin on his face that tells me not to believe what he is going to say. I also know when he's done my mother will scold him for leading me on, but I don't know where she thinks he is leading me. What I've learned is that when she really scolds him, my father has told me what grandpa calls a real whopper.

Actually, what grandpa says is if a yarn's worth telling, it's worth telling big. Only I'm not sure what a yarn is, except it's some kind of whopper. Yet, I think what Grandpa's talking about is something different from what my mother uses to knit sweaters.

So when I ask my dad why it is called a wake, he gets this funny little grin on his face and says it's because people make enough noise at them to wake the dead. Yet this time my mother doesn't scold him. She gives him that look I hate to get and then doesn't say anything. She just stares straight ahead and when my dad tries to kid her out of it, she tells him she is not amused. Then she turns and stares out the passenger window and I know my dad is in real trouble. When my mother raises her voice it is bad enough, but when she gets quiet, it's worse.

My dad looks at her for just a moment, then shrugs and lights a cigarette. I want to ask him all kinds of things, but my mother's silence tells me I better not. I know she will get over it soon, and so does my dad. So we drive along in silence for a while until a deer runs across the road in front of us. My dad brakes hard and I hit the back of his seat, bumping my nose. He pulls the car off the road and turns around to see how I am, but my mother has already turned to see. My nose is bleeding so she makes me lie down in the back seat of the car. My dad gets a piece of ice out of the cooler in the trunk and puts it in a handkerchief. When he puts it on my lip it feels good and the bleeding stops.

When my mother sees I am all right, she kisses me on the forehead and tells me to stay down for a few more minutes just to be sure. Then she asks my dad for a cigarette. This is strange because she never smokes outside the house. What is even more strange is how her hand shakes when my dad lights it for her. Then she puts a hand over her eyes and starts crying. When my dad reaches out to hold her, she clings to him, sobbing. This is something I have never seen. It scares me and I start to cry.

My mother throws down her cigarette and turns to me. As she reaches into the car to pick me up, I see my dad frown and step on the butt to put it out. Later, after I have seen what a range fire can do, I will understand why he does this without thinking. Now I think he is upset with me and I cry even harder. Yet he is soon by my mother's side, gently stroking my head and telling me things are all right. "It's over now," he tells my mother. "We all came through it in one piece."

My mother nods and smiles, then gives me a kiss and sets me down. She hugs my father and kisses him, too. "Thank God he was sitting down," she says. My father nods and we all get back into the car. As we drive away, I see the deer watching us from the edge of a wooded fence line a hundred yards away. I point it out to my parents and they laugh. I don't see what is funny, but I laugh, too. It feels good.

My dad turns on the car radio and we drive on for a while, singing along with the music. It's an old song my parents know well and I quickly pick up the refrain, clapping my hands with the beat. Then another song comes on and they start to teach me that one, too, but something happens. The music stops and a man's voice comes on the air. I don't understand everything he is saying, but he sounds scared. Something bad has happened. I think someone has been shot, but I don't understand what that means.

Suddenly, my mother is crying and my dad is sitting there, white faced and silent. I want to know what is going on, but I am too scared to ask. I have never seen my dad's face look like this. I have never seen him this silent. He pulls the car off the road again and sits there a long time, listening to the radio.

"Does this mean war?" my mother asks. She is very frightened.

"I don't know," he answers. "It depends on who did it."

"You think it was the Russians?" she wants to know.

"I didn't think they were that stupid," he tells her. "It's probably some kook." His voice is very sad when he says this. "I just hope he doesn't get the rest of us killed."

"Do you think we need to go home?" she asks. "Sissy will be scared."

My dad is silent a minute. "No," he finally says. "She's with my folks, so she'll be all right." He shakes his head. "No, I think we may as well go on. They are expecting us and I don't want to insult them."

"Surely, they would understand," my mother answers. She gives him a strange look.

"I don't know," he tells her. "They might or they might not. After all, he's only a white man, even if he is a chief." He lights another cigarette, hands it to my mother. "No, I don't think anything major is going to happen that quick. Even with that crazy sumbitch from Texas in charge. We'll keep an ear on the radio."

The image of my father bending over the radio with his ear pressed to it tickles me and I laugh. A sudden fury comes over my father's face and he snaps his head around to speak to me, but my mother stops him. "Junior!" she tells him. "He doesn't understand."

My father stares at me, hard. Then the fury is gone as quickly as it came, and he nods. He tries to say something but all that comes out is a loud sob and he begins to cry. This is even scarier than his fury, and I begin to cry, too. My mother reaches over the seat and pulls me to her, pulling my father in, too, holding us each with an arm. "It's going to be all right," she tells us. "No matter what happens, it's going to be all right. As long as we have each other, we're going to be all right."

When we arrive at Corn Creek, the news has traveled ahead of us. I see a group of men standing around a pickup truck with its doors open, listening to the radio. Their faces are grim and hard to read, but somehow I know they are scared. They are scared the way my father is scared, and some of them look very sad, too. As we pass by I see that none of them are smoking. They are just standing there, like sad statues around the pickup as they listen, all looking at the ground. None of them look up as we pass by, not even the old man who sang to me yesterday, but I see tears running down the cheeks of one young man. He is better dressed than the others, and I have not seen him before.

We enter the house and the women are gathered in two small groups, mostly in the kitchen, talking quietly. My father nods to Johnny's grandmother and shakes her hand. Then he goes back outside to stand with the men around the pickup. I start to follow him, but my mother stops me, shakes her head. Then my father turns, holds out his hand, and she releases me. I run to him and we walk outside to the truck.

The radio is full of static and I have trouble hearing what it is saying. One of the men reaches into the truck and tries to tune it but the sound only gets worse. He raises his head to look at the sky and then says something in Lakota. The others nod, looking up and around. Another storm is moving in and as we look up, we see small drops of rain begin to sprinkle around us. Even though it rained yesterday, the wind has dried the soil and the first heavy drops raise puffs of dust as they strike the dirt path to the house.

A sudden flash of intense white light blinds me, and the loud crash of thunder is right behind it. I see one of the men pointing and look in that direction. Lightening has split a tall pine not fifty yards from where we stand, and the half of the tree lying on the ground is burning fiercely. Two of the men grab shovels out of the back of the truck and start toward the fire, but the old man says something and they stop. A moment later there is another bright flash as a second bolt of lightening hits a rock outcropping half way between us and the tree. The two men throw their shovels back into the truck and climb in it. The rest of us rush to the house as a heavy rain begins to pour.

I see my mother standing in the doorway, looking out. Her face is white and tight, but when she sees us coming in, she smiles and takes me from my father's arms. I was so scared I don't remember him picking me up, but he must have when the first bolt hit. My mother dries my hair with a dish towel and kisses me on the cheek. Then she kisses my father, too, which causes some of the women to laugh. They are speaking in Lakota, but I know they are teasing her because my father grins and she flushes.

Once we are in the house, I stop being afraid. I go into the front room, looking for Johnny. He is standing in the corner listening to a young man tell a group of girls all about the lightening. I am surprised he is not speaking Lakota. I'm also surprised how different it all sounds when he tells it. I only remember two lightening strikes, not four. Later, as we are driving home, I tell my father about this and he laughs. He tells me that by next week it will be six or eight lightening strikes. I don't understand and ask him why, but he tells me a time will come when I will. He tells me stories grow with age, just like people, and some day I'll see what he means. He says that a lot, too.

When Johnny sees me, he runs over to me and asks if I saw the lightening, too. I tell him I saw the second flash and he wants to know all about it. When I tell him nobody was struck, he seems a little disappointed. Then he asks me all kinds of questions about the tree getting split and I tell him all I saw. He looks puzzled when I tell him I only saw two flashes, but after a while he gives up. He goes back to the corner where the young man is telling the story again.

I look around and see the old man who sang to me going down the stairs, so I follow him. When I get there, the room is almost empty. There is only the old man and another two old men there. One of them is very tall and slim, and dressed all in black. He is not wearing skins but a black suit with black cowboy boots. Even this man's shirt is black, but there is a little white square in the middle of his collar. Around his neck he is wearing a beaded necklace like the one on Willie, except this one is black and has a gold cross at the end, not a medallion.

The old man sees me looking and says something in Lakota to the tall man. The tall man in black nods and turns to me. He stoops down and offers his hand. He tells me he is Father Alex from Sisseton and I tell him my name. He sees me looking at his cross and holds it out for me to see. At the center of it I see something that looks like a shield. On it there is a cross with some funny writing, and around the cross are four tipis. The man in black asks me if I would like one like it and I nod my head. He tells me that some day someone will give me one like it, only silver and not gold. I ask him why I can't have a gold one like his and he laughs. He tells me I have to be an Indian priest for twenty-five years to earn a gold one.

The old man says something else in Lakota and the man in black looks at me again and nods. He hold out his hands and I go to him.

For some reason I am not afraid like I am most times with strangers. He lifts me up and turns to the white box, and he begins to tell me things. He tells me Willie looks like he is sleeping because he is. He asks me if I ever dream and I nod. Then he tells me Willie's spirit has gone to the place our spirits go when we dream. Only this time, Willie's spirit is not coming back. This time it is staying in the other place with a great warrior. He tells me the white man's name for this great man is Jesus, but he has many names. What is important is that he will take care of Willie, just like he will take care of me when I go there to stay. He tells me the great warrior takes care of all good people and he protects them from the Bad One.

I tell him I sometimes go to a scary place when I dream. I ask him if this is where the Bad One lives. He tells me it is not. Only bad people go to the Bad One's camp, and little children are never bad people. Little children are the favorite people of the great warrior, Jesus, and he would never let the Bad One have them.

I look down at Willie and I ask how long he going to have to sleep in the box. The man in black tells me this is not Willie, only the body he lived in while his spirit was here. He tells me that in just a little while we are going to give Willie's body back to the Earth Mother. She gives us bodies for our spirits to live in, but when we go to sleep the last time, we must return them to her.

I ask him why she needs them back, and he tells me she uses them again and again to make bodies for all the creatures of the world. He takes one of my fingers between his and shakes it gently. He tells me this may have been a feather on an eagle's wing the last time she made something with it. Or it may have been a cone on one of the tall pines on the mountains.

I don't understand, but I can't think of anything to ask him. I look around and my father is standing right behind us. I reach out to him and the man in black puts me in his arms. My father shakes his hand and smiles. "It's good to see you again, Father," he says and I am confused. I thought my grandpa was his father.

When I ask my father about this a little while later, he tells me this is something people say to honor their priests. He tells me Father Alex doesn't have any children at all because he is a Catholic priest. This confuses me even more. Then he tells me the Indians do the same thing when they call their old people grandfather or grandmother. It is a way of honoring the elders.

I start to ask my father to explain, but Johnny runs up and wants me to come to his room. He doesn't say this, but somehow I know this is what he wants. My father does, too, and he tells me not to leave the house. The way he says it I know I better not.

When we get to Johnny's room, there are three other boys our age already there. They look like Johnny and Willie, but I have never seen them before. Johnny doesn't tell me their names or introduce them, and when they see me they begin talking in Lakota. I can't understand what they are saying, but I don't like the way they look at me.

One of them is taller than the rest of us and he stands in front of me and stares in my face. He smells like bubble gum. When one of the others I don't know says something, he laughs and shoves me so hard I fall against the bed. "You don't even know what we are saying, do you, *wasicu*," he says, almost spitting the last word. He shoves me again.

Suddenly, Johnny is between us, shoving the bigger boy back, telling him to leave me alone. He tells them I am his friend. For a minute I think the bigger boy is going to push him back, but he leaves with the other two. But as he goes out the door he says something else in Lakota. All I understand is the same word he said to me, *wicasu*. The way he says it is very ugly.

I am relieved, but Johnny is angry with me. "Why didn't you fight back?" he asks me. "Why did you let him shove you like that?"

"I don't know how," I tell him and he gives me a strange look, like I've told him I don't know how to talk.

"Everybody knows how to fight," he says, still unable to understand.

"I don't," I answer.

"Don't you have any brothers or sisters? Didn't they teach you?"

I shake my head. I tell him my sister is older than me, more like a second mother, and I don't have any brothers.

"Don't you watch movies?" he asks. "They fight in movies. Haven't you seen that?"

"Yeah," I tell him. "I watch movies. I've seen it, but I don't know how to do it. My mother tells me it's bad to fight."

Johnny looks at me a long time. "Then I'll teach you how to fight," he says. All of a sudden he shoves me like the big boy did. This time the bed is not behind me and I fall down. "Come on," he says. "Get up. Push me back."

I get up off the floor and push him a little. "Come on!" he says, pushing me so hard I almost fall down again. "Push! A little baby can

24

push harder than you."

Suddenly, Johnny is on the floor and I am standing over him. His eyes are wide in surprise, and I am surprised. I am not sure how he got there. Just then my mother walks in the door. "Randy!" she says to me. There is iron in her voice. "What are you doing?"

I am so scared I can't talk. Johnny jumps up. "I'm teaching him a game," he says and I nod dumbly. I can see my mother doesn't believe this for a moment. Then Johnny starts yelling and beating his chest. "It's called Tarzan," he says.

My mother looks at us a long while. Then I see the corners of her mouth twitch and I know we are all right. "All right, Tarzan," she says to me. "But don't play so rough. We heard you all the way out there."

We nod and my mother leaves. I am amazed at my new friend. When I am caught doing something wrong, I freeze. I can't think of anything to say.

"You learn quick," Johnny tells me. "You sure nobody ever taught you that before?" I shake my head. "All right," he says. "That's what you do next time that big guy pushes you. Knock him down." I tell him maybe the big guy won't push me again, and Johnny looks at me like I am crazy. "Yeah, he will," he answers. "You let him get away with it once, so he will do it again."

The way he says it is like saying the sun will come up tomorrow. I know he is right. "Why do I have to fight him?" I ask. "Why can't we just be friends?"

"I don't know," Johnny answers. "Some people you just have to fight. They don't want to be friends."

Does memory fail me here? As I write these words, they seem far too old for boys so young. Yet I remember them so clearly. Why is this? Am I confusing the day of the assassination with another trip to Corn Creek? I don't know. There are so many funerals in Indian Country every year. There were many, many trips to Corn Creek to bury friends of my parents. I know that in one year after I was grown I covered over forty different funerals, all people known to me well. I imagine it was no different for my father. I also know we were riding in the car on the way to a funeral when we heard the news that JFK was shot. I remember the deer running in front of us just before.

Or does it matter? Growing up in the newspaper business I learned very early that while facts are the Holy Grail for news people, they are often used to obscure a deeper truth. This is commonly called politics, the world of nuance and slant. What is important to me here is telling the truth as best I can, not getting the facts in line. So what if the details are dis-remembered if the truth is told? God may be in the details, as someone once said. Yet, I believe God is even more in the greater truth.

What is the truth? The gentle rabbi could have answered the governor even as he answered Martha when the facts were so unclear. "I am the truth." The point is, there lies within each of us a reality of who we are that is the highest truth, and I believe that for me, this gathers around the memory of my friend, John K. This may be right or wrong in a religious sense, but I don't care. It was Johnny who so often showed me the deeper truth about myself. Was that not what the Teacher did?

So was it at Willie's funeral I first saw the balloons go up? Or was it at another funeral at Corn Creek? I honestly don't know. What I remember is the rain, but so many funerals happen in the rain. If it never rained on funerals, Corn Creek would be the driest place in the world. Sadly enough, that is the greater truth, not just about them, about the folk who live at Corn Creek, but about us all.

When we get to Corn Creek for the day of the burial, someone has draped a large blue tarp over the back porch of Johnny's house to keep rain from blowing in the kitchen door. My mother goes on into the house and I stand with my dad outside under the tarp as he visits with the men. The rain is steady and the tarp acts as a big basin, catching the rain as it pours off the roof. One place near the far edge of the tarp bulges heavy with caught water, and when one of the men tries to adjust a corner pole to let it go, he is soaked. The rest of the men laugh and one of them throws him a towel. He is laughing as hard as they are.

Then someone puts a long pole up in the middle of the tarp. The problem is solved, at least for the moment, and the water drips evenly off the edges. Some of the men clap and the problem solver holds up a clenched victory fist. Then a gust of wind floats the tarp, dropping the pole, and a couple of men spend a long time trying to get it fixed for good. Nothing works until one of the men lowers one of the outside corners so even the wind cannot lift it up. Yet this leaves little room for standing under the tarp and the men go inside. One of them starts to wipe his feet, but the feed sack used for this is wet and muddy as the kitchen floor. So he gives up and walks in.

There are more people here today. This is the third day of the burial and the tiny house is crowded, even the basement. Long benches have been set up along the basement walls but these are crowded with old people and the smoke from their cigarettes is so thick I can hardly see. Yet the smoke smells different, and as I walk down the steps I see the old man who sang to me standing in front of the white box. He is singing again and in his hand there is a thick twist of grey-green weed bound tightly with red thread. Later my father will tell me this is sage mixed with sweet medicine grass. The very end of it is smoldering and gives off thick puffs of pleasant smoke as the old man waves it over, under and around the white box. Then he picks up the eagle feather and fans smoke into the box where Willie lies sleeping.

When the old man is done, Father Alex steps up to the front and begins speaking in Lakota. At first, his eyes are closed and his face is lifted up, and I know he is praying. I have seen the people do this at our church. They usually have their hands up when they do this but Father Alex is holding a little red book in both hands in front of his chest. When he is done praying, he opens the book and says something. Other people have books like his and they open them, too. Then someone in the corner starts playing an accordion and the people start to sing. I know the tune because it is a song we sing in church, too, but the words are different and sung much slower. When I start singing the words I know, Father Alex looks at me and smiles. I feel my father's hand gently squeezing my shoulder. Without looking up I know he is shaking his head the way he does when he wants me to be quiet, so I stop and just listen. There is something very sad and very beautiful about the way the people are singing. To this day the words still come to mind whenever I hear the tune of Sweet Hour Of Prayer. I must have heard them sung in Lakota a thousand times. *Jerusalem, wakan kin he....*

After the hymn, Father Alex speaks for a long time. When he is done a group of men in the back of the room begin singing a drum song, and everyone stands and turns in the same direction. They do this three more times before the song ends. This is a Song of the Four Directions, but long before I understand the words, I know it is a very sacred honoring song. What I see right away is that no one talks or walks around while this song is being sung. Some of them will when Father Alex is talking or praying, but not while the drum group is singing this song. Not even the little children.

Other people get up to talk and after a while I grow sleepy. I am sitting on my mother's lap, so I put my head down for a while and fall asleep. When I awake, Father Alex is standing in front of a small table. He has a wide, rainbow colored strip of cloth around his neck hanging down to his knees, and there is a loaf of bread and a cup between two candles on the small table before him. As I watch, he lifts up the round loaf of bread and breaks it in two. Then he says something in Lakota and people answer. He breaks off a little piece of bread and eats it, and then he gives a small piece to another man in black standing by his side. Then they both drink from the cup and Father Alex begins to walk around the room giving everyone a little bread. The other man follows, giving them all a sip from the silver cup. After he passes they touch themselves between their eyes, then on the tummy and each shoulder. I have never seen this before and I wonder what they are doing. I also wonder how there can be enough in one cup for so many people.

When Father Alex gets to us, my father makes the same gesture as the other people and holds up his hands. Then Father Alex breaks off another bit and hands it to me. I start to take it, but my father holds back my hand. He tells Father Alex I am not yet baptized. Father Alex gives him the same look my mother sometimes does and says very softly and clearly, "That is not his fault. Are you forbidding him to come to Jesus?"

My father is lost. He looks at my mother, but she is no help. She is smiling and yet she is somehow giving him the same look as Father Alex. There is nothing my father can do or say, so he smiles and nods. Later he will tease my mother and call this his personal Little Big Horn, but faced with God and mother, he surrenders with grace. When he does, Father Alex smiles and offers me the bread. He says very clearly, "This is the Body of our Lord Jesus Christ. Receive what you are." When he says this, my father gives him a very strange look.

I eat the little piece of bread, which is very good. Then the other man in black is standing before me, offering the cup and saying, "This is the Blood of Christ, the cup of salvation." Hearing this scares me, but I take the cup anyway. I see it is half full and I take a big sip. When I swallow I am surprised how it warms my mouth and throat, and I can feel it burn all the way down to my stomach. I am suddenly dizzy and my eyes start to water from the heat of the wine. Yet, somehow I know it is very important not to cry or make a sound and I do not. I take a deep breath and the man with the cup smiles. "The blood of Christ is powerful medicine," he says in a rich, musical baritone so common among the Lakota men.

Then the man moves on, and I know something very special has just happened. I do not understand what it is that has taken place and it will take many years for me to even begin to understand what it means.

I have heard it said that catholics are born, not made. I don't know how true that is but I do know nothing has ever been the same for me since. I certainly have thought of myself as catholic from that point on, even though I am nominally Methodist. Sometimes I wonder. Was this something which was meant to be? Would my life have been different had Father Alex not insisted, violating Canon Law in the process?

A very wise priest once told me that what could happen that day did happen. I am not sure I can accept this. This raises as many questions as it answers. What I do know is that I will never forget the exact date. It is carved in stone for me to see any time I visit the grave of Willie Lyons. It was at his funeral I received my first communion.

Rosebud Wacipi

4 April 3, 1977. Someone said something good about me the other day. At least I think so. Seeing who said it, I think it was good. He said it to my face and I am bigger than him. The guy's name is Buddy Boudreau, and that's strange because it's not just a nickname. He says that is the name his mother gave him when he was born. Not Bubba or Bud, just Buddy. He says she named him after his dad, who people called Bud, even though his name was Homer. The reason they called him Bud is because his daddy was also called Homer. I guess Cajuns do this, but it seems strange. Why not give him his own name? I guess in a way she did.

Buddy is shorter than me by an inch or two and he is lighter built. He is also a lot darker than me and could pass for Lakota except for his eyes. I have never seen eyes like his, bright blue. They grab your attention and he's got all the *wiyonan* after him. You would think he's Ricky Nelson the way the *wiyonan* and the white girls go on about him. They do just about anything to get his attention, but it doesn't do them much good. He laps up the lime light but I don't think he does much about it. I wouldn't call him queer because I have no reason to, but he seems to like hanging out with guys better than girls. Nobody else has said anything, at least not to me. They all seem to think he's a real lady killer and envy his luck, but not me. Maybe he doesn't come on to guys, but something tells me he is about as straight as a three dollar bill.

Anyway, it was Buddy that said it. His family moved to Winner around the first of the year and he came out for track. Built the way he is, he's a long distance runner and he is damned fast. I guess he took state champion in Louisiana last year, both the eight-eighty and the mile. He was telling us all about it, so after warm up, the coach put him up against me in the mile. There is no one around that can take me in the mile, and I guess the coach thought he'd see just how good I am against real competition.

I was kind of curious what Buddy has, so I let him set the pace. I stayed behind him a step or two until the middle of the third quarter, and I knew I could take him. So I started dropping back to made it look good, and when we finished the third quarter I was fifty yards behind him.

Of course, everybody but the coach thought I met my match and they started cheering and yelling for Buddy. I guess they had never seen anyone that fast. The coach wasn't fooled, though, and as I crossed the start line for the last four-forty I saw him thumb his stop watch. I don't know what happened, but when I saw him do that something exploded inside me. I began to run like I have never run before and by the time we hit the middle of the quarter I was hard on Buddy's tail. Not knowing how he played, I went wide and when I passed I saw him poring it on. We went neck and neck, with me on the outside until the last turn. Then I found some reserves I never knew were there. I was running free and easy and I kicked it in the ass. By the time we crossed the finish line I was twenty yards ahead.

Later, the coach told me how last that last quarter was and I didn't believe him. If it had been at an official match, I would have set a new record. When I did later on, my time was only twenty-three hundredths of a second faster. Yet, I don't believe I ever ran faster than that afternoon. I think the coach's watch was a little slow.

After the race, I took a half lap to cool down. When I got back to the start line, Buddy was there catching his breath and waiting for me. He said, "Man, I'm glad you wadn't at state lest year. You run like a scairt nigger!"

Like a 'scairt nigger'. I was so shocked I didn't know what to say. Nigger is not a word we use up here. Yet, somehow I knew Buddy didn't mean any harm. So I told him something like 'not a scared nigger but a red nigger,' and everybody laughed.

Of course, I don't know if what he said is true or not because I wasn't scared. If I had been I would never let him take the lead. But the name stuck and for a long time the guys called me Chief Scairt Nigger, or Red Nigger, even though Buddy didn't. I think that is fighting words where he comes from. Then one day I got tired of it and bounced one of the bastards off the wall. I wasn't really mad, I was just tired of it. After that they didn't do it to my face, but they kept at it until the coach made them quit. The last time was when one of them wrote it on my locker with red paint. A long time after it happened, I found out it was RD's dad who got that stopped. I guess he had what Buddy calls a real come-to-Jesus meetin' with the coach.

On the other hand, I think what I said that day is true. I think Indians are red niggers to people around here, and I think the white settlers did the same thing to us as they did to black people. The only difference is that we didn't make good slaves and they didn't put black people on the reservations they way they did us. They forced them into ghettos, but at least those were in the cities where people could get jobs. These may not have been very good jobs but even scut work is better than no work, the way it is now on the reservation. No matter how good you are at whatever you do, there are no jobs for most people on the reservation.... (From John K's high school journal.)

Late August, 1970. We are on the way to Rosebud this morning and I am excited. I love *wacipi* and the one in Rosebud is one of the biggest. People come from all over to see it and to dance, and you can hear the drums miles away. Last year my dad stopped on our way here to see somebody near Soldier Creek and we could hear the drums when we got out of the car. They give cash prizes for the best drum team, but my dad says that's not why the teams come. He says the prizes will not even cover their travel expenses. The drummers come because drums are honored here. The prize could be a single eagle feather and that would mean more than the cash prize. "Not that they turn down cash," my father adds, laughing. "That comes in handy, too."

I like the drums, but that's not why I am excited. Johnny will be there and I have not seen him since summer started. We were going to summer camp together but someone in his family died and he couldn't go. So I want to tell him all about it. It was the first time I was ever away from home and I really liked it. They have a big swimming pool and horses and archery, and I made Johnny a long whistle lanyard in craft class. It's red and yellow, his favorite colors, and I think he will like it. My dad got him a new silver police whistle to go on the hook in the end. He said he didn't think he was doing Johnny's parents any favors. I am not sure what he meant but he was smiling when he said it, so I know it's all right. I wanted to get Johnny a real Scout knife with all the different blades, but my mother didn't think that was a good idea and my dad agreed.

When I saw Johnny last, he told me he was going to dance this year. He said he was going to enter the fancy dance contest, but I told him he was too young. Most of the guys who enter are as old as my sister and a fourth grader doesn't stand a chance. Well, almost a fourth grader.

We both finished third grade this year, although he goes to school in Parmalee. That's where his parents live, his grand parents, even though his dad works for the BIA in Rosebud. He drives a truck and bosses a road crew. He promised to take me with him on a road grader sometime and I hope he does. I watched one day when we were passing by and I think it would be fun to sit up high like he does and grade the roads. My dad says it is a very important skill. People have to know what they are doing. If they don't, the roads will wash away.

Even though it's very early, the sun is already up when we get to Rosebud. Not many people are up yet, but I hear a drum group singing over toward the arena. There are lots of cars and pickups parked all over the *pauwau* grounds, and a dozens of tents are set up all around in family groups. A few people have even put up tipis, and I tell my dad I want to go look at them. He laughs and tells I better wait until the people are up.

We park the car and get out, and my dad tells me to stay close. While I wait for him and my mother to get their stuff I read the sign by the entrance to the grounds. It is hand painted in red and black and green, and the words go all over. " NO ALCOHOL OR DRUGS ALLOWED HERE," it says in bright red. Then in black it says, "VIOLATORS WILL BE PERSECUTED!" Then at the very bottom someone has painted in green, "AND PUT IN JAIL THIS MEANS YOU!!"

I think this is funny since the trash barrel next to the sign is full with beer bottles and pop cans spilling over the top. I point it out to my dad and he takes a picture of me by the sign pointing to a beer can on the ground. "Surely you're not going to publish that?" my mother says and he tells her it's only for the album. He has a whole album full of pictures he won't ever print in the paper. When I asked him why, he said it's because he wants to keep printing the paper. I guess he thinks some of his pictures might make some people pretty mad. One of my favorite ones is a picture he took of a sign someone threw away at the Okreek dump. It was propped up against a whole pile of trash and said "YARD SALE TODAY."

I can hear the drums start up again as we walk down a wide walkway from the parking lot to the arena. There are canvas booths set up on both sides of the walkway selling about everything people will buy, tee shirts, bead work, fry bread and Indian tacos. Some of this is good stuff and some of it is what my dad calls cheap crap. There are trash barrels set up along the walkway, but most of these are full and the whole area is littered with napkins, old paper cups, hot dog wraps and cigarette butts. Since most of the booths are still closed, we walk on by until my dad sees one selling coffee. He buys coffee for him and my mom, and he gets me a can of orange juice and a big donut. There is a table nearby and we start to sit down, but someone has spilled catsup all over it and there are dozens of flies buzzing around.

We walk on to the arena and take a seat on the bleachers with our backs to the sun. It is already too warm for a jacket and I take mine off, tying it by the arms around my waist. Then I watch the line of old men in Army hats dancing in a line across the arena. I ask my dad what they are doing and he tells me it is an honoring dance for veterans who have died in the wars. He points to flags flying around the arena, one for each veteran being honored. As I watch, the line of old men turns slowly, facing each flag for a while before turning to the next one.

Except for us, there are almost no people sitting in the bleachers. We are sitting high enough that I can see quite a way over the tops of the tents, and I see people stirring. Some of them are sitting in lawn chairs drinking coffee, and others are cooking. I see one lady washing her hair at a cold water spigot, and when she is done, she strips the tee shirt off her toddler and begins to give him a shower. The water must be cold and he doesn't like this at all. I see him running up and down in place, crying and screaming as she washes him off, but I can't hear him over the drums. I wonder why she hasn't taken him somewhere where they have hot water.

The drum song changes and I look back toward the old men. They seem to be doing the same thing and I look back at the toddler. His mother is drying him off now and he has stopped crying. As I watch, she puts his tee shirt back on and he runs off to join some other children who are playing by the tent. His mother goes after him and puts on his shoes, but that's all she dresses him. He has no pants or skivvies or diaper and I feel embarrassed for him. What happens if he has an accident?

When I ask my dad about this, he laughs and tells me he guesses they will have to rinse out his tee shirt. He tells me I am a chip off the old block asking questions like that. I ask him what block and he raps his knuckles on his head. I don't understand, but my mother tells me it means I'm a born reporter just like he was because I ask questions. This makes me proud. I want to grow up to be like my dad.

Something else is going on now. I see two men in black setting up a table on one side of the arena and another man setting up a music stand.

I recognize the third man as the same one who played at Willie's funeral and I ask my dad who is getting buried. He gives me an odd look and then smiles. He tells me that we aren't burying anyone today. The men in black are setting up for Mass and the man setting up the music stand will lead the singing.

I can see right away he is right. Father Alex comes into the arena carrying a small black suitcase and a bright colored blanket. He spreads the blanket on the table and then opens the suitcase. I see him take out a bottle of wine and a couple of candles. Then he lays a small white square cloth in the middle of the blanket and sets out a silver cup and a small silver plate. Then he sets the two candles on each side of the white cloth and lights them with a match. They are big and round and I can barely see the flame from where I am sitting. What I can see clearly is heat waves rising in the air above each candle.

When he is done with this, Father Alex walks over and begins to talk with the man with the accordion. The man has a small red book in his hand just like the one Father Alex has and as they talk the music man writes something down on a paper. When he is done, he tears the paper in half and gives one piece to Father Alex. Then they all walk to the riser behind the table and sit down to watch the honoring dance.

Nothing else is going on and I look around, hoping to see Johnny. I see a pickup like his grandfather drives and a group of tents gathered near it, but no one is moving around the tents. Yet, I see heat waves rising under a big coffee pot on a gas stove and I know someone will be around soon. Sitting here watching is boring, so I ask my mother if I can go over to the tents and see if Johnny is around. My father leans across and tells me to wait until after Mass. I am not sure what Mass is, but I know if Father Alex is doing it then it will take a long time.

I start to argue, but the honoring dance comes to an end and the announcer begins talking so loud into the microphone on the stage my words get lost. He is speaking Lakota with a few white words mixed in and I understand most of what he is saying. I even know the Lakota for the white words he uses. Then the announcer repeats what he has said in white talk, but I know this is not for the *wasicu* or the tourists. Johnny told me once that there are lots of Lakota on the reservation who don't know their own tongue. This is why the announcer is using white talk.

The announcer keeps going on so loud it hurts my ears. So I put my fingers in my ears. My mother smiles when she sees this and shakes her head. Then she puts an arm around my head and pulls me close. When

I take my hands down she smiles and nods, and I understand. What I was doing might be seen as disrespectful to the speaker and we are guests here. My parents tell me this every time we come to the reservation. Remember we are guests here. Mind your manners.

What I don't know is why the speaker doesn't turn the sound down. Can't he hear how loud it is? If I was hurting his ears talking too loud in my home I would be expected to speak more softly to respect our guest. Why aren't we being respected the same way as guests here? When I ask my dad about this later on, he tells me different people have different customs and this is particularly true of the Lakota. What makes good manners to us doesn't necessarily make good manners to them.

My grandfather is listening to this and snorts when my dad tells me this. When he snorts like this I know what he means is "bullshit" but he doesn't like to say that in front of my mother. "Come on, Junior," he says. "Tell the boy the truth."

My mother gets a strained look on her face when he says this but says nothing. She is very careful to respect my grandfather, even when she does not agree with him. I know she wants me to drop the subject, but before I think, I ask, "What truth?"

My grandfather looks at my dad, who shrugs. I know he is telling my grandpa that since he lifted the bale, he needs to kill the snake under it. I can see my grandpa wishes he hadn't opened his mouth, at least not in front of my mother. He thinks a minute before he speaks, choosing his words carefully. "The truth is, son, the man was probably being deliberately rude."

"You don't know that," my mother says quietly. "You weren't there."

"No," the old man sighed. "I wasn't there and I may be wrong. But I've been there a lot of times and I know deliberate bad manners when I see them. I also know racism."

"Why did he do that?" I asked, not able to help myself. This was very curious and something I had never heard. Except for the big boy at Willie's funeral and a few others, all the Lakota were very kind to me.

"He's angry," my grandfather replied. "The white race gave his people a terrible beating a long time ago, and he is angry about that."

"The white race is still doing it," my mother said softly.

"Racism is racism," my grandfather insisted. "Skin color doesn't keep anyone from being racist."

"We didn't do anything to him, did we?" I asked. This was all very strange.

"That's the point," my dad broke in. "He was rude to us because we are white, not because we did anything bad." He looked at my mother. "I was there, sweetheart. Dad is right. The man was being rude. That particular man always is to anyone who is white."

I could see my mother did not like it, but she didn't argue. "Well," she said, "Well, you may be right, but it's his garbage. I for one don't intend to take delivery."

"That's very wise, Susan," my grandpa said gently. I would later learn this was his way of apologizing to her. "We don't have to take it personally, do we?"

"Well, who would like some more tea?" my mother asked and I knew the subject was closed, at least for the moment.

The announcer is still talking in a very loud voice and I can understand him better with my mother's arm over my ear. Then Father Alex gets up and walks to the table with the chalice and candles and puts on his stole. The announcer keeps on talking but after a moment, Father Alex turns and stares at him until the man finally runs down. Then Father Alex nods and someone rings a big bell near the stage, and the announcer tells the people in the whole fairground it is time for Mass. I see some of them moving out of their tents and coming to the arena, but I can't spot Johnny.

When the bell stops ringing, Father Alex says something in Lakota, crossing himself and then repeating it in the white tongue. Most of the people seated around the arena rise and answer him, some in Lakota, but most in white. I see them cross themselves and I do the same. Out of the corner of my eye I see my dad give me an odd look and frown but I don't look at him. I do see my mother raise a finger to her lips as she turns to him.

This scares me. I do not like to make my father mad, but my mother is on my side and I know it will be all right. At first, it feels strange to cross myself the way Father Alex and the others do, but it also feels like I am doing something right. There seems to be something more powerful than my fear moving my arm up and down and across in this strange motion. Yet what I am even more aware of is being surrounded by a love warmer than my mother's, even more fierce than my father's. It wraps itself around me like a blanket and I know I am safe. No matter what happens, I am safe.

The Mass moves along faster than it did at the funeral and Father

Alex does not talk as long. When it comes time for the people to take communion, they move forward out of their seats and form two long lines in front of the table. I feel my father's hand on my shoulder as I start to move forward. When I look at him, he shakes his head. I see he is ignoring the look on my mother's face.

I feel my eyes begin to sting but I fight back my tears. I am not a baby any more, but I am very sad. Despite my effort, I feel tears making tracks down my cheeks as I watch the people taking the bread and drinking the wine. Oddly enough, I feel no shame, only a deep sadness.

As the lines begin to grow short, I see Father Alex looking around. When he sees me, he smiles and beacons, but my father's grip on my shoulder grows tighter. Then I see Father Alex shift his gaze, looking at my father with the same strange intensity as he did with the announcer. I hear my mother murmur, "Please, Junior. Please."

My father sighs and releases his grip. I do not give him time to change his mind. I run down the stands so fast I trip and fall face down in the dusty arena. I am stunned and I feel strong hands lifting me, dusting me off. It is my father and he stands me up on my feet. Then he smiles and walks with me to get in line. I feel my mother's presence behind us and I am surprised to hear her sniffle.

Out of nowhere, I sense Johnny at my side in the line. "You sure are in a hurry to come to Jesus," he whispers and my father snorts. I hear my mother clear her throat loudly and Father Alex looks up and grins. When we get to the front of the line he tells me the same thing he did at Willie's funeral, "The Body of Jesus. Receive what you are." My father looks at him in a strange way again but says nothing.

After communion there is a long prayer in Lakota, and then we sing two or three numbers from the little red hymnals everyone seems to have. By now I know many of the words to the favorite hymns and Johnny and I sing these together, trying to outdo one another. Several people around us smile and Father Alex shakes his head. I can see he is trying to hide a grin.

When the Mass is done it is time for breakfast and Johnny asks us to come to his tent to eat. When my mother hesitates, he says his mother really wants to see her and my dad shrugs. "I can see the others later," he says. "Maybe we can eat supper there."

Even though it is breakfast, the food is pretty much the same as what people eat at funerals, but there is not so much of it. Mostly it is beef stew with fry bread and cold tea, but there is also coleslaw and a Jell-O salad I really like. Like most of the other people around, we eat off paper plates but eat with metal forks and drink out of tin cups. I really like the cups. They remind me of Gabby Hayes when he drives the chuck wagon for a trail drive in the movies.

Just before we eat, Father Alex arrives and says a blessing over the food. Then Johnny's mother serves him first and serves us next, before the family. Johnny's grandpa has made a large table out of saw horses and a sheet of plywood and it is covered with a large white sheet. When we sit down around the table, my dad takes a seat next to the priest and begins to ask him about some things going on down at St. Francis. There was a big wind there last week and one of the church buildings was damaged. We all laugh when Father Alex tells us an outhouse blew away, too, but fortunately no one was in it. My dad says that would be really uplifting if anyone was in it and Father Alex says it would be a very moving experience, all right. Everyone laughs while they go back and forth like this for a while.

Johnny is sitting next to me while we eat and we talk quietly. He tells me there is a race he is in later this morning and a fancy dance not long before supper. I ask him what he will be wearing and he takes me to one of the tents to show me his costume.

Over the years I've seen thousands of costumes, but I think Johnny's is the most beautiful I ever saw. Johnny tells me his grandfather made it in the old way and it took him almost all winter. He shows me the first thing his grandfather made, which is a roach cut out of porcupine fur. This is cut to fit across Johnny's head from front to back with three soft leather straps coming together just in front of his ears to hold it on. These are beaded in red and yellow, and tied together with the chin straps against two small beaded rosettes. The beading is mostly red and yellow against a deep blue background. Later when I see these very same patterns in a museum of Indian history I realize they are probably handed down from generation to generation in Johnny's family.

The next thing Johnny shows me is a chest plate of hollowed bones tied together with sinew and large pony beads. He tells me this was put together from an old chest plate his grandfather picked up in a pawn shop in Rapid City. The thing was so old he had to replace all the sinew and some of the cowry shells used to space the pieces of bone. I ask if I can try it on and he tells me to take off my shirt. The old bones make a strange sound and feel cool against my skin as he ties them on.

Then Johnny shows me his medallion and hangs it around my neck.

It is the same swirling logs pattern of the rosettes on the roach and it hangs from a chain of shell and bone like those on the chest plate. When he does this, Johnny steps back and laughs. He tells me I look like an Indian.

The breach cloth is made out of beaded buckskin and I have to take off my pants for it to fit right. Then Johnny fastens a belt studded with harness bells around my waist to hold it up and ties leather straps with smaller bells around my knees. The sound they make when I move the least little bit is bright and cheerful, and they jingle as I put on the beaded moccasins Johnny will wear in the dance.

The next thing to go on is the big round butt bustle with two cloth tails hanging down behind and the matching bustles for each arm. Each of these is made of a circle of eagle feathers bound in red cloth at the quill ends and tied together in the center with a leather thong. A large bead rosette in the same swirling logs pattern holds the bustles on my arms and around my waist.

Then Johnny picks up the roach and ties it over my head. He laughs and tells me all I need is war paint. I tell him I want to show my parents and we run back to the table.

When Father Alex sees us he laughs and speaks to my father. "Looks like you have a fancy dancer in the family." To me he says, "You been learning to dance this summer?"

I tell him about summer camp and everything I did there. This reminds me about the lanyard I made for Johnny and I run back to the tent to get it out of my pocket. He really likes the whistle and tries it out. It's so loud everyone has to cover their ears and an old man in the next camp asks where the cops are. Johnny's grandmother says she has a special place by the door to hang it so she can call Johnny when it's time for supper. His grandpa says he can practice blowing it behind the shed, too, and everyone laughs again. My dad takes our picture together, me in the dance costume and Johnny with the whistle.

When the women start cleaning up the dishes, Johnny's grandpa says he needs to see about something he is supposed to do. After he leaves, Father Alex and my dad sit and smoke with their coffee, swapping news until my mother joins them. As Johnny and I put away his dance costume I hear them talking quietly even though we are inside the tent. Something strange is happening in St. Francis and their voices sound worried.

I go back out to ask them if I can go with Johnny to the race, but before I can ask, Father Alex sees me and says, "A little child shall lead them." Then he turns and asks my father, "Have you christened this little hellion yet?"

My dad gets a strange look on his face. "No, Alex," he says. "We are waiting for him to make his own choice about that."

Father Alex looks at my mother. She is busy studying the hem of the table cloth.

"I think he already has. Haven't you, RD?" Father Alex looks at me and I nod. "We could take care of it right now," he says, looking at my mother.

"Right here?" my dad asks. He laughs but I can tell he doesn't think this is funny.

Father Alex looks around. "Yeah, this is as good a place as any." He smiles at the ladies who are finished cleaning up and join us at the table. "You're among friends... and family, too." He looks at my father.

I can see my dad is uneasy. "You don't understand, Father," he says. "Our family are all Methodists."

Father Alex laughs. "Is that so? You know, I'd like to be one of those, too, Randy. My bishop won't let me marry!"

One of Johnny's aunts speaks up. "You could always become Episcopal, Father. They let their priests marry."

Father Alex laughs again and says, "For you, Alice, it's tempting." Everybody laughs. "But you already have a husband."

"I know," Alice tells him. "But Nancy doesn't."

Father Alex turns to my mother. "See what I'm up against around here? They are all out to marry me off!" Then he turns serious. "What do you think, Susan?"

My mother looks at my father and shrugs. "As you said, it's as good a place as any, but I need to honor my husband." My dad's face is very still, the way it gets when he and my mother disagree. I know he is being very careful what he says.

Before my father can say anything, Father Alex says, " I know I am pushing, Junior. I'll shut up and respect your decision if you're really against it. Baptism at this point is a little redundant, anyway. RD has already come to Jesus and made him part of himself."

My dad nods. I can see him relax. "Why do it then?" he asks.

"That's a good question," Father Alex says. "To me, it's like getting married. All two people need to do to be married is make a covenant with one another and God. It doesn't take a license or a priest or even a judge. What the ceremony does is make their marriage a part of the community. It also asks the help of the community in preserving the marriage."

"I am not sure I follow you, Father," my dad says. "What does this have to do with baptism?"

Father Alex smiles. "There's no doubt in my mind that RD has been joined to God already. He received the body and blood of Christ, literally took it into himself. What he felt this morning was God pulling him back again." He shrugs and smiles. "To use an old Baptist term, he answered the altar call."

My dad nods. "Methodists call it that, too, although they don't do it very often. I still don't see where you are going."

"I'm a long winded old priest," Father Alex says. "The point is, by making his vows in this community of faith, RD would be asking his family and friends to help him keep the vows he makes. So it becomes a covenant with the community, too, not just one between him and God."

My father smiles for the first time since this conversation began. "Damned if you don't sound like a flaming Congregationalist, Alex. RD's great grandfather was a preacher from Massachusetts."

"My bishop tells me that, too," Father Alex says. "Anyway, it's your call, my friend."

My father looks at my mother a long while. "You really want to do this, don't you?" he asks so softly I can barely hear. She nods and he turns to me. "This is what you want, too, RD?" I don't give him a chance to ask twice, I nod and tell him yes. "All right," he says. "Do you want to do it here or back home?"

"Here," I tell him. "Can Johnny's grandma be my God-mother? That would make me and Johnny God-brothers."

"Out of the mouths of children," Father Alex says, shaking his head. I wonder if I have said something wrong. Then he says, "Talk about Blood-brothers! Wow!" I don't know what he is talking about, but I know it must really be something.

What is amazing to me is how Father Alex's words stay with me over the years. As an adult, one piece of the puzzle will fall into place when I hear a gospel choir sing "Are you washed in the Blood of the Lamb". The other will fall into place when I remember a movie where two guys, an Indian and a white man, cut their hands and bind them together to become blood brothers. I don't know if real Indians ever really did this, but I will know then in my mind what I knew in my heart as a child. I will know that somehow Johnny and I are brothers in the deepest sense, brothers in the Blood of Christ. We eat the same Bread and drink the same Cup, and somehow the sacred elements become part of each of us, in body and an in spirit. This is what binds us together, the same Blood running in our veins. Nor does it matter that I am Celt and he is French-Lakota. Despite differences in the culture and history we are born into, this is our common union, our communion, and this is what Father Alex understood so clearly.

An hour later, with Johnny standing at my side, I find out why the toddler was so upset. I am baptized at the faucet where he got his morning bath, and even though I have all my clothes on, the water is very cold, so cold it almost burns. Somehow, though, it also makes me feel very warm, too, warm the way I felt when I took communion.

The whole thing doesn't take very long and when we are done, Johnny and I head off the foot race. When we get there, the man on the PA system is the same fellow that talked so loud at the arena. This time he is not talking so loud. Something is wrong with the system and he is having to use a megaphone. What he is trying to do is to group those who will be racing into age groups.

Like all things in Indian country, it takes a while to get the race organized. When the racers began gathering in different areas, someone has the PA system working again and the announcer turns the volume up so loud the system howls. Off to the side I see one of the men standing around pull the plug and the whole group laughs as the announcer tries to get it going again. When he picks up his megaphone again, the man plugs the power line in and the system feeds back.

The announcer throws the megaphone down like it is on fire and the man at the side unplugs the power again. By now people in the stands see what is going on and begin to laugh and cheer. Some of the men down front begin teasing the announcer. Then one of them jumps up on the stage and does something to the dials. The man at the power plug connects it again and the system works fine. The man on the stage laughs and tells the announcer it might help to maybe not talk so loud. He seems to be scaring the microphone. Everyone laughs again.

By now the race groups are forming and I notice Johnny joins the group of older kids. The announcer notices this, too, and tells Johnny he needs to get in the ten to fourteen group. The younger kids will race first. Johnny shakes his head and stays where he is. Then the announcer tells him he's supposed to be fourteen years old to run with the older kids, but Johnny ignores him and begins warming up. Someone yells something at the announcer and he shrugs and tells the youngest kids to line up.

The first race is only fifty yards and it doesn't take long. The kids are six to eight years old, but some of them are pretty fast. Others can hardly finish the race. Then the two middle groups run, both a hundred yards and the crowd cheers the winner. Then it is time for the oldest group and I see Johnny take his place at the far end of the start line. I climb as high as I can into the stands to watch since this is a full quarter mile race.

When the gun sounds the big kids take off, bunching together as they approach the first turn. Johnny disappears into the crowd, but then I see him falling, holding his foot. Someone has tripped him and he falls into the cinder track face down. Then he rolls to his feet again and takes off, following the pack, and people in the stands start cheering.

Johnny has lost thirty yards, but by the time the main body of racers has come out of the first turn, he has almost made it up. Then I see him cut wide, to the outside and he begins to pass older boys. When he enters the final turn, Johnny is in seventh place and he manages to pass three more runners in the turn. The people in the stands are on their feet now, cheering him on.

Then it happens. As he is passing the first runner, the bigger boy bumps Johnny, almost knocking him down. This time Johnny staggers, but does not go all the way down. Yet, the finish line is only fifty yards away and the older boy gains a five yard lead.

What happens next is a story I will hear told on the reservation for years to come. Rather than trying to pass the older boy, Johnny runs directly toward him. With just ten yards to go he grabs the older boy by his braided hair and leaps onto his back, riding him like a horse across the finish line, and throwing him face forward into the dirt five yards beyond. When the people see this they go wild, stamping their feet on the wooden risers and letting out the scariest sound I have ever heard.

The older boy jumps up and starts to come after Johnny, but two men standing by grab him and hold him off. Then there is silence as the race judge comes forward. He looks at Johnny and the older boy, then points at Johnny. He tells the crowd Johnny's arm was wrapped around the older boy's nose and crossed the finish line first. Once again the crowd cheers and someone begins to beat a drum. The older boy looks at Johnny for a long time. Then he shakes his head and makes the same hand motion the old man made at Willie's funeral. Johnny nods and does the same. *Waste!* It is done. Throwing back his head, the older boy lets out a whoop and begins to dance. Within moments every man in the crowd is on the field dancing with him.

I jump down onto the field and begin dancing with the crowd. When I look up I see my father coming toward me through the crowd. He looks worried until he sees that I am all right. Then one of the men says something to him and he nods and begins shuffling his feet along with the drum, too, but he looks funny and I laugh. Then my father laughs and the men start laughing, too. Pretty soon everyone around us is laughing so hard they can barely stand up.

When we talk about this that night at home, my father tells me he's never seen anything like it before. Lakota are quiet people most of the time. Yet when they let out the scary yell, he heard them all the way to the arena and came running. He knew I was there with Johnny and he knew something was wrong. When I ask him about the scary sound, he tells me he thinks what we heard was the old war cry. My grandfather is listening to us and nods. He says he has heard about these things but never seen them. Then he says something strange. The old ways are in the blood.

As a man I remember my grandfather's words. I think about them often and I believe he is right. We foolishly think we are in charge of our lives and the way we are. Then something happens and the old memories are there, strong as the day they were formed. Then we find ourselves walking along ancient ways we never imagined ourselves taking, and doing things which seem familiar but which we've never done.

Never in all the years which have passed since that have I heard that terrible cry by so many voices again. In some ways I hope I never do again. Yet I know I will never forget it. Nor did Johnny. I came across something he wrote when he was in the Marines years later. Somehow it fits into all of this and into the craziness which would come later on. I think when he wrote it he was remembering that day at the Rosebud *wacipi* when he ran with the older boys and counted his first coup.

> There seems to be this wild thing within me
> which cannot be caged or housebroken
> or truly tamed that howls within my sleep

to be released to roam wild and free
among these hills and mountains
I know as Home
As with all wild things, this wild One
whom I call Coyote or sometimes Condor
and is brother to the wolf, to the eagle and the fox,
the badger and the crow, can only be honored
and allowed to give life to my soul
or destroyed, taking me with it....

The old ways are in the blood. And those of us who think we have control over our being are sadly mistaken. I am convinced the very best we can do is learn who we really are and come to terms with it. I heard Father Alex tell my father once that he believes our demons and our angels are one and the same. When we try to subject them to our own will they become the devils which plague us. Yet when we surrender them to the tender mercies of God they become the guardians who seek us out and lead us Home.

The Winner of Our Discontent

5 July 4, 1976. They call this place Winner. That's what the *wasicun* call it but the Lakota know it by another name. I have heard some of the men call it *cesli,* which means Stinker, or what the *wasicun* call dung. So to us what the whites call the city of Winner is what we call a pile of shit.

I don't like it here. Nobody knows who I am. They don't know of my grandfather or my mother, and they don't care what family I'm from. All they see is another Indian, and it isn't just the whites. The Indians are just as bad. Most of them are from Milk's Camp and they look down on anyone who isn't. Even with my own Sicangu, those who claim to be pure Lakota look down on us who they call half breeds. They don't know who I am or what kind of man, and they don't care. I'm not one of them and that's what matters.

The people from Okreek are all right, though. Some of them are my relatives and know my family. They helped my mother get started here after my grandfather was killed at Pine Ridge. They helped when other people turned away. My mother says all the others were afraid of AIM. She says our family from Okreek lived far enough away to feel safe, but I don't care. Family is family, and they wouldn't help. They wouldn't even help us stay in my grandfather's house when the tribal council kicked us out. The council said my mother wasn't on the tribal rolls and they gave our house to someone else, even though my brothers and sisters are on the rolls. So we had to move. On top of everything else, we had to leave and this was the only place we could find, Shit City, South Dakota.

The strange thing is we never knew what happened or who did it. All we know is my grandfather left one morning headed for Pine Ridge. He was taking food to some relatives of our neighbor, the one who was always getting drunk and fighting with his wife. Then he didn't come home, and it wasn't until late the next night one of the tribal police showed up to tell us he was found shot dead in a ditch near Porcupine Butte. Whoever shot him took his wallet and everything but his shirt, which is why it took so long to identify him. They never found his beat

49

up old pickup.

Then the stories started. The BIA police said it must have been a simple robbery, but word got out he was shot by mistake by the FBI. They made it look like a robbery to keep it quiet. Things were tense enough with the siege going on at Wounded Knee and the FBI didn't want more trouble. Then the FBI came and talked to us. Their questions made it sound like my grandfather was one of the radicals. They said he was smuggling supplies to the people at Wounded Knee but I know he wasn't. I know because I was there one day with another guy, and when my grandfather heard about it he came and told me doing that could make trouble for the family.

I guess it did because that was when all the stories started that it was AIM who shot him for being an Apple Indian, red on the outside but white all the way through. Maybe that's why they didn't let us stay. They didn't want trouble with AIM.

Not long after that the tribal police told us we had to move and no one from our *tiospaye* stood up for us. None of our relatives in Parmalee lifted a hand to help us find another place, and none of them helped us move. They knew my grandfather was a good man and they knew my mother most of her life but they wouldn't help a damned bit. That was almost as bad as his getting shot, maybe worse. They made our whole family outcasts and our clan let it happen... (from an early journal of John K. Lyons)

I do not remember when it happens, not the month or year or even the season. Is it cold or hot, or is it spring or fall? I do not remember exactly, but I think it must be in the fall of our second year of high school. It may be September or even November, but what is remarkable is that even after all the years, I see each detail quite clearly, just as clearly as if it happens this moment. This surprises me, but I don't know why. Students of the human mind tell us time has no real meaning down deep where we live. The ticking of the clock only matters to the thinking part of ourselves, to the mature persona we like to think is who we really are. This is what we present to the outer world, the definition of ourselves which lives and moves and draws its being from the order we try to impose on the universe and on ourselves. This is the I of our conceit, those of us who believe we are in control of our own being.

Yet there is another side to us, the child we are and were and ever shall be. This is the dark, unknown side which lives in the long shadow cast by our self deceit, and to this eternal child, time is meaningless.

There is only the eternal now, and the fright which happens yesterday is as present now as it is then. There is joy here and great delight in all creation, but there is also fear of the bogey man who might hurt us and the dreadful things which go bump, moaning through the night. To that child we ever are, the world is ever new and our history is never ended.

Speak of the devil! This is not where I want to go with this. What matters is not me, but John K. This is about him and the whole idea is to tell his story. Yet, the strands of our separate lives are so intertwined so early on it is hard to draw them apart. No, we were not born joined at the hip. Nor do we see each other that often growing up. We never go to the same school until his dad is killed by an angry AIMer at the second siege of Wounded Knee. Yet ever since that first meeting at Willie's funeral there is a bond so strong that what happens to each of us separately seems to affect us both. Nor do I understand this completely. I am a hardheaded newsman and don't have much truck for spiritual crap. John K and I come from very different worlds, different cultures. In many ways we are quite different. Yet, it is like we were twin spirits formed in the same fire of a cosmic forge and welded one to the other through eternity.

No, I'm not religious, either, though Johnny grows up that way. He is Roman Catholic, one of Father Alex's altar boys. I don't even see myself as very spiritual, either. I tend to side with H.L. Menken, the journalist. Like him, I hope that if I'm wrong, the God I meet after death is a forgiving one who accepts apologies. Yet I am not an atheist, either. Atheism is too absurd for words. I have seen too many self proclaimed atheists who protest too much. Their lives are centered around whatever He Or She Or It Who Does Not Exist. The God they deny claims their lives as surely as Jehovah consumes a shoutin' Methodist!

No, I call myself agnostic, in the fullest sense of the word. I look it up in Greek and it is the exactly the right word for me. A-gnosis literally means without knowledge. To put it another way, I simply don't know. There may be a God or there may not be, and if there is, the jury is still out whether or not this is a kindly being, or even one who gives a damn. I don't know and I don't think the bishop of Rome does, either. Not for sure. The best anyone can have is hope, not knowledge. What little hope I claim is based on the integrity of Father Alex himself, on something he told me after Willie's funeral. "Randy," he tells me, in that solemn, gravely voice I remember so well. "You have received the body and blood of Jesus. You have taken it into yourself. Now it is part of you, and you are his forever. Don't ever let anyone tell you that's not true."

Somehow those words touch the scared little kid I was and am. This comforts the frightened child who lives way down deep in the darkest shadows. I know that since he said that, I have never been afraid like I used to be, not ever again. No, what scares me now is not whatever is out there, but what is in here. What scares me is who else lives in the dark corners of my heart and soul along side the eternal child. Like the Shadow on the old radio show, I know what evil lurks in the hearts of men. I see it looking in a mirror and seeing my own. It scares me to death.

I know. I'm getting ahead of my story telling you this, but please bear with me. You will soon see what I mean. What you need to understand is how important it is, even though it is only a passing incident to the others. Yes, it is not one they are likely to forget, but it is one of many which were part of growing up in that time and place. To the others it just happens and passes with the ebb and tide of our youth. Yet in hearing the story, I think maybe you can understand why I now remember each detail so clearly, why it became so important. God knows, I'd like to forget. At the time I shut it out from memory as quickly as it happens, but how did I think I would not remember?

I do know the incident takes place during high school. It has to for me to do what I recall. For the three summers following grade school I work on my grandfather's ranch, helping out with everything from building fence line to bucking bales. Every year I take on more and I come to the full strength of a grown man very young. My father and mother are tall and slender, and he tells me I am a throwback to an older line of the family. As a matter of fact, he tells me there were many times he felt like throwing me back and I am sure he did. I have children of my own. The point is, I carry the ancient Celtic genes from my mother's father, who I never met. Like him I am stocky and uncommonly powerful. I carry his fire of a Celtic temper, too, although I never discover this until my own inner Rob Roy leaps out of the shadows, kicking ass and taking names. Old Rob may be a good one to have on your side in a brawl, but he is flat scary. I rarely see him, but I never know when I will. This worries me.

Anyway, when the scene goes down, we are in the locker room cleaning up after football practice. I guess it could be track season but I'm almost sure it's football. Jenny knows for sure, as women do, but I'm not going to ask her. Not for all the tea in China. Call it male pride and

I'll answer, "Amen, brother, alleluia!"

What I do know is we are hot and sweaty, standing around outside the locker room the way we do. We carry our towels slung over our shoulders and we joke around. While we wait to shower we play teenage grab-ass, each of us very careful not to touch, or be caught looking directly at, the naked manhood of another. So even if we seem relaxed and are fooling around, there's an uneasy tension which lies among us. None of us wants to be considered queer, and we're very cautious in our vulnerability, even as we put on a good show that fools no one. The only acceptable touch when we are naked is that which causes pain, a punch or a slap on the arm or back. Never on the naked buttocks. Naked buttocks are way too sexual to be treated casually, and the only acceptable touch there is the stinging lash of a wet towel, snapping an angry welt. Nor is towel snapping done lightly. It is an article of faith among us that a hit in the wrong place with a snapped towel could unman us, so we are careful how we dodge. A sore welt on the butt for a few days is one thing. Pissing through a straw for life is another.

This is how we usually are, but today there is very little kidding and no towel snapping. I am one of the last players off the field. It was a tough practice for us all today, especially for me, since I cost the whole team extra laps. So I slump on the bench for a while before stripping off and storing my gear. When I get to the shower room, most of the guys are already done, but there is a cluster standing by the entry. As I approach, I see them looking at something, passing it back and forth, but I don't join the group. The shower is still half full of people taking a long time and horsing around. So I sit on a bench in the hallway to wait. I want solitude, not grab-ass.

I hear the guys by the entry laughing, but I don't look up. My mind is still on practice. I cannot believe how easy I was to fake out or how many balls I dropped in passing drill. I have good hands and a strong grip, and if I can reach a ball, I can normally bring it in. But not today. Today I am all thumbs and my eyes are on the floor as I recall the coach's cutting words. What hurts is I know he is right. I am not in the game today. My mind is on other things, on the dance Saturday night and on Jenny, who I have known all my life and who I just saw clearly for the first time Saturday.

Sweet Jenny. How did I miss her growing up? Last year she was a skinny little kid, a sister of one of my friends. Johnny introduces her as his sister, but that's the Lakota way. She is his first cousin in the English way of reckoning kin. Unlike Johnny's mother, her sister married a white man and Jenny grew up on a farm near town. So she's not full Lakota, not even as much as Johnny. They are what full blood Lakota call breeds, and this is not a term of endearment. She is a member on the tribal rolls, as are our children, but she doesn't look Indian. Growing up, I know her only as a scrawny little white girl from one of the German farms. Even though her mother looks very Indian, somehow it never quite computes that Jenny is, too.

As a matter of fact, I do not remember paying Jenny much mind at all. She is just there, one of the many kids who live near by. Then over one summer something happens and she becomes a woman. Yet, I never really notice until Saturday at the dance. There is no reason to notice her. She is two classes behind Johnny and me, and the girls in our class have blossomed into distractions, too.

I am talking to her brother, not paying much mind to anything and I hear them call a Sadie Hawkins round. This means it is lady's choice, and I try to duck out before I get asked. I don't mind being a gentleman, and I really like to dance, but there is a girl in my class who goes out of her way to be in my line of vision. Not that she's bad looking, just a little pushy. I don't want to hurt her feelings, but I don't want to dance with her, either. So I try to slip away.

Then there she is, Jenny, asking me to dance. I am so taken back I can hardly talk, but she laughs and hauls me out onto the dance floor. Out of the corner of my eye I see she has rescued me from the clutches of my not-so-secret admirer. When I tell her this later, she laughs and says what I didn't see was how fast she moved to get ahead of the other girl.

When we arrive on the dance floor, the song is a slow dance. It's a two-step, and as we move around the floor I'm painfully aware of the gentle curves of her body pressed close to mine. I feel her warmth through layers of light cloth which are almost not there. I am overcome by the scent of her perfume and my imagination goes wild. I know she is the sister of a friend. I know she is Johnny's cousin and I mean no disrespect. Yet, we are in that season of life filled with hormones which tell us it is time to mate, and this daughter of Eve is full of grace. I wonder what it would be like to kiss her full lips, to feel her arms holding me tight, her tawny skin pressed against mine as I....

Suddenly, I am aware just how much I am responding to her, and I feel my face grow hot and flushed. I close my eyes, curse my body for betraying me like this. I try to think of something else, but when I close my eyes, I am only more aware of Jenny's warm presence. I see us dancing in the moonlight, clothed only in smiles. I open my eyes and look down, and her eyes meet mine. They are deep wells of mystery drawing me into them. She smiles and I am so relieved. There is hope. She is not offended. Maybe she thinks it's my pocket knife pressing her leg so insistently.

Then the music ends. I stand there not knowing what to say. I am dressed in poplin trousers and a light shirt, and if she moves away, there is no hiding the evidence of my attraction. I feel like a deer caught in the headlights. What if she looks down? And if I move away, everyone will surely notice my shame. They will laugh and I will never live it down. So I hold her for a long moment, looking into her eyes. I hear my voice thanking her for asking me to dance and telling her how nice she looks. She laughs and I realize she knows. She knows I am not carrying a pocket knife and she understands my shame. She is defending my pride, and when she smiles again, I am overcome with gratitude.

Then the band fires up again, this time with a fast polka. Without asking, I swing Jenny out onto the dance floor in a wild whirl. She is almost as tall as I am and far from skinny, but she moves as lightly as a feather as I take her through the spins and turns. Half way through the dance the band picks up the pace and I am dimly aware there are fewer and fewer others on the floor. We begin whirling faster and faster, dancing with wild abandon out onto that thin edge which lies between grace and catastrophe. Yet she never falters, never tightens with fear. She is with me every step of the way. I have never known such trust. Never have I held a partner so bold, whose every move anticipates mine.

When the music ends I am thunderstruck. We are alone in the middle of the gym floor, surrounded by cheering crowd, but they seem far away. I don't know what has happened, but I know the universe has changed. We have crossed a boundary, Jenny and me. We have just made love for the first time. While the pooling of our genes will take place much later, this wild moment is when our first child is conceived, and I cannot speak. I stand there stunned, looking into Jenny's eyes, holding her in my arms.

Then she is gone. She gives me a warm smile and thanks me, but I am speechless. I see in her eyes she knows something has happened between us, but I am in shock. I hear her sweet voice tell me she has to go now. Her brother is leaving and she came with him, so she has to go. Before

I can find my voice, she is out the door. Before I can stir my feet to go after them and offer her a ride, they are off and away. I am left standing in the middle of the dance floor with what Johnny tells me is a stupid look on my face. Nor do I remember leaving the dance floor, driving my date home, or much else which happens in the days between.

So I miss plays. I drop passes and stumble into people and things. Only the bitterness of the coach's wrath cuts through the fog and after extra laps around the field I am sitting on a bench outside the shower room. I am wondering what has happened to my well ordered life.

Then I hear someone say my name. I look up. Three members of the team are standing in front of me, all looking at me oddly. I realize I have just missed something else, whatever it is one of them just said.

"You've really got it bad, don't you?" one of them asks. His name is Ronny Teal but we call him Duck. He is big, a fullback, one of the fastest runners we have. I have known him all my life and we are friendly.

"Yeah," I admit, trying to fend him off. Duck is like a bulldog with a rag when he gets a football in his hands or an idea in his head. Pull him off the floor by his teeth and he still won't let go, which ain't all bad. This is one reason we'll go to State this year. My hands are another, even if I'm not worth damn today. But right now I don't want to mess with Duck. All I want is to be left alone. "Yeah," I admit, trying to throw him off the scent. "I've had a shitty day. I owe you one for the extra laps."

I see from their grins I haven't fooled them a bit. They know. "That's not what I hear," Duck says. "I hear you got a new girl friend."

Normally, I could act mad and Duck would back off. I may not be the fastest man on the team, but I am certainly the strongest. That's how I make the all state team three years in a row as a tackle on defense. I've been known to move two guys twice my size and still make the tackle, so they don't mess with me. Especially when I get mad. That doesn't happen often, not off the field, but when it does, it gets pretty hairy. So people don't go out of their way to piss me off.

Today the anger deserts me. I feel a deep flush rising up my neck and I know I can't fool Duck and the other two. All I can do is take whatever ragging they dish out and hope they get tired of it soon. That's how bad it is with me. I can't even defend myself.

Duck sees the flush right away. For an instant I see something like compassion flicker in his eyes. Were we alone, he would back off, honoring the bond men share in their vulnerability to their deepest feelings. Yet the others are there. They are not as aware as Duck. Seeing my vulnerability, they grin. One of them nudges Duck.

"Yeah," he says. I can see Duck is embarrassed, but he can't back off. "Well, here," he says, thrusting something into my chest. I grab it by reflex. "Maybe this will cheer you up."

The others laugh as I look down. What I am holding is a skin magazine, one as famous for its articles as for the quality of its photos of nude women. It is opened to the trademark center fold, and as I take it, this falls open. Nor is it the normal centerfold. I have seen those, but I have never seen one like this. In one of those moments shrouded in serendipity, the photographer has captured his subject in the fullness of her being. The long legs are perfect, as are the graceful arms and hands hanging naturally her side. Long auburn hair hangs over one shoulder, hiding a perfect breast. The other is in full view and magnificent. The long line of her stomach is breathtaking, ending in a wisp of auburn below a delicate navel, and as the photo is snapped, her full mouth is slightly open, as if she is about to greet an old friend.

Yet is it her eyes which capture my attention. It is the eyes which speak of the mystery which she is. They are like deep green pools, full of the innocent assurance of a lioness. Strangely enough, I understand that while she is not dressed, she is no more naked than any other creature of the wild. Within the innocence of her beauty she is better clothed than the best corseted matron, and what the photographer has produced is a work of art. Setting out to capture her beauty, he has revealed her soul, and it is as if I am looking into the depths of her being as a woman. I see within the eyes of this young woman exactly what I saw in the depths of Jenny's eyes, all I could ever want as a man. Without ever seeing her undressed, I know this is how Jenny will look, and I respond with all my heart and mind and soul.

Then I hear the others laugh. One of Duck's companions points out the obvious. "Hey, R.D.'s got a 'ard on!" I feel blood rising along my neck as fire ignites within my belly. Even so, I get up slowly, drop the magazine on the bench and turn to walk away, hiding my erection with my towel. As I do so, I am trembling.

That could have been the end of it. I walk away and cool off. Then I make peace with Duck at some point, maybe, and rack the shit of all of them on the football field. Yet the other kid is new to town, trying to work his way into the crowd. Out of the corner of my eye I see him pick up the magazine and leer at the picture. "Hell's bells!" he crows. "This looks like Jenny!"

This time the fire in my belly is rage, an intense blue flame burning away all emotion. I am not aware of feeling anger or hurt, or anything at all. I am strangely cold and detached, as if I am watching a movie of my actions from a great distance. I feel myself spin faster than I can imagine. I see my hand fly out, shove Duck in the chest so hard he slams into the shower wall with a loud boom. Then, before the others can respond, I am on them like a cat. I grab each of them by the neck, slam their heads together and throw them to the floor. Somewhere far away in the background I hear someone shout my name, but I pay no attention. A moment later I have lifted each of them by the neck and thrust them against the wall over the bench. I see my fingers dig into their flesh so deep their faces turn red and their tongues protrude, and a detached part of my mind notes how strange they look as I meet out justice like an avenging angel.

Suddenly, I feel something slam into my back. Someone is trying to pin my arms and neck in a full Nelson. As my head goes down I see dozens of hands pulling at my arms to free my prey. Then knowing hands find a pressure point in my neck and the strength goes out of my arms. Those I am holding against the wall drop like sacks of flour, collapsing on the bench.

"What in the hell is going on!" someone demands. It is the coach. I hear him tell Johnny to let me go. The pressure on my head eases, but not completely. I hear Johnny's voice in my ear. He is asking if I can control myself if he lets go. I nod and he helps me to my feet.

Again the coach demands to know what is going on. I open my mouth, but no words come. I hear Johnny tell the coach they insulted my girl. I hear Duck tell him this is true. The other two are still trying to catch their breath. The coach gives me a long hard look, then nods and I know it is over. He tells us he wishes we would grab-ass as hard on the field as we do in the shower room, then gives the four of us ten extra laps for tomorrow. Duck tries to get me off, telling the coach they are the ones who started it, but the coach shakes his head and I know he's right. I did not have to respond. Not that way. All they hurt was my pride.

Johnny looks at me intently. Without asking he knows where I am. Nothing like this has ever happened to me, before or since and I am scared thinking where it might have gone. I believe I would have killed them both if he did not intervene, right there and then. The strange thing is I bear no malice toward any of them, neither today nor back then. They are not bad fellows, and both have become good friends of mine. We go after walleyes together every year on the Missouri, Tom, Hank, and Duck whenever he's in town. Johnny comes with us, too, every once in a while, until he's too far gone. Yet, none of this would come to be except for Johnny. I would have killed them without mercy and this is not a comfortable thing to know about myself.

Johnny knows this and he's waiting for me when I walk out of the locker room. Nor does he say anything about it. He just jumps down from the wall where he's sitting and gets in the truck. I give him a ride all the time, so there is nothing unusual about this. Except today there is. He is here because he knows I need him and he's good at waiting, like most Lakota are.

We drive around for a while. I swing by the Dairy Queen and get us a couple of shakes, vanilla for me, chocolate for him. We never have to ask. It's always the same. He reaches for his change, but I won't let him pay and he nods his thanks.

This is the way it usually is, and it's not a big deal. I know how tight things are at home for his family. Except for what Johnny makes pumping gas, I don't know what they live on. So when I go to visit I try to take along a sack of groceries for his mom, and I try not to get there at dinner time, either. Not because it's another mouth to feed. I always bring plenty. No, the reason is I don't like the way his mother cooks. I'd never tell her this, but good cooking isn't that common among the Lakota. Or maybe it's more fair to say they have a different way of preparing food, one that I don't really like. They like it, and that is what matters. Maybe to them the way we cook tastes like fried dog scat. Not that I've sampled that recently.

While we sit drinking our shakes, Johnny builds himself a smoke. He knows the risk he is taking. The coach will suspend him if he sees him. It doesn't matter that Johnny is our fastest man and ball carrier. Duck is the only one on the team who stands a chance of catching him if Johnny gets into the secondary. Even so, he will have to sit out the next game if the coach catches him, and maybe I will, too, for being in the same car. At the moment, I could give a shit, and when he fires it up, I hold my hand out and take a couple of drags when Johnny passes it over.

I don't know what Johnny is smoking, but it tastes terrible and smells funny. I ask Johnny what the hell kind of rope he's smoking. He laughs and tells me it sure ain't sisal. I tell him I'm going across the street and get us some decent smokes, and he laughs again. I wonder what is so funny. When I open the door and try to walk it's like I had a couple of beers. I ask Johnny what the hell, and he laughs again and tells me it's wildwood weed. Hemp. Grass. Mary Johannah.

"Jesus," I tell him, looking around. Nobody is paying us much attention but I can see the local cop inside the Dairy Queen having coffee with the mayor. I start the engine and pull out slowly trying to avoid attracting attention. They may want to legalize it on the West Coast, but possession of marijuana is still a felony in South Dakota. A lot of people passing through are given long vacations by the state for possession. So I head west out of town on a county road, scared and pissed at Johnny. I ask him why the hell he didn't tell me what he was smoking. He shrugs and tells me it won't hurt me. He says he picks it himself on the rez and there's nothing else in it. Pure grass.

I'm not convinced, but I head toward Dog Ears Butte. There's not much out there but miles and miles of wheat, and that's where we go at times to have a beer. Even with the lower drinking age, we're too young to buy it or possess it, and out there you can see a car coming a long way off. So there is plenty of time to ditch the booze if we see the sheriff or the game warden headed our way.

When we get there I park the truck so we can see a long way in every direction. Johnny rolls a couple more cigarettes and hands me one. He tells me it works better if I hold in the smoke for as long as I can. I ask him if he is sure this isn't addictive and he tells me it's not. He tells me he has been smoking for two or three years now and he can take it or leave it. Sometimes he runs out and doesn't smoke for weeks. He tells me it will help me mellow out. Then he laughs and tells me there is no hangover, either. That's one of the best parts, he says. No hangover.

I'm still scared but I decide to try it. I know Johnny would never do anything to hurt me, so I watch what he does. At first it feels funny when I do it, and I get the same feeling I get when I hold my breath swimming underwater a long distance. That first gulp of fresh air makes me a little light headed. I'm a little disappointed, but even straight vodka takes a minute or two to produce a buzz. So I do it again, sucking the smoke deep into my lungs and holding it in as long as I can. I don't feel much different and I wonder what the big deal is. Then all of a sudden it's like stepping on the express elevator. I feel my body rising like a helium balloon and I grab the steering wheel to keep from floating out the open window of the truck.

Johnny sees this and starts laughing. He asks what's happening and starts laughing again when I try to tell him. Then I start laughing. I don't know why, but what we are trying to tell each other is the funniest thing in the world. We are laughing so hard we are folded up on the truck seat with tears running down our face. Later this will scare me. The sheriff could arrive with red lights and siren and we wouldn't know it until he busted us. We'd think it was funny as hell and laugh all the way to jail.

After a while we calm down and smoke some more. This time Johnny turns on the radio and we tune in the local station. There is a special show on, featuring a jazz band coming to Sioux Falls, and we listen. I don't care for jazz or blues, but tonight it sounds different. There is a sax player that is very good and I get caught up in the music. Time slows down and I can see each musical note as it floats out of the speaker, like balloons floating in the wind. The notes look like they do on paper but they are three dimensional. As they move through the air toward me, I feel them touch my body and float into it, becoming part of me. Then the song ends and I feel incredible sadness, as if someone I just met and really like died.

I feel Johnny touch my arm, hear his voice speaking from far away asking if I am all right. The question surprises me. I tell him I am feeling great and he lifts my hand to my cheek, asks why I am weeping. I am surprised to find my cheek wet with tears, as if I have been crying for hours. Then I notice my eyes are full, too, and suddenly it is over. At that moment I am clear in my mind, no longer stoned. There is still a warm glow which surrounds me and I feel better, as if I have been purged, but nothing has changed. A thought drifts through my mind. I have seen the face of my Accuser and I am he. Yet, I don't understand what this means. I say it out loud and Johnny gives me an odd look, then shrugs. I'm sure he thinks it's the weed talking.

I think I am on the threshold of a major epiphany, but I don't know what it is. I cannot quite get my mind around it, so I put it aside. I begin to talk about Jenny and what took place in the gym. Not that I'm talking to Johnny. We have not had a chance to talk much since early last week, but I am not filling him in so much as I am trying to make sense of it myself. We do this a lot, Johnny and me. We listen while the other one tells himself what he needs to know. I know it sounds strange, but it works.

When I first start talking, Johnny seems kind of vague. I realize he is still stoned, but I know he is listening because he always listens. Even when I'm shoveling out manure. Now as I talk, he comes more and more into focus. By the time I am done, he is back on planet Earth. Somehow, he seems uncommonly sad. I start to ask why, but don't. When it is time, he will tell me. He always does.

We sit there silent a long time. What I don't know is that he is bleeding to death inside, his heart cut to shreds with my words. What Johnny doesn't tell me then, Jenny tells me years after we are married. She is his first cousin, but he is in love with her. She has a crush on him, too, and growing up she dreams of marrying him some day. Yet he never tells her how he feels, and then we dance. We fall into each other's lives and into each other's hearts, and she only learns the truth from his mother long after he is gone.

I don't know this, of course. I don't know that the sadness I sense grows from a choice he just then makes, a tragic choice he takes with the two people he loves most. I would like to think I could make the same choice in his place, but I don't know. There are things which go far deeper than friendship, and in Jenny I have met bone of my bone and flesh of my flesh. Would I sacrifice my love of her for his sake? No. I am sure of that, just as I am certain his love is far greater than mine.

After a while I need to whiz, so I get out and stand by the truck. The wind is out of the southwest and I turn my back to it. Looking out over the prairie I can see the lights of town and the moon coming up, maybe a week past full. It is clear tonight, no dust in the air, and even in bright moonlight, the stars are tiny lights on a deep blue-black sky. I think of Jenny, wonder where she is. I have not seen her since the dance. When I tried to call on Sunday, her brother said she was out of town. When I tried again last night, he said the same. That's a strange thing for him to say. Where would she be out of town to on a school night?

When I get back in the truck, I ask Johnny. He tells me her brother is telling the truth. There is a family crisis in Corn Creek. One of their aunts is sick and Jenny is gone there with her mother to help out. I ask him if there is a telephone. He says the closest one is at a neighbor's house two miles away. I tell him I need to talk to her and he says he will take me tomorrow, or tonight if I want to go now.

I am torn. I have never missed a day of school in my life. Not unless I was sick. Nor have I missed a football practice. This week is a by, so we won't miss a game, but I would miss practice tomorrow. What do I tell my parents?

Johnny knows what I am thinking. He reads me like a book. He says to tell my parents there is a family problem in Corn Creek and he needs a ride there right away. His mother's car is already there and he can ride back with her. I tell him my dad will ask why he didn't go with her already. Johnny shrugs, says tell him the truth. Johnny has to work all night tonight and can't take off. He needs the job and the family needs the money.

When I tell my dad this an hour later, he frowns. He tells me Indians don't normally let things like that stand in their way. He says something else must be going on between Johnny and his family. As usual, he is right on both counts, but I don't know this right then. I tell him I am not aware of any problem Johnny is having with his family, and my dad nods. He says I'd never know if there was. He is right about that, too.

Then my dad looks at me. He is a very observant man. He asks how I am and I know he is aware of the fight at school. I shrug and tell him I got in a shoving match in the shower. He nods and tells me he's glad I clarified that. The way he heard it I took out Duck and two offensive linemen. I agree they were pretty offensive, all right, and add that a young lady's honor was at issue.

Dad smiles at my play on words and nods. "So you need to get out of Dodge for a few days, then?" he asks, more like a statement than a question. I nod and he wants to know if I will be back by Monday morning. I tell him I will and he says all right, he will cover for me. This means he will send a note to school and keep my mother off my back. I thank him and tell him I need to get packed. He nods and goes back to his paper. As I am about to leave the room, he calls my name and I turn back. He tells me to drive carefully and to give his compliments and best regards to Jenny. And her family, of course, he adds. As I walk down the hall I hear him chuckling to himself. Offensive linemen, indeed!

The next morning Johnny and I are on the way early. Normally, I'd head through Mission and up to White River the way my dad goes, but Johnny wants to stop and see someone in Wood. So we head up to Witten and across through Moser. There's not much to see in either place, just some farms and a few homesteads closer together than usual in this part of the world, but when we get to Moser, Johnny tells me to turn south. There's something he wants to show me.

A mile south of Moser we turn east on a dirt road. It looks like it leads into a cow pasture, although I see the roof line of some buildings over a small rise. When I stop at a wire stretch gate a half mile down the road, Johnny jumps out and opens it. Some cows near by raise their heads to watch us so he closes it again after I pass through. Then some of the cows begin to come toward us and Johnny laughs. He says they think we're going to feed them.

I start to go toward the buildings, but Johnny tells me to follow some ruts leading south from the gate. When we turn I can see something ahead of us but it takes me a minute to recognize it as a cemetery. I ask Johnny why we are coming here and he tells me he heard some of his relatives were buried in the Episcopal cemetery near Moser and wants to see if he can find their graves.

When I park by the cemetery gate I can see someone has been taking care of the place. The grass is high all the way to the fence, but inside it is cut short and trimmed back next to the stones. While Johnny wanders around looking for his relatives I begin to look at the grave markers.

Some of the graves have wooden crosses painted white but most of them are faded and peeling so bad I can't see the name or dates. Others have plain white military stones with block letters that are easy to read. And some of the stones are very old, so worn by rain and wind and snow that I have to stand to the side and close one eye to make it out. These are mostly simple slabs but one or two are tall square columns tapered in to a small square point at the top. One of these is leaning to one side and the way it is weathered, it looks a little obscene from where I am standing. I point it out to Johnny and he laughs. When we look at the delicate script writing on the side he tells me this must be one of the relatives he is looking for, a great warrior who had lots of children.

I notice a large new stone nearby and go to look at it. It is a flat polished slab over three feet tall, a couple of feet wide and almost a foot thick. When I get around to the other side I see the inscription cut in relief in large block letters, and I am surprised at what I see. The stone says this is the grave of Old Blind Woman, who was born 1833 and died on June 15, 1895. There is also a crucifix carved in relief at the top of the stone and behind the crucifix is what looks like a bow case. The case is decorated with ivy vines cut in relief, and what looks like three feathers or strips of braid hang from each end.

I ask Johnny who this is, but he doesn't know. I point out it must be someone who is pretty important for someone to spend so much money for such a large stone. He nods and says either that or important to someone who came up with the money. I don't really understand what he is saying until a long time later, but the Lakota are like that. When it comes to honoring the dead they will make all kinds of sacrifices. They may not have the money to buy winter coats for themselves or their kids, but they spare no expense when it comes to honoring the dead. Yet it's not just the Lakota. I have seen Hispanics and Irish and Poles do the same. There is always money for a good funeral, and it's almost like those left behind are trying to make up with a funeral what the dead were deprived in life. I can almost hear someone say, "Well, at least we gave her a good funeral."

Or maybe I am wrong. Yet, the good rabbi was quite clear on this point. Let the dead bury the dead, and come follow me. I take this to mean we are to tend to the needs of the least among us and looking around at all the money poured out into carved stones I cannot help thinking what it could do for the living. And I think the Muslims have it right. Even the Prophet is buried in an unmarked grave.

Even so, I have to admit there is something very moving about visiting the Vietnam Memorial when I am in Washington years later. There is also something deeply spiritual about coming to this country cemetery, which has survived the passing of the church next to it, and seeing such a monument to someone known only as Old Blind Woman.

These thoughts come to me as I am writing this years later, not as I stand there in the middle of nowhere wondering who this is who is buried here. What strikes me at the moment is what a strange name she carries, even among Indians. Other stones here have unusual names, some French and some translated from Lakota. Kills In Water. Medicine Blanket. One Horn Bull. All these names have stories behind them and the one I like best is First In Trouble. Was this someone who was always there when people were needed to fight, or was this someone who was always messing up? Indian names can go either way.

I don't know how long we stay at the cemetery, but it is getting warmer by the time we leave. The cows we saw came running after us and are all gathered around the truck. I try to wave them away and step in a fresh pile one of them has left behind. My foot goes out from under me and I land butt first on the pile. When I get up, I see Johnny laughing so hard he is bent over and almost falling down.

I yell and run after the cows, but they take off and am conscious of dung soaking through my pants. So I strip them off and try to clean them on the high grass, but all I do is smear it in worse. I hear the truck start and in a moment Johnny pulls up and tells me to get in the back. He says there's a place I can wash up down near the gate. I can see he's having a hard time keeping a straight face and I'm tempted to pick up a fresh pie and let him have it.

Then it hits me how funny I must look standing there on the prairie bare ass naked from the waist down, holding my pants in my hand, and I start laughing, too. By the time we get to the water trough by the gate, I am guffawing so hard I can hardly get a breath, but the icy water sobers me up pretty fast. I rinse out my jeans and shorts, and wipe my boots. Then I toss it all into the back of the truck and change into dry jeans. I'm lucky I brought a clean pair along, especially going to see Jenny. Some might think eau du bull is a romantic scent, but not me.

Johnny is pretty well recovered, too, by the time we get going. Yet, when we are half way to Wood he starts laughing and this sets me off again. Then he tells me he has a new Lakota name for me, Falls In Dung Bull.

When we get to Wood, Johnny tells me to turn north through town and then takes us on a series of turns that completely confuses me. I know which way we are headed but not exactly where we are and it doesn't look like many cars or trucks come this way. The last turn takes us to a stretch gate and across a hay field before it suddenly drops off into a deep coulee draining north toward the White River. Even then, all there is to see is a set of ruts leading up the coulee, until we drive around a stand of sumac. Then we see a cabin and a couple of outbuildings. The cabin is small, one large room, and built out of cut logs fitted so closely they need almost no chinking. The roof slopes up toward the center and is covered with shakes, but it takes me a minute to realize what I am seeing is built like the Navajo hogans I saw one summer in New Mexico. I can see three sides at once and there are no windows, only a covered doorway in the eastern wall. An iron chimney pipe sticks up from the center of the roof and I can see smoke drifting up from it.

As we drive up someone comes out of the cabin and watches us from the doorway. A lanky gray dog with fur like a coyote comes around the side of the cabin, but doesn't bark or approach the truck. Like the man in the doorway, it simply stands watching. The only sign of interest it shows is that its ears are pointed toward us. Then I see its eyes. They are dark yellow, not brown, and I realize I am not looking at a dog. What I see is a coyote, and I have never seen one this close. Then movement catches my eye and I see a large black bird settling on the bare limb of a tree across the coulee.

I start to get out of the truck, but Johnny's hand stops me. When I look at him, he shakes his head and puts a finger to his lips. Then he gets out of the truck and I see him crumple a cigarette into the palm of his hand and lift it up, letting the light wind take the spirit weed to itself. Then he say something in Lakota, but I cannot make out the words. I think it is a greeting, but it is one I have never heard before.

The man on the porch answers and steps out from under the cover. I see it is the old man who sang at Willie's funeral and I am surprised how easily he moves, almost like a young puma. His face looks a hundred years old, but he stands tall and straight, and when he sees me watching he waves a casual greeting, signaling me to get out.

When I do, I see the coyote has disappeared, but glancing to my right I can still see the raven sitting on its dry branch. It croaks and the old man says something. Again I cannot catch the words he says, but the raven flies away and the old man chuckles. "Nosy bird," he tells me. "All he wants is more corn." He reaches into a barrel by the door and throws a handful of golden grain out onto the ground. A moment later the raven is back on his branch. "He's waiting for us to go inside," the old man chuckles. "He doesn't want us to put him in the pot for supper."

Johnny and I follow the old man into the cabin. When I get inside I am surprised to see how light it is and how comfortable. The light comes from small windows set high in the southern walls and the large open room is heated by a heavy iron stove set in the very center. There is at least a cord of wood carefully stacked all the way to the roof line on the north wall, and on the west wall I see a single bunk covered with a woven wool blanket. There is a simple wooden table under window of the most southern wall and there are low shelves covered with different things on either side of the door. When my gaze comes back to the door I notice a lever action Winchester leaned against the portal, and I know it is loaded.

The old man is watching me look around. "You're surprised to find a Navajo up here, neh?" he murmurs and chuckles at the expression on my face. I tell him I didn't know he was Dinee, and he chuckles again. "I'm not," he tells me. "I'm Cherokee."

Johnny laughs politely at the joke, but the old man doesn't join him. He nods at him and says, "What Johnny doesn't know is I'm really Pawnee. That's why I keep a gun loaded by the door, with all these crazy Sioux around." The way he says the white name for the Lakota has a cutting rasp and I see a shocked look on Johnny's face. Then the old man begins to laugh and Johnny looks confused.

I wonder what in the world is going down and when I ask my dad about it later on, he laughs, too. He tells me the Pawnee are hereditary enemies of the Sioux and the old man was having some fun at Johnny's expense. He says the old man is Johnny's great grandfather, which would make Johnny a full eighth Pawnee if what the old man said were true. To a Lakota, this would be like someone from the deep South finding out his great grandfather came straight off a slave ship.

The old man asks us if we have eaten. There is a large enamelware pot on the wood stove and he dishes us each a large bowl of soup. When I taste it I find it very good, very tasty, unlike some of the soup they serve at funerals. There is a particular taste to it I cannot quite make out, though it seems familiar. When I ask the old man what it is, he says something in Lakota and points to a braid of herbs hanging near the stove. These look like garlic but he tells me they are wild turnips, gathered together at a particular time of year and braided together in long ropes, like chiles. He says the reason they taste familiar is that they are ground up and used in fry bread. Not all fry bread is made with them, he tells us, but the best is.

When we are done I feel very content, even sleepy. The old man gives us a cup of coffee and takes out a tobacco pouch from his shirt pocket. He begins rolling a cigarette. When Johnny sees this, he gets up, says he forgot something in the truck and goes out to get it. While he is gone, the old man looks at me and something strange begins to happen. I feel like I am transparent to his eyes, that he is peering into the deepest parts of my being, into places within my soul even I am unaware exist.

This happens so quickly I do not have time to pull back, to hide my thoughts. I find myself talking, pouring out my heart, and I am strangely not afraid. What I feel within the old man's gaze is a warm light that surrounds me and holds me safe, like a baby in his father's arms, and I find myself telling the old man about Jenny and the offensive linemen and the rage which almost left them dead on the shower floor.

At some point in the telling, Johnny comes back into the cabin. He has a carton of Pell Mell cigarettes he brought to give the old man, but when he sees us talking he sets them on a shelf by the stove and takes his seat at the table. I am sure the old man is aware of his presence, but his eyes never turn from mine.

When I am done, the old man nods. He walks to the shelf and takes a pack out of the carton of cigarettes and nods his thanks to Johnny. Then he sits down again, and even though he is present in body, I sense he is somehow in another place, too, and he sits so still I cannot see him breathe. The only sign of life is his hand holding the cigarette half a foot from his face. His elbow is propped on the table and he holds the butt between his thumb and forefinger, with the lighted end up. This is the first time I have seen tobacco used this way, and when I ask him about this later, Johnny tells me the old man was not smoking the cigarette. He was making giveaway offering of spirit weed.

When the cigarette is burned almost all the way to his fingers, the old man is back with us as suddenly as he went away. The butt has stopped burning and he carefully sets it beside the salt cellar. Then he lights another cigarette and begins smoking it.

We sit there in silence a long time. I begin to feel a little stupid unloading so much of my soul to this old man I hardly know and I wonder what he thinks of what I have told him. Something keeps me from asking, and when he finally speaks, I am glad I kept quiet.

"You carry much anger," he tells me. "This is useful. When you need it, it can help you." He stops speaking to take another puff of smoke. "Anger is a two edged knife. It can cut your enemy, but it can cut you, too, and your friends. I think you discovered that and it makes you afraid."

I nod. He has spoken the truth and told me what I knew without knowing. "Fear is your worst enemy," he goes on. "Not your anger. Anger is simply power. Fear is the dark side of your spirit, the side which destroys. What you fear holds your spirit in its hand, and you cannot be whole. When you fear your anger, you give its power to your worst enemy. When you respect it, you keep its power for yourself and are whole."

I hear the words, but it will take many years before I begin to understand them. "I want to control my anger," I tell him. "How do I do that?"

The old man chuckles. "If I could bottle that, I would own the world. Not that I would want to." He is quiet a moment. "Anger is power, what the old people call medicine. Medicine is not something a man can own. It is a gift he is given by the Earth-maker, the one who you call God. It is not something you can control."

I am confused. This flies in the face of everything I have been taught, but I sense the old man is saying something very important for me to understand. "So what do I do? How do I keep it from destroying me?"

The old man smiles and nods. "That's a different question. Every man must find his own way, but the path he follows must be *wakan*. " He frowns and shrugs. "I am not sure what the right word is in English," he says. "Maybe sacred, or holy, but it's not something you do. It's something you are, something you become."

I am more confused than ever. "But what do I do?"

"You do sacred things," the old man tells me. "You look on the inside of things. You do things of the spirit. This is what Indians call the Medicine Way."

Johnny speaks up for the first time. "You mean like sweat lodge and Sun Dance?"

The old man frowns. "There is no traditional word in Lakota for Sun Dance. This is something new. I am not sure how *wakan* it is."

"What about the pipe?" Johnny asks. "What about drum songs and vision quest?"

"Those are very traditional," the old man answers. "Those are the Medicine Way of the people of the plains. Other people, like the Dinee, have their own medicine. They call it the Rainbow Road, or the Way of Beauty. The Jews called it the Way of Holiness."

"So I become religious?" I ask. Something of my distaste for church must come across because the old man laughs.

"No, my friend, you become what white people call spiritual." When I ask him what the difference is, he thinks for a long time. "What I have seen of white man's church and religion seems to be about rules and rewards. Do this and God will reward you. Don't do that or God will punish you. Believe this and God will save you. Don't believe that or God will burn you in hell forever."

He pauses and I nod. This pretty much fits what I have seen. "What I have seen studying your sacred writings is something else. What I see there and in the teachings of Jesus is about being connected. It is about being in harmony with the Creator and with yourself and with all the rest of creation. This is what being spiritual is, being connected and in harmony."

"So it doesn't matter what way you follow, as long as it's sacred?" Johnny asks.

The old man shook his head. "No, it matters very much. Every man must find his own way. My way is not your way and your way is not Randy's way." He looked at me. "I think a man can learn a lot from every way, but he has to find one that fits him best."

"So there is nothing wrong with me following the Medicine Way?" I ask. "I can do sweat lodge and the pipe?"

The old man thought for a long while before answering. "Yes. You can do these things. You will find a great deal of power in them and you will find food for your spirit. Yet you will not find the healing you seek. I think you will have to follow the Jesus way for that." He turns to Johnny. " I think this is true of you, too."

Johnny looks surprised, but nods. I know he has accepted what the old man says with reservations. He will wait and see, but I am so surprised I am in shock. This is just too much. I don't say anything but I think the old man is as full of shit as a Christmas turkey. There is no way I will agree to be like one of those mealy mouthed hypocrites I see in church.

I also think the old man knows exactly what is going through my mind because he laughs and shakes his head. "You young guys. So full of piss and vinegar." Then he looks thoughtful. "I'm going to do a sweat this weekend, Sunday afternoon," he tells us. "You're welcome to come."

Johnny looks at me and I nod. "Sounds good to me. I need to sweat out a couple of offensive linemen."

Sweat Lodge

6 November 12, 1983. "The only good Indian is a dead Indian." I've heard this all my life and I looked it up the other day to see who first said it. The man was General Philip Henry Sheridan, but this isn't exactly what he said. When the tribal elder told him the Indians camped around the fort were "good" Indians, a witness wrote that the general actually said. "The only good Indians I ever saw were dead."

Things were different back then, but I wondered why he would say something like this. I wondered what Indians had done to give him such a thirst for their blood. So I went to the library and looked him up to find out more. The reason he said this was not because of what Indians did to him or his family. No, the reason he said this is and did what he did was because he was mean or crazy. Or maybe both.

The record shows Philip Sheridan may have been a brilliant general, but he was a very harsh one, even to his own men. Many things happened during the Civil War to show this, and when he was military governor of Texas, things were no different. He did things to his men no Lakota war chief could do and still have followers. To be harsh to your enemy is the way war is fought. To be harsh to your own people is crazy, and I think Sheridan was crazy. So even if these were not his exact words, I think this is exactly what he meant. "The only good Indian is a dead Indian."

Yet, this does not answer my real question. I've heard this said since I was a child, and I do not understand it. Why do the white people hate us so? What did we ever do to them? Most of them do not have ancestors who fought against the Lakota. They moved here later on. So why do they say this? Why do they hate us?

The strange thing is that whenever someone says this in my hearing they are quick to tell me they don't mean me. But who do they mean? Who are they talking about? Do Indians not have faces for them? Are not some of us good and some of us bad, just like them? Do they believe we all think alike and do exactly the same things? When they look at

73

me they say they see John Lyle, and not an Indian, but how can I believe them? I have a face. I have a name. And I am an Indian. How can they say this and not mean me? (excerpt from John K's journal)

Johnny and I get back to Winner late Monday night. When we do, I am a different man. I have been to sweat lodge. I have claimed my love, and I am no longer a child but a man. While I am still young, with much to learn about being a man, I am no longer a boy.

I think Johnny knows this. We do not talk about it, but I think he senses a change in me and I think he knows it is connected to seeing Jenny. Nor does he ask. He knows if I wish him to know, I will speak, and there are some things a man does not ask a brother. To ask is to be a child, and neither of us are children any more.

The strange thing is that I cannot remember a specific time when Johnny crosses this river, when he changes from a child into a man. I don't know how to say it, but even as a very young child, there is a part of him which is very old. I don't give much credence to what I have read about reincarnation or transmigration of souls, but if I did, Johnny would be the best example I know. It may be something as simple as genetic memory, but there is a part of him who was there when the buffalo roamed the Plains in large herds. There is part of him which was already ancient when the Lakota first migrated to the area now called Minnesota. There is a part of him who suffers the bitter winter and dies in the snow at Wounded Knee.

While I do not see this part of him often, I believe it is always there in each step Johnny takes. I believe it is there in every decision he makes and sometimes I see it in the simplest and most unexpected ways, like the way he strokes a horse or stokes the fire. Yet, I think what is extraordinary is not what he is doing at these moments, but the utter clarity with which I see my friend. Within those short epiphanies, I believe what I see is who he really is, a proud warrior from another age. Then the moment passes and I see the friend I grew up with and I wonder if I was dreaming.

I keep getting ahead of my story. Yet, telling is the father of understanding all these things and there is healing here for me. I seem to remember things in the order I need to recall them to make vital connections, and there seems to be something beyond my conscious effort at work here. I feel foolish even writing this thought down, but it is true and the whole point of telling this is to find the truth. I think the gentle rabbi was right when he said, "You shall know the truth, and the truth shall set you free." I think what I see in my moments of utter clarity is the truth about myself and about my friend. Then it slips away and I wonder if it is real because it seems so strange. Yet, I believe it is and I believe it is somehow tied to the vision I saw when I first met the old man. I see myself as a down-to-earth newspaper man and very hard headed when it comes to facts. Yet there is also this other realm which keeps intruding into the fabric of ordinary life. When it happens it is this experience of "The Twilight Zone" which seems most real.

When we leave the old man's house that evening, we head for Corn Creek. Maybe it is getting away for a while, or maybe it is talking to the old man, or maybe it's slipping in a pile of shit and laughing like a fool. Whatever it is, I feel relaxed for the first time in two weeks. I want to see Jenny, very much, but I'm no longer driven crazy by it. I seem to understand whatever takes place between us will happen in its own time. Call it fate or call it karma, I understand that whatever will be will be. This is the sense I have of that whole afternoon as we drive to Corn Creek, the sense of a deep peace within which comes through talking with the old man.

This sense of peace stays with me, despite the craziness we find when we arrive. The family emergency which brought us here has passed but another has taken its place. This is how life is among the Lakota on the reservation. One crisis comes to replace the one before it with no time between, as if life is a constant state of war. This is why some believe the people there drink so much. There's no time to get through the grief of one loss before another claims its place, and each man, woman and child on the reservation carries a well of grief which is overwhelming. So many of them drink to dull the pain.

This may be true, but I met someone else who told me something which makes a lot more sense. I met him doing a story on the recovery center in Rosebud. He is Lakota, a counselor there, and he has been without a drink for over ten years. He said most Lakota look at the thing backwards, the same way white people do. They say they drink because of their problems. Yet, it is the drinking which is the source of most of the problems, not the other way around

This sounds very strange and I asked him about it. He told me that using alcohol to kill one's pain only works for a while. With continual use, people build up a tolerance and have to use more and more to get the same effect. Eventually, what was once the solace from pain becomes a source of pain, and people discover they cannot live with alcohol or without it. It is only when they begin to come to terms with the attitudes they have about life and themselves, the same attitudes which lead to their drinking, that they find healing and peace. It is only then they can put the bottle down.

I don't know if the man is right, but he is sober now for a long time. He faces the same losses others experience without drinking, without the temporary amnesia of getting too drunk to remember, and he is a source of strength to others. When I ask him how he does this, he tells me he draws on basic spiritual tools from both the traditional Lakota way and from his Catholicism, which is rooted in the same basic understanding as the Twelve Steps. Each has something he needs and he finds no conflict between them. When he says this I think of Father Leo. To him the *wakan* is *wakan*, the sacred is sacred, the holy is holy, and he, too, draws on the power of both ways. Through this he finds peace in a world that never rests.

I think this is the same kind of peace I have driving on from Wood. When we arrive in Corn Creek, Jenny's aunt is past immediate danger and is doing well in the hospital in Rosebud. Yet, while the family is still at the hospital, a cousin comes in with a sick child. Little Noah Three Bulls is not four months old and he has severe pneumonia. No one knows he is allergic to antibiotics, and when he is given an injection, his small body reacts to the medicine like a bee sting. Everything the hospital does aggravates the problem and within twelve hours little Noah is dead.

By the time we arrive in Corn Creek, the family is gathered at Jenny's family home and Father Leo is there. Despite everything, he smiles and greets me warmly and Jenny's mother does, too. She gives me a hug and thanks me for coming. She tells me Jenny is in the back room making preparations for the wake and sends one of the children to let her know I am here. I wonder how she knows I am here to see Jenny.

Then Jenny comes out and she is very shy. She stands by her mother, looking down, and offers me her hand. I hear a murmur from the back of the room and a quiet chuckle. The old people know exactly what is going on, but it doesn't matter to me. Tired as she is, Jenny is the most beautiful sight I have ever seen. When my hand meets hers, the touch is electric, as if she were coming into my arms, and when she looks up, there is nothing between us in her eyes. I know she is glad I am here, and her glance promises there will be time for us later. For now, family must come first.

Jenny gives Johnny a brief hug, then excuses herself and returns to the back room where she is needed. Johnny and I greet the rest of the people there and take our seats with the men. They ask after my father and mother, but after this very little is said. We mostly sit in silence, and even Father Leo is subdued. While the loss of a child is nothing new on the reservation, it is no less devastating for being so common. I believe it is more so. To lose so many children is like having a tornado roar through town every week, leaving nothing standing. One might think the Lakota would give up after a while, but they never do. I am told one of the historic keys to their survival is having so many children and this may be true, not just now, but even before Columbus. They have children faster than they lose them, but I cannot imagine the collective grief they carry, not only as individuals, but as a people, too.

The wake begins that night and I have a sense of deja vu. This is the same house where we came when we buried Willie, and many of the same people are there. I wonder when the old man from Wood will arrive and why he has not heard, but I hear someone say he will be coming in the next day. I wonder why the old man said nothing to us while we were at his house, but Johnny answers my question even as it arises. He tells me the old man doesn't have a phone and someone went to let him know he is needed. He would be here tonight, but he has to prepare.

This is strange to me. Even though I grew up next to it, I cannot imagine someone so important to the life of a community not having a phone. Yet there are many people on the reservation who do not have them. Sometimes this is because they cannot afford it, but there are others who see it as an intrusion and choose not to have one. I suspect the old man is one of these. When I was at his cabin, I cannot remember seeing power lines or even a refrigerator. The only modern thing I remember seeing was a rusty old pickup in the back, and I am not sure it was running.

Yet, I also remember something else my grandfather once said when I asked why one of his neighbors didn't buy a new tractor instead of constantly repairing his old one. He said, "Son, a poor man has poor ways." Then, when he saw I did not understand, he added, "He has more time to spend than money." What strikes me about this now is how true this is of the Lakota. They have more time than money and the way they live their lives reflects this. Some of them turn this abundance into creativity, producing fine art and craft work of great beauty, or creating opportunities for themselves to break free of the constraints of poverty. Unfortunately, many others find they have more time than healthy ways to spend it, so they brood and drink and fight and betray one another, creating even more pain to carry.

As the afternoon grows into evening, a meal is brought in by relatives and shared. I notice Father Leo does not eat much but the fry bread and the *wateca*, a fruit sauce like pudding, but not so sweet. When I ask him about this later when we are alone, he laughs and tells me he attends so many wakes and funerals his waist cannot afford for him to eat more. Then he gives me an odd look and looks around to make sure no one else can hear him. He tells me the truth is this is what he tells his hosts to not hurt their feelings. He says he once became so very ill from eating some of the food at a wake that he had to be rushed to the hospital and could not perform the funeral. So he stays away from things which spoil quickly, especially salads made with mayonnaise or chicken, and sticks to fry bread and *wateca* and certain kinds of soup. He looks at my plate pointedly when he stops speaking, and I find I've lost my appetite for the potato salad and tuna salad heaped over it.

When the meal is done, the women put away the food and clean up the kitchen. I see it growing dark before Jenny comes to the doorway between the kitchen and the living room and catches my eye. She doesn't say anything and disappears back into the kitchen. Yet, I know she is telling me she is done and after a few moments I get up from the bench where I am sitting and go into the kitchen. She is not there, but the only other door is open, the one into the back yard, and I go out onto the porch,

Jenny is not there, either, and it takes a few moments for my eyes to adjust to the low light. A full moon is just rising and its light casts deep shadows around the house and in trees to the south, but somehow I know this is where I need to go. It is only when I come into the first group of trees I become aware of Jenny now close by my side. She reaches out and takes my hand, and I follow as she leads me along a path through the trees my eyes can barely make out.

I wonder where Jenny is taking me, but I say nothing and we walk for a long while. Then we come through an opening in the trees and we are suddenly walking on soft grass along the shore of a large pond. When we come to a spot on the west shore where the moon is just now being reflected off the still surface of the pond, Jenny stops and turns to me. Without a word, she wraps her arms around my neck and pulls my mouth to hers. When our lips touch for the first time, I am startled at the intensity of her passion. Yet, I respond with all my soul and we stand, fused together for a long while.

When Jenny pulls back, I am surprised again. Yet, she smiles and begins to unbutton my shirt. I start to help, but she gently pushes my hands away, and when her fingers have released the last button, she pushes my shirt off my shoulders and drops it on the grass. I start to respond, but she puts a hand to my chest and begins to unbuckle my belt.

I am thankful I am wearing moccasins this night. I do not think stopping to pull off boots and socks would matter, but I am glad they are not there. So when my love lowers my trousers, I simply step out of them and onto the soft grass. Then she reaches out and touches me, takes me gently in her hand, and it is almost more than I can bear.

When she releases me, she stands quietly and looks deep into my eyes. Without words I know what she wishes me to do. With trembling hands I begin to unbutton the man's shirt she is wearing for a blouse. When it falls from her shoulders I see there is nothing beneath it, and when my hands touch her stomach, seeking the top button of her jeans, a soft moan escapes her lips. Then she is standing naked before me in the light of the full moon, and she is the most beautiful thing I have ever seen.

I do not remember how many times we make love that night. What I remember is how each held its own sweetness. At first I am reluctant to go on, knowing I have no way to protect her from conception. Yet, when I try to tell her this, she shushes me, tells me it doesn't matter. So I take her into my arms and we sink into the soft grass. Time stops and there is nothing else in the universe, nothing but me and Jenny and a silver moon who sheds her light, blessing our love.

Three days later Johnny and I are on the way to Wood for the sweat lodge. It is middle afternoon and neither of us has much to say. The funeral this morning was sad and somehow beautiful, too. Father Leo spoke of little Noah meeting his grandfathers for the first time in the spirit world and how he is free now from all pain and sickness, free from all the demands of the human body. I cannot remember how he said it but the image what he said left in my memory is little Noah spreading the wings of his bright spirit and flying up from the earth to the spirit world where he will soar forever.

Now in my middle years, the memory brings tears to my eyes as I write it. At the time, though, it was simply a beautiful memory which imprinted itself in my mind. There is no way I can understand, as a young man, the depth of what that image means now, or why Father Leo's eyes mist when he speaks of being set free from all the things which plague the physical body. Now, as a man of ripe years, I know why, and tears wash my cheeks as I write. For what I hear Father Leo saying down all these long years, and hear as clearly in my mind's ear as if it is yesterday morning—all this echoes the words of another man of God. "Free at last! Free at last! Great God, Almighty, I'm free at last!"

Johnny and I are young men. We know death is all around us. We have seen it all our lives. We know it comes to every living creature. Yet, somehow it is not real, at least not to me. Johnny lives with it more closely than I do, and I know he sees it differently from me. We never talk about it, but somehow I know this. Even though it death is so present, I am still in that strength of youth which thinks itself immortal. Somewhere down deep where there is no thought, only feeling, I believe death is something which happens to other people. With no reason except the life force erupting within me at this marvelous springtime of life, I believe I am bullet proof, like Crazy Horse or Wyatt Earp. I am just now reaching the fullness of my strength as a man and I cannot imagine being any other way. I cannot imagine being old or frail or facing the end of my days. I cannot imagine my strength not being there to carry me through.

So as Johnny and I drive to Wood, I am not thinking death or the funeral we went to in the morning. I am thinking about Jenny and the last two nights. I am remembering the soft grass, the warm, smooth texture of her skin. I am recalling the surprising way we join our bodies and souls, as if this were not the first time. I marvel at the strength of her passion, the way she moves, the beauty of her breasts in the moonlight, the soft warmth I feel....

I am suddenly aware I am becoming aroused. Were I alone, I might allow myself to drift along in the warm, pleasant stream of desire, anticipating the joy of our next union. Yet, Johnny is driving and I feel awkward, almost ashamed to be thinking these things. I feel my throat start to color and I look out the passenger window, hiding my face from my brother. This is strange, for we hold nothing back from one another, Johnny and me. Yet, with Jenny, it is oddly different. To talk of her, even with Johnny, would be dishonor.

I spend a lot of time looking at nothing. When the flush fades, I turn back toward the front window. Out of the corner of my eye I see Johnny watching me, looking at me strangely. I make myself turn, meet his gaze. Yet, as soon as I do, I wish I had not. He knows! I tell myself, but I say nothing. He knows. Then I see something happen in Johnny's eyes, some deep movement I have never seen before or since. He turns his eyes back toward the road and the moment passes, but not before I see something I will never forget. Later I will recognize it for what it is, but now it passes to quickly for me to recognize.

Even as the moment passes, a great sense of sadness comes over me. Just a moment before I am on top of the highest mountain, and now I am plunged into the depths of the earth. Many years later I will read a poem Johnny wrote while he was in high school, and when I read it for the first time, I will remember this moment. I will know this passing instant was what he was writing about, and I will understand what I saw. The first lines of his poem say it all:

> The vision's lost, the mountain's high
> the birds are gone, the winter sky
> grows dark with rain and winter night
> sets in your soul....

Yet, when this dark night comes on me on the road to Wood, I have no idea what it is or where it is coming from. I cannot imagine why I am feeling this way, but I am caught in the depths of utter despair, and for the first time in my life, I wish I were dead. The feeling is so sharp, so overwhelming, I can hardly breathe. The shock is so sudden I cannot even cry out and even the bright blue sky outside turns black as shadows gather around me and I sink deeper and deeper into utter darkness. As the final verses say,

> Cold and lost and all alone
> time hangs heavy, is a stone
> that crushes hope and renders bone
> to dust upon the wind...
> Then face to face, eternity
> casts its shadow on the sea
> that reaches down and down to be
> where darkness ever grows....
> And from the night, the raven's cry
> My soul bespeaks the mindless lie

I live each day until I die
A vain and pointless death....

Yes, I am sure of it. This is the moment that poem is conceived. Yet, it is only when I read it some twenty years later that I come to understand the pain my brother is suffering. I realize what I was seeing deep within his eyes was the breaking of his heart. At the moment I am simply overwhelmed by something so vast and empty I shrink within myself. I shrink to the size of a grain of sand, a single grain of sand, alone in a universe of despair.

Yet, as soon as the sense comes over me, it passes on. The darkness clears, the bright light returns and it is as if nothing ever happened. What I hear in the voice of my brother is joy, pure delight in the momentary gift the universe has given. "Hey, look, RD! There's a bald eagle! It's a good sign for our sweat!"

What amazes me now is how this whole memory simply disappears for twenty years. I am riding in the pickup. I am swamped with despair for less than a minute. Then I am riding in the pickup again, excited about the sweat we are going to. The memory is like a photo lying dormant on undeveloped film. Twenty years later, there it is, as sharp as the moment it happened. This seems very strange. Yet, there it is, and I believe with all my soul this touches deeply on how it is to be Lakota. It is to experience joy within despair. Perhaps this is what keeps them going, despite their burden of pain. At least, until the millstone grows too heavy.

There are a half dozen cars and pickups parked at the old man's hogan when we get there. It is still early, a long time until sundown. There is faint smoke coming out of the chimney. No one is standing around and when we go into the lodge, it is empty. There is a large enamel canner simmering on the wood cook stove and I can smell tobacco and sage mixed with the aroma of whatever is cooking.

Johnny looks around, then goes to the wood stove. "Bean soup," he says, looking into the pot. "It's going to be a windy night." I tell him it's good that we are going to be eating after the sweat and he laughs. "I hope they didn't have this for lunch!" Then he nods for me to follow and we go outside.

There are several dry coulees coming together in the basin below the old man's hogan. Most of these are narrow, choked with brush. I catch the smell wood smoke but I can't tell where it is coming from.

The hogan is behind us and the wind is in our faces, so it has to be from another fire. We stand there listening for a moment or two. Yet, all I can hear is the rustle of the wind through the brush.

Johnny's hearing is much better than mine. Sometimes he hears things even a dog does not, and now he suddenly takes off toward one of the coulees. The one he heads for looks more narrow than the rest and completely blocked with brush. To me it looks like a dead end but I follow. Johnny sometimes seems to know things not tied to human senses. Maybe it is intuition or racial memory, but those are simply two other ways of saying we don't know. What I do know is that this sense he has is always right. Later on, in Honduras and other dangerous places, it will save our lives.

I see an opening in the brush when we get to mouth of the coulee and the whole thing is much wider than it looks from the old man's house. Once we enter the brush I can see a faint path, but it looks even more faint than a game trail. No one seems to have used this path in months or years.

I notice Johnny is walking to one side of the pathway, so I move to the other. When I do, I see the faint imprint of a western boot where the grass has been crushed next to a patch of dust. I look back and see no sign of my tracks. I know without looking there will be no sign of Johnny's steps, either. We are wearing moccasins with soft soles. While we are not trying to sneak up on the lodge, we are not trying to signal our arrival, either. We are moving quietly, the way the native people learned to survive. As we do, I have a sense of time slipping back to another age as one of those epiphanies unfolds. We are warriors, Johnny and I, Lakota warriors moving quietly through the brush. We come in peace, prepared for war, and it is a good day to live or to die.

Then this sense fades as quickly as it comes. The brush gives way to a clearing and there it is, the sweat lodge. What strikes me seeing it for the first time is how it looks a huge mushroom growing out of the ground or like a large rock covered with lichen. I don't know where he found them, but the old man has used buffalo hides to cover the wooden framework. The hides look old, stained with smoke, and there are small wooden pegs holding them together. There is still woolly hair on the hide covering the very top, and at first I cannot see any opening to go in. Then I see a small flap with pins, facing the fire pit, and I see a distinct track leading from the pit to the flap.

There are more than a dozen men sitting in a large circle around the fire pit. The old man looks up when we come into the clearing and motions us to take places in the circle of men. I start to greet him, then stop. This is not a time for words, so I simply nod to him and sit down next to Johnny.

Most of the men in the circle are strangers to me, although some of these look familiar. Then I remember where I saw them. They are members of a drum team and I know them from funerals and the Rosebud *wacipi*. I do not know their names but I have seen them many times and they recognize me, too. A couple of them nod, but say nothing. I know the others see me, but their gaze is fixed on the fire.

As I look at the fire, I see there is more than wood burning. Logs are stacked like a rough cabin with an open center and large round stones fill the opening. These are black from smoke, used many times before, but some of the ones toward the top have a distinct ruddy glow. I realize that someone else must have started the fire, for the old man left the funeral lunch only about an hour before us.

Then another man comes into the clearing and I recognize him. I guess you could call him the old man's apprentice. I have seen him helping the old man at funerals and on a couple of occasions when the old man was not there. I have no idea what his name is but Johnny tells me later that in the white way of looking at kin, he is the old man's nephew. Now he is carrying a shovel and I watch him use it to tend the fire. As I do, I wonder what the Lakota used before they had shovels to pick up the hot stones. When I ask the old man this at supper that night, he laughs and tells me, "A big stick!"

There is a clear pathway through the circle of men. This leads straight from the fire pit to the lodge and I notice it is rounded at the bottom like a track. I can also see there is a gentle slope to the path which grows deeper as it nears the lodge. This puzzles me for a while until I see the fire tender using his shovel to clear ashes away from where the track enters the fire pit. Then I realize the track is used to roll hot stones from the fire into the lodge to make steam.

I see a what looks like a red serape spread on the ground across the pathway and there is a buckskin bundle tied with read strips of cloth lying across the serape. I see what looks like a twist of sage and a braid of sweet medicine grass lying on either side of a large flat seashell below the bundle as you face the fire. There is also a leather pouch lying directly below the seashell, side by side with an eagle feather fan. I can see from where I sit that the bead work on the handle of the fan is very elaborate and matches the rosette on the large medallion the old man in wearing. It also matches the colors of the bone and bead necklace which suspends the medallion.

To one side of the red serape there is a small branch stuck into the ground. This has been cut off just beyond a fork in the branch, making a Y for something to rest six or eight inches above the ground. Next to the fork is the only thing which seems completely out of place, a red and blue box of kitchen matches.

However, one of the things I have learned over the years observing the Lakota is how adaptable they are. With certain things they stay with traditional ways, but other things don't seem to matter. So right next to the symbols of an ancient way of life here is something which reflects a level of technology far beyond the Neolithic culture which produced the understanding behind the ceremonials we are about to engage.

Despite my best intentions, I find myself thinking I probably should be grateful it is a box of matches and not a Zippo. I know even then that my reaction says a lot more about me than the Lakota. I understand from many talks with Johnny that any expectation things might be different stems from a romantic noble-red-savage way of thinking about Indians, from me wanting them to be the way I expect them to be and not as they are. And I find myself ashamed. To even think this way surrenders to racist, patronizing stereotypes I abhor. The greatest violence these do is to the unique individuality which makes each human being who she or he is.

I become aware of the soft music of a flute. Gently, it calls me, draws me out of myself. Without words it surrounds my soul, healing the self inflicted wounds of rebuke and calling me into itself. Fly with me, it sings. Take my wings, let yourself be lifted from the earth, feel the wind in your face, reach out your arms, feel the power beneath your new wings. Rise up! Come with me! Let your spirit walk the rainbow way to beauty.

Walk the rainbow way. Somewhere in the dim recesses of memory the ghost of a Navajo poem I once read comes alive. Walk the way of beauty. Walk the way of harmony. Walk the rainbow way. As I sit staring into the fire, waves of memory I never knew I had wash over me and deep within the fiery coals I see something moving. At first it is tiny, no larger than a dime seen across the room. Then it grows and I can see bands of vivid color arching from the desert floor toward a cobalt sky. A small white cloud forms at the base of the bow, then begins to move upward. As it does, pieces break off and become clouds, growing into thunderheads and giving rain to a thirsty earth below. Plants spring up and the desert blossoms, bringing forth bright flowers from spiny cactus and thorn bush and mesquite. As the rain falls, it gathers in deep pools and trees spring up around these, cottonwood and willow and desert ash.

Then I raise my eyes to the rainbow and I see the source of the clouds and the rain. There is a tiny figure dancing over the bow and each time his feet touch down little puffs of white steam rise. These gather to make clouds and I know I am looking at the Rainbow Man. Within one hand he holds the lightening. Within the other there is a stalk of fresh corn, the tassels newly formed. Yet it is his eyes which catch mine. They are as deep blue as the evening sky, and I feel their gaze sinking within me. Around them a face forms, and below the broad bands of ceremonial paint I can see a distinct features. Somehow I am not surprised to discover it is the face of my brother, Johnny. Then the features of the Rainbow Man change. I am shocked to see my own face looking back at me.

The shock breaks the vision. When I come back to here and now, I find myself looking across the fire. staring directly into the eyes of the old man. He smiles and nods and I find myself trembling. This is crazy, I think. Yet, even as the thought crosses my mind, I am aware of the absurdity of my denial. Shock is replaced with a strange sense of calm. No, I think, it is true. Yet it seems so strange. Many years later I will remember this moment when I unexpectedly come across the lines of an ancient Hebrew song. It is one I have read many times, but only at that moment does it connect to the truth of the vision I am given while staring into the fire.

Blessed are those whose strength is in thee,
Whose hearts are set on the pilgrim's way....
As they go through the desolate Valley of the Weeper,
They make it a place of springs....

What is strange about all this is that I can see Johnny as a Rainbow man. What I cannot see is myself. So for many years I discount the sense of truth I am given. I look at that part of the vision as my own need to be important, my own ego, intruding. Then one day I am talking to Father Leo and I mention this. I mention it to illustrate the insidious way our egos force their way into even the most sacred things. Yet, when I tell him this, Father Leo laughs and looks at me, astonished.

He shakes his head. "You really don't know, RD, do you? You really don't have a clue who you are." Then he pisses me off refusing to explain. All he will say is that I should trust the truth within the vision.

Yeah, right, I say to myself. Johnny Rainbow is one thing. There is some poetry to that. Whoever heard of a Randy one? Randy Rainbow sounds like something from Alice in Wonderland, or the mascot of a bread company. Now, I am not so sure.

The old man nods again and holds up his hand. The flute is no longer playing and one of the men picks up a large flat drum and begins to strike it softly, making a sound like a beating heart. When he does, the men all stand as he begins to sing. It is the Four Directions Song, one I know well, and I turn with the rest of the men to face each cardinal point as the singer sings his prayer. When we are done, the old man sits cross legged on the outer edge of the red serape, and the rest of us take our places in the circle.

The old man opens the bundle on the serape and takes out a red stone pipe with a long, curved stem. The stem is not joined to the pipe when he takes them out, and he sets them aside for a moment. Taking the large flat seashell, the old man breaks off an inch or two of the sweet medicine braid and spreads it in the shell. He does the same thing with the sage, and when he is done, he opens the leather pouch and mixes in two or three pinches of tobacco. Then he nods to the fire tender, who gently reaches into the pit with his shovel and drops a large live coal in the middle of the mixture.

Smoke begins to come up immediately and the old man hands the tender the fan of eagle feathers and the shell. The tender begins to lightly fan the smoke toward the old man, who pulls it over himself with his hand, starting at his head and covering his whole body. Then the tender moves to each man in the circle.

I notice some of the men say a prayer aloud as they purify themselves, and others do not. I have never been to one of the old man's sweats before, so I simply do as I have seen him do. When the tender moves by, my eyes lock with the old man's once more and I see something I have never seen there before. Nor am I sure of my understanding, for what I see in the depths of his eyes is laughter. There is also a playful challenge, as if he is saying, Don't take yourself too seriously, my friend. This is to be enjoyed.

Even as this thought comes to me, I feel a sense of delight rising up into my bare legs from the ground. Without thinking, I jump to my feet and begin dancing around the outside of the circle. The drum picks up my rhythm and it spreads among the men like wildfire. Those who went before me with smudge jump to their feet and fall into step behind me. One by one, the others join in as they are purified, and soon we are all dancing in a large circle around the old man and the fire.

What amazes me about this now is how natural it is at the time. I am normally so reserved off the football field it takes a beer or two to get me on the dance floor. Yet, here I am, the only white man around, leading the dance. Talk about brass! Yet, it is the only thing I can do and when we talk, Johnny tells me he believes it is one of the reasons I am led to the sweat. To lead the dance.

The most remarkable thing, however, is the clarity I have looking at every man who is dancing. Some of what I see is very frightening, not for me, but for them. Some of it is simply very strange. Nor is there any sense or continuity. Time and space fold in on one another, and with some of the men I see the ancient past. With others I see what must surely lie in the future, and it is this which is frightening. For I see some of the men there being born and I see others dying violent deaths.

What I am spared is seeing myself, what lies in my future and what the future holds for Johnny. I think the grief knowing then what I know now would be too great. Yet I don't know this then, and when I look at Johnny, I see him riding across the plains. The horse he is mounted on is a big buckskin, and I know he is on the way home from war. There are fresh scalps hanging from his belt and blood from a long wound across his chest has congealed into a thin scab. Yet, while he is victorious, there is a strange sadness in his eyes, and I know that in killing his enemy, he is aware he has killed part of himself. There is great sadness within his joy.

I am not going to write about what the old man did in the pipe ceremony. I have seen it done a number of ways, and there are some things which need to go unrecorded. This is heresy for a news reporter, but it is true. Some things need to remain recorded only on the fabric of the human mind, mostly because there are not words to do them justice. Such mysteries are beyond time and space, and there is no other way of recording the unique inner truth they give except to remember and to give thanks for the great gift of having known them.

What I will say is this. I am quite fluent in Lakota, but I understand only part of what the old man says in his prayers. What he is using is the ancient Lakota tongue, and I am told that very few contemporary Lakota can understand it well. I am also told that each medicine man uses his own special language, and one common to other medicine men. I am not alone in not knowing exactly what the old man says. The others are as much in the dark as I am. Yet, my sense of it, based solely on my relationship with the old man, is that what he utters are prayers beyond words.

The same is true of the experience of the sweat lodge. What I am told is that it is a way of not only purifying not the body, but also renewing the spirit. I am also told it is a way of returning to the earth, to the one who gives us life. When we emerge it is like being reborn. Our bodies are purified of the poisons they accumulate and our spirits are renewed by being reconnected with the source of life. This is captured in the American Indian expression, the earth my mother, my father, the sky. Prayers are offered at the altar of the pipe, rising up with the smoke of tobacco, which is called the spirit weed. Then the body is given back to the mother earth, and the circle of life is somehow renewed. It is a mystery.

What has always puzzled me about the sweat lodge is how so many men can crawl into such a small space and stay there for so long without consuming all the oxygen within the lodge. Those who attribute the mystical experiences of a sweat to oxygen deprivation may be right, but in my gut I do not believe this for a moment. I know that when I am in the lodge, time goes away, and I wonder if the body does not slow down, too. This is another of the many mysteries of sweat lodge.

What I remember of this sweat is that the sun was just down when we entered the lodge, and it was just rising when we came out. I believe I was awake the whole while, for I remember the times when the flap was opened for more hot rocks to make new steam. I remember seeing the fire stones, bright cherry red with heat to my light starved eyes, roll down into the deep pit in the middle of the lodge, and I can still see the old man's hand reflected in the red light as he sprinkled water on them. I hear the crisp sound of new steam and feel the heat as it caresses my body, and I feel the cool earth against my naked buttocks. I can hear the whisper of the breathing of the men on either side of me and I feel their flesh pressed against mine where we touch.

Through all this, I wonder how I, who am so claustrophobic, can do this. This is nothing like my first sweat experience. Now there are too many men in too small a place and my mind knows there is too little air. Yet, the momentary panic I feel when I first enter the lodge quickly goes away and I feel strangely calm. Maybe it is because of the prayers I hear the old man whispering or because of the songs we sing. I am not sure about this, but what I am sure about is even more strange. After this sweat lodge, my claustrophobia is healed. I never experience it again.

Years later I run into a psychologist who tells me I must be mistaken. He says that phobias cannot be completely cured, so what I had must have been a deep seated fear, not a phobia. When I hear this, I wonder how he would respond to a deep seated fist in his gut, and the thought tickles me. When he asks what I am laughing about, I tell him I'm tickled about something someone said, and I ask him a question. Since it is about his latest work, the conversation moves on in another direction.

When the old man tells us it's time to come out of the lodge, it surprises me. I emerge through the flap and the first thing I see is the early light of dawn. Johnny is right behind me and we stand together beyond the fire pit, looking at the line of soft light coloring the eastern horizon. A gentle wind is blowing in our faces and the morning star is hanging bright over the distant hills. I believe that very moment is most peaceful ever in my life.

Suddenly, a great shadow swoops low over us. I look up over my shoulder and see the largest owl I have ever seen flying over the sweat lodge and into the brush on the other side of the clearing. Then my gaze catches the face of the old man. He is standing by the entrance of the sweat lodge looking at Johnny. For a moment, I see his eyes fill with grief. Then I look at Johnny and his eyes are filled with joy in seeing the great owl. I glance back at the old man and his features are calm.

I know at the time that I have just witnessed something significant. Yet, I do not know what it is. Only years later, when I spoke to another medicine man, did I begin to comprehend. The owl is the most deadly of predators. It is called the night eagle and its wings make no sound as it flies. So it is not surprising that among some Indians the owl is considered the messenger, what some call the angel, of death.

Niobrara Gathering

7 June 19, 1973. They were fighting when I woke up this morning. I could hear them in the kitchen, cussing and yelling and banging pots and pans. Or maybe they were throwing them at each other. Whatever it was, they were making a hell of a noise. That was what woke me up. It wasn't the screaming. They're always screaming at each other, and I've learned to tune that out, but this morning they are in the kitchen and she's slamming the skillet or something against the stove. It's too damned loud to be the table or his head she's banging, although she did that last year. Laid him out like a corpse, right there on the kitchen floor. It was lucky for her she didn't kill him. We thought at first she did. There was blood all over the place. Then two weeks later he is out of the hospital and they are at it again.

I wonder what set them off this time? Or maybe it's the same fight they were having last night when I went to bed. I could hear them yelling through the open window. Maybe they got tired and stopped to rest a few hours. Or to go get more beer. They can't fight without beer. Hard liquor gets them drunk too quick and they pass out before they really get started. But give them enough beer and they can carry on a war all week.

I wonder why they stay together? They seem to hate each other, so why don't they split up? Why don't they call it quits and get on with their lives? All they are doing now is making each other miserable. And keeping the rest of us up, too. The police have been called so many times now they won't even come out. The last time mom called they asked if anybody had been hurt. She told them no and they said they would be out after a while, but they never came. That was two years ago and I guess people stopped calling.

So why don't they split up? I know their kids need a family, but what are they learning from their parents, to get drunk and fight all the time? It can't be much fun living there, either. It is bad enough living next door, but it must be awful for those little kids right there in the middle of it day after day. We feed them half the time, but that's about all we can do. When my mother gave their oldest daughter a coat, her mom traded it for beer the next day and the same thing happened when we gave them some extra commodities. They are always broke, but they always seem to find money to buy beer and cigarettes. I know he owes my dad a lot of money. Every time it's payday, he is over here borrowing what he can. Only it's not borrowing. He doesn't even pretend to think about paying it back. It's begging, but for some reason my dad is always good for a dollar or two. When I ask him why, he just shrugs and shakes his head.

I'm glad my parents don't drink. If they fought like that I think I'd run away. Yet, where would I go? I'm too young to go in the army. Or even to get a driver's license. So where would I go? I'm an Indian and I hear that as bad as it gets here on the reservation, it is even worse in Rapid City. A friend of my dad's told me this. He said it's even worse now after the big fight down in Pine Ridge. He doesn't live here. He lives in Rapid and has a job there. I guess that's why he stays. He's a cop, and I guess he ought to know. He says that every week somebody from the reservation gets cut up or killed, and nobody wants to hire Indians. He says it's no better in Sioux Falls or Denver or in Minneapolis, and Montana is even worse. Down south they think you're a Mexican and out west he told me the Mexicans hate us worse than the whites.

So where would I go if I couldn't stay here? What would I do? There doesn't seem to be anywhere an Indian is welcome.... (excerpt from John Lyons' first journal)

There is an early memory which haunts me and I need to go back a few years. I'm not sure what year it is or how old Johnny and I are. It is before we are in high school and maybe a year or two before he moves to Winner. Nor did I understand what it meant until later on, although it stuck with me and reading Johnny's journal brings it to mind.

When it happens, we're on the way to Lower Brule. At least, that's where I think we are headed. My dad is driving his pickup and pulling a pop-top camper for us to stay in for the week, and Johnny and his grandfather are riding with us. His grandfather is in the cab, with one of Johnny's sisters between him and my dad, and Johnny and I are riding in the back. We can see my mother and the rest of Johnny's family in their car behind us, though it's a little hard to see over the camper. My dad tied his fishing boat on top to use on the lake if the wind isn't too bad and it's as wide as the camper, almost.

We're headed for Lower Brule so my dad can write a story for the paper about the thing we're going to see. It's called the Niobrara Conference and people come here from all over the United States to visit. When I ask my dad if it is like a *wacipi*, he laughs and tells me it's more like an old time revival meeting than a *pauwau*. He says it's some kind of thing the Whiskey-palian people do every year, but the way he says it I didn't believe him. Especially when I see my mom roll her eyes. I know he is waiting for me to ask him what a Whiskey-palian is, but I just nod. Later I heard him pull it on someone else and when they ask, he tells them it's his name for Episcopalians. He says wherever two or three of them are gathered together, there's always a fifth. Even then I don't really get it until Johnny explains that a fifth means a bottle of whiskey. I ask why it's called a fifth but Johnny says he doesn't know, it just is.

Even though it's June, Johnny and I have our jackets on. It's still very cool when we start out this morning and we have to wrap a tarp around us to stay warm. Now the sun is up and we're sitting on the tarp so it won't blow out of the truck. It's not very comfortable, not like sitting in the cab, but I don't mind. I like to feel the wind blowing through my hair even if it is a little cold and I like to be able to see all around us. Just before we cross the White River we spot a red tailed hawk soaring way up over a field, looking for game and we watch him until he is out of sight. Then we see a herd of antelope grazing a hundred yards from the road. They look up when they hear the truck passing by but they don't run. Johnny and I pretend we have rifles and are shooting at them.

When we pass through Reliance and come to the turn-off to Lower Brule, my dad stops the truck and walks back to check the trailer hitch. When I hear him swear softly I look over at him but he isn't looking at the hitch. He's looking back up the road. Johnny and I stand up but I can't see what he's swearing about. Then he asks Johnny's granddad if he thinks we should wait or go back and find the women, I realize the car with the rest of our families is not behind us any more.

Johnny's granddad says we better go back. The water pump on the car is making noise and maybe it went out. So we turn around and go back the way we came.

We don't go very far. A mile from where we turn around we come around a curve and see the car pulled over to the side of the road. The hood is not up, but the trunk is and I can see the flashing lights of a police car parked behind it. When we pull up the women and children are standing around and a policeman is digging through the stuff in the trunk of the car.

My dad parks the truck and walks over to the policeman. I follow along behind. He asks the man what he is doing and the policeman gives him a hard look. He asks my dad what he needs. My dad tells him he needs to know what the policeman is doing, and the policeman tells him it's none of his business and to return to his vehicle.

I can see this steams my dad, but he doesn't move. He tells the policeman it's his wife he stopped and it damn well is his business. The policeman glares at him but my dad doesn't back down. He adds that it is a public road and he is a news reporter. He takes a pen and pad out of his shirt pocket and asks the policeman what his badge number is.

I can see this really torques the policeman off, but he shrugs. He says the car was weaving on the road and he stopped it to see if the driver was drunk. My dad writes this down and asks him why he was looking in the trunk. The policeman tells him a car like this was reported fleeing from a burglary and he was checking it out.

Somehow I know the man is lying. I think my dad does, too, but he nods and tells the policeman that makes sense. Then he asks if he's done so we can get on down the road and the policeman says he is. He gets into his patrol car and does a U-turn, heading back the way we came. When he does I see my father write the license number of the patrol car in his notebook.

My mother comes up to us. I have never seen her so angry. Her whole face is pinched so tight her lips are white and she is trembling. I am glad she is not mad at me. "That was a complete lie!" she tells my father. He nods and she asks, "Why did you let him get away with it?"

"There's no one here but him and us and it's his word against ours," my dad tells her and shrugs. "There wasn't much I could do. He's the man with the gun."

I seen Johnny's grandfather nod, but my mother isn't buying. "Well, you could do something! The reason he stopped us is that he saw a car full of Indians."

"You don't know that," my father answers, but he doesn't believe it, either.

"It's all right," Johnny's grandmother says. "It worked out. We don't have to let it ruin the day."

"It's not right!" my mother says. "He shouldn't be able to get away with things like that. He's a public servant."

"I'm not sure pointing that out would have helped," my father says.

"Besides, who says he's gotten away with it?" He holds up his notebook. The look in his eyes is one I know very well and I am glad I am not the policeman.

"All right, then," my mother says, looking around at the mess the policeman made searching the trunk. "We seem to be unpacked. Who would like a sandwich?" Pretty soon everyone is sitting around the trunk of the car, laughing and talking as we eat the food the women set out. No one says anything about the policeman and I wonder why. They act like nothing happened.

After lunch we head out again for Lower Brule. Johnny's sister decides to ride in the car with the women and other kids and Johnny and I are squeezed into the cab of the truck with my dad and his grandpa. My mother decides it's not safe for us to ride in the back of the truck and my dad goes along with her. I don't like riding in the cab as much as in the back, but I'm in the middle and Johnny is sitting on my lap with a seat belt fastened around both of us. Nobody wears seat belts much on the reservation, but my dad had a set mounted in his truck and he makes us wear them when we ride with him.

Neither my dad nor Johnny's grandpa have their seat belts on now. This surprises me because my dad always wears his, and I think he forgot. Yet, when I point this out, he gives me a stare. I don't know what's going on but I know it has something to do with my mother. When I glance at Johnny's grandpa, he is staring straight out the window but I get the feeling he is trying not to smile. After a minute or two my dad glances over at him and says, "*Wiyonan!*" This is Lakota for women and Johnny's grandpa laughs.

We drive along a while after that. The men are silent and Johnny and I talk in low whispers. Then my dad says to Johnny's grandpa, "You know, I've heard about that all my life, but I've never seen it before."

Grandpa Lyons shrugs. "It happens all the time. Not so much around here but all the time in Rapid." He is talking about Rapid City. "Not so much East River, either. "

My dad nods. "I hear Rapid City gets pretty bad for Indians."

"It's worse than you hear," the old man tells us. "Lot of stuff happens there that never gets in the paper."

"Lots of stuff happens around here that never gets in the paper, too," my dad tells him. "Mostly because there's no proof."

Johnny's grandpa shrugs. "It would just stir up trouble if you put it in the paper."

"I don't mind doing that," my dad answers. "But I've got to see it or have proof to take it to press. When I try to get proof, no one wants to talk."

"They know it won't do any good," Johnny's grandpa says. "It could make trouble for them if they do."

"So the real story doesn't get told." My dad sighs. "I can't say I blame them. I'm not sure what I would do in their place." Then he grins. "That's the nice thing about being the only paper in the county. Some people don't like what I have to say but they can't pull their ads, not if they want to stay in business."

"They might if you told the real story," Johnny's grandpa says.

My dad chuckles, but I can tell he is not amused. "Yeah, you're right. I don't think they want to hear the real story, mostly because it's about them. They don't want their dirty little secrets made public, like how their police harass Indians."

"You might be better forgetting it, Randall," Johnny's grandfather says. He sounds worried. "It's over. Let it go. It wasn't personal."

My dad shakes his head. "Oh, it's always personal with me, John. It was my family and my friends that yokel messed with. That makes it personal. Besides, if we just forget about it and go on, then nothing will ever change. They'll just keep doing it. Look at what's going on down South. People stopped taking it and things are changing."

The old man nods. "Yes, but people are getting killed, too. Good people, like those children in that bombing."

"Do you really think that could happen out here?" my dad asks.

Johnny's grandpa nods. "It does happen out here. You remember that man who was shot over on Pine Ridge last year? They one they never figured out?" My dad nods. "They said it must have been an Indian who shot him but it wasn't."

My dad looks at him sharply. "Is that what they say or what you know?"

"I talked to a man who knows. I believe him. He doesn't lie."

My dad shakes his head. "I'm not doubting what you say, John, but why hasn't the FBI come up with anything, then? They are normally pretty thorough. Did your man tell them what he knows?"

Johnny's grandpa nods. "They didn't listen to him. They don't listen to anyone they don't want to hear. He tried to tell them, but he's just an Indian. What does he know? I think they didn't want to believe him. Cops take care of each other."

"It was a policeman!" my dad asks. He is shocked. He thinks a moment. "You said it wasn't an Indian. So it was a white policeman? He came on the reservation?"

The old man nods. "Or shot him someplace else and dumped him there. You saw it yourself this morning. It happens all the time when it comes to Indians. Any car with Todd county plates gets stopped outside the county, unless the driver is white."

My dad is quiet a long time, thinking about what Grandpa Lyons just said. "It's not right, John," he says. "It's got to stop."

"It's been that way for a hundred years," Johnny's grandpa tells him. "Maybe more. People say they don't like it, but I think they are wrong. The people who try to stop it get killed. They get shot at from both sides."

My dad nods. "That sounds like the Irish. When they run out of common enemies, they fight each other. No one seems to want peace enough to do what's necessary to have it and they always blame the other side."

"Sounds like the Irish and the Lakota must be kin," Grandpa Lyons says. His face gets very sad. "I think we're our own worst enemies. No white man treats us as bad as we treat each other."

"Well, they're alike in more ways than one," my dad answers. "Indians can't handle liquor and the Irish can't, either. They only drink to get drunk."

Johnny's grandpa gives my father a strange look, as if he wants to ask why else one would drink. Yet he doesn't say anything and my dad misses the look. Somehow I seem to know it is time to keep my mouth shut, even though I want to ask questions. This is a very different way of looking at things, one I don't understand. My dad drinks without getting drunk, and so does my grandpa. They have a beer on a hot day and they even give me a sip when they do. After the first time, I don't take it any more. It tastes awful, like panther piss, I guess. That's what my grandpa calls it when my mother is not around. Or when he wants to get her mad.

Then, at Christmas time they drink eggnog, too. My dad makes it with rum but his dad likes it better made with Canadian whiskey. *Usgebaugh* is what he calls it. He tells me this is a Celtic word for "water of life" but I don't know why they call it that. The time I sneak a sip from my dad's rum bottle I think I'm going to die. It feels like it's burning a hole through my guts and I get real dizzy and barf. Sometimes my dad takes a drink straight from the bottle when it's just him and grandpa, but I don't see how they do it. I like wine, but I think beer and liquor are barf juice. It even makes eggnog taste real strange. I like it best without anything in it at all, not even nutmeg.

About this time we come to the Lower Brule turnoff. The road we were on goes on until it crosses the Missouri River near Ft. Thompson, but the pauwau grounds where the thing we are going to is in Lower Brule. At first, Johnny and I watch the road ahead to see when we arrive, but the turnoff is several miles from Lower Brule and we get bored seeing nothing but the same scenery we've looked at all morning.

Johnny's grandpa sees us getting tired from riding in the truck and begins to tell a story about Sinte Gleska , the last great leader of the Rosebud Sioux that white people call Spotted Tail. He tells us that Spotted Tail is not exactly right because sinte gleska is what the Lakota call a banded tail hawk. It's the same bird, but the Lakota description is more accurate.

The story he is telling us is about why about half of the Sicangu are Roman Catholic and the other half are Episcopal. He says that a long time ago two missionaries came to convert the Rosebud Lakota and Red Cloud's people gathered with Spotted Tail's people to listen to them and decide which way they would follow. The missionaries talked all day and when it got dark, Spotted Tail said to Red Cloud, "They are both saying much the same thing. I am done listening. Why don't you take one of them home with you and I will take the other?" Red Cloud agreed and took the Roman Catholic missionary to camp with him that night. Sinte Gleska took the Episcopal to his camp and that is the way it has been ever since. Red Cloud's people are Catholic and Spotted Tail's people are Episcopal.

I ask if that means the people we are going to be with are Spotted Tail's people, and Johnny's grandpa tells me this is mostly true. Since everybody is pretty much related to each other, though, there may be some Catholics here. A lot of the families married into one another, so it depends on which way the couple decide to go when they marry. On the reservation, it doesn't make a difference the way it does with white people. He tells us Father Alex told him he may be coming to Niobrara this year to see some people he has not seen in a long time.

By this time we are coming into Lower Brule and I am a little disappointed. From all the talk I expect it to be a different place, but it looks just about the same as Mission or Rosebud. A lot of the houses are run down and need paint, and there are a lot of old cars and other things around many of the houses. I remember asking my dad once why there is so much stuff piled up around houses on the reservation, and even around Indian houses in Winner, and he tells me it's because the people who live there like it that way.

My mother is listening and says she can't understand why poor people let it get like that. It doesn't take money to keep things looking neat and kept. My father tells her it's the psychology of poverty. When I ask him what psychology is, he gets a strange look on his face, like I've asked him something so simple he can't explain. Then my mother laughs and tells me psychology is about the way people think and feel. My father nods and says she took the words right out of his mouth, and my mother tells him that's why he couldn't think of them. She'd already taken them. Adults talk very strange sometimes.

Things change when we get through town and head out to the *pauwau* grounds west a mile or two. The arena is freshly painted bright white and there is a big blue tent like a big top set up right in the middle of it. When I see this I ask my dad if there is going to be a circus here this week. He laughs and says that's one way of looking at it and Johnny's grandpa says some of the priests are as big as elephants. He is serious when he says this but somehow I think he is teasing me. Then my dad asks him isn't Will Bill Hickock supposed to be here with his Wild West Show and they both laugh. Grandpa Lyle says he doesn't know if Wild Bill will show up or not, but there will be plenty of Indians.

Johnny and I pile out of the truck when we stop near the arena and my dad hollers after me not to wander off. The first thing we do is look in the big top tent, but that is disappointing. All the chairs are set up in rows facing a podium in front, just like pews in church, and there is no center ring. By now it is almost the middle of the afternoon and it is warm in the tent. The side curtains are rolled up except on the south side keeping the wind from blowing through. There are small groups of people standing around talking and someone is trying to get the sound system to work. I wonder why things like this always have trouble with the sound system.

I hear Johnny call and run over to where he is. Someone is laying out the lodge poles for a tipi on the other side of the tent and we stand and watch. Pretty soon the guy setting it up asks one of us to hand him a rope and we stay to help him out. He ties three of the poles together at the small ends and then pushes them up to make a tripod. When he is satisfied with this, he adds the rest of the lodge poles, stacking them in a circle between the short upright ends of the tripod. The long rope he used to tie the first poles together is dangling inside the circle made by the bottom of the poles and when they are all in place, he grabs the dangling rope and begins walking around the outside of the circle, wrapping all the lodge poles together at the top.

When he is done tying the poles together, the guy grins at us and tells us the easy part is done. Then he turns to the people who have gathered to watch and tells them any help they may care to offer is welcome. Several young men come forward when he says this and begin unrolling a large bundle of canvas and laying it around the poles.

What makes this hard is the wind, which has picked up and keeps tugging at the edge of the canvas. When the young men begin to lift it off the ground, it gathers wind like a sail and only the upright poles keep it from blowing away and dragging the guys along after it. By now enough of them are holding onto the bottom to keep it from blowing away and the guy in charge shows them how to walk forward so the wind wraps the canvas tight against the poles. When the ends come together on the other side, he begins to fasten them together with long wooden pins and pretty soon the tipi has taken shape, except for the very top. To fasten this together, a really tall guy goes into the tipi and gets Johnny to fasten the last two pins from inside. Everyone laughs when this happens because all we can see is a tipi with an arm sticking out the top, fumbling around for the pin holes.

There is not much going on after that until time for supper and Johnny and I look around. There is a small rise south of the *pauwau* arena and this is covered with tents. A small bunch of outhouses are set up a good way to the east of the tents, and from the rise I can see a few more scattered around. There are also a couple of big pavilions covered with brush off to one side and Johnny tells me these are where we will sit to eat.

I ask him how he knows since he has never been here before, either, but he just grins and tells me to wait and see if I don't believe him. Then I see something I didn't notice before. It is a couple of covered pickups backed up to another shed next to the pavilions, and I can see people unloading coolers and roasters and large tea barrels.

I can also see that one section of the tents seems to be newer than the others, and Johnny and I go over to check this out. When we get there we see a bunch of older white kids standing around. Most of them look like they're high school kids and when one of the girls walks by, Johnny asks her where they are from. When she answers, her voice sounds kind of funny but I like it. The way she says her words is very gently, with the edges sort of blurred, like she dipped them in honey before she offered them to us. It's strange, but the way she says them makes me feel warm inside, like each one is a hug every bit as warm as my mother's, and meant just for me.

I see Johnny giving me a strange look and I look down at my feet. My face feels hot, like I've been out in the sun and wind all day, and I can't think of anything to say. I just stand there dumb as a fence post, listening to that beautiful voice and feeling it surround me like a blanket.

I hear her tell Johnny her name is Lou Ann and she is part of a youth group from a church in North Carolina. I'm not sure where that is, but I know it is a long way from South Dakota, even farther than Kansas. And I know she sure doesn't talk the way people do from Kansas.

Then she asks who we are. I hear Johnny tell them his name and that he is from Corn Creek on the other side of White River. Then it is my turn and I can't say a thing. I hear Lou Ann ask me what is the matter, does the cat have my tongue. I want to say her cat can have my tongue any time it likes, but all I can do is stammer. "My name is Randy," I hear myself croak. I feel my cheeks burning.

"Why, he's shy!" Lou Ann says, touching me lightly on the arm with her hand. When she does it feels like liquid fire coursing through my whole body. I have never felt anything like this in my life and I think I am going to die. "Well, how sweet! Where are you from, Randy?"

I somehow manage to get Winner out between teeth that seem to have melted. She laughs. "Randy from Winner. My goodness." Then she winks at me. "I guess that makes you a randy winner, hum?" I don't know what she means by this but Johnny laughs. I know this means he doesn't know, either, because of the way he laughs.

Lou Ann seems to know this, too, because she laughs and says it is nice meeting us but she really must get back to her group. When she walks away, the way she swings her hips makes me ache in a way I never have before. Then I hear my dad's chuckle. I turn to look at him and he is grinning. "Looks like you guys found a red hot mama," he says. "Come on, it's time for supper." As we walk back to the arena he gives me an odd look. "I think you and I may need to have a talk one of these days soon."

I guess it is about a month later when the sheriff comes by to talk to my dad. We are back home in Winner and I am still out of school for summer vacation. I am down at the newspaper office reading a book in the workroom across the hall from my dad's office and we are alone in the building. We put the paper to bed on Tuesday, like we always have, and my dad lets the office help have the afternoon off. I am with him because my mother and sister have gone shopping in Mitchell and Sioux Falls and my dad promised to take me for an ice cream when he is done making a few phone calls. He promises a double scoop if I am as quiet as a mouse while he makes his calls, so I am trying not to make any noise.

I hear the front door open and close. I guess my dad has forgotten to lock it. He always locks the door when he is working alone in the office. He says it is the only time he can be sure he's not interrupted, and Wednesday afternoon is when he writes his piece for the next edition. Today he is making an exception. Next week is Frontier Days and the whole paper will be about that.

I hear footsteps coming down the hall and I duck under the table where I'm sitting. I don't know why I do this, but I do. There's something scary about the way the footsteps sound in the empty office. Not like someone is tiptoeing, but walking so quiet I can barely make it out. I hear a murmur of my dad's voice talking on the phone, but I don't think he can hear the steps.

I listen while the steps stop outside the room where I'm hiding, then move on down the hall to my dad's office. I am scared and I don't know what to do. I wonder if I should yell to warn my dad. I am just about to do so when I hear his voice speak up, "Why, hello, Sheriff. I wondered who that was slipping up the hall."

There is a deep chuckle and a voice I don't know answers. "I should know by now I can't sneak up on you. Randy. I swear, you can hear a gnat fart a block away. You got a minute to talk?"

"Sure," my dad answers. He says something into the phone and I know he has been talking to my grandpa. I hear the sheriff laugh and tell him he won't need bail.

I listen while my dad and the sheriff talk about the weather and how the crops and pheasants are doing. Then they turn to the election coming up in November and my dad asks how the sheriff thinks he is doing. This is the first time someone else is running in a long time, too, and I hear the sheriff complain he's forgotten how to politic.

I hear my dad make a rude noise and say, "Horse shit!" They both laugh. Then my dad says, "I guess that's why you came by, isn't it?"

The sheriff laughs again, but I can tell he doesn't think it is really funny. He tells my dad the article last week really got some folks upset.

"That's what I intended," I hear my dad say. "There are some things that need to change, and treatment under the law is one of them."

"You know, I try to be very fair," the sheriff says. "Sometimes it isn't easy, but I do try and I make sure my deputies do, too."

"I know," my dad tells him. "I tried to make it very clear that who I was talking about was that asshole of a patrolman who gave us a hard time."

"Yeah," says the sheriff. "I know and I do appreciate that. It was the patrolman who asked me to come by and have a talk. You were pretty rough on him in what you wrote and he was pretty stung. I told him it wouldn't do much good, but he asked me to do it as a personal favor. So I'll tell him we talked and you told me to shove it. Or am I putting words in your mouth?"

I hear my dad laugh. "Yeah, you are, but at least they're the right ones, but I can't imagine having to have to tell you to shove it. You're too smooth for that."

"Thank you, I think," the sheriff says. "The problem is, it wasn't just the patrolman who got upset. I had to talk pretty straight to some of my deputies, but even that wasn't what brought me here. You pissed a lot of private citizens off, too."

"Most of who have made a point of telling me about it," my dad chuckles. "Don't worry, Sheriff. It will blow over. It always does."

"I guess so," the sheriff answers. He is quiet for a moment and I hear my dad ask if there is something else. When he answers I can tell the sheriff hates having to ask for what he wants. "Look, what I was wondering is if you might be willing to tell the other side of the story, too."

"The other side?" my dad asks. "What other side? The fellow abused his authority and got caught doing it. I was there. I saw it."

"Yeah, but you were directly involved," the sheriff says. "How about how people in law enforcement might look at it? How about that other side of?"

It is my dad's turn to be quiet. "What do you have in mind?" he asks. "You want me to interview that trooper, too?"

"Wouldn't be a bad idea," the sheriff says, "but I don't think you could be objective with him. Why don't you talk to some of my deputies? They'll tell you how they see it."

"Interesting idea," my dad says. He doesn't say anything for a minute. I can hear his pencil scratching and I know he is doodling, the way he does when he's trying to figure something out. "Well, if I do, I'm making no promises," my dad goes on. "I print the truth as I see it and they might not like what I say. It doesn't sound like they would be too open my point of view."

"Why don't you get to know them as people?" the Sheriff asks him. "Let them get to know you the way I do. Talk to them on the job if you want, but talk to them at home with their families, too. I think you'll see a whole different side of them then. I think you would understand where they are coming from."

"I print it as I see it," my dad says. "No promises and everything is on the record."

"All I'd ask is for you to be fair," the sheriff says. "And no details of any current investigations printed, either."

"All right," my dad decides. "I'll start with you. You got time now?"

"Sure," the sheriff says, and I see my ice cream melting in the sun. When my dad gets to talking he doesn't know when to stop and it is already getting late. By the time he gets done the drug store will be closed.

I make a decision. I know I promised to be quiet, but my dad promised me an ice cream, too. So I crawl out from under the table and walk across to my dad's door. I don't say anything, though. I just look in.

"Well, where did you come from, squirt?" the sheriff asks. He is surprised to see me. "I didn't hear you come in."

My dad laughs. "He was so quiet I forgot he was here. You mind talking over an ice cream cone?"

The sheriff laughs, too. "Over a beer is more my style, but I bet they've got some coffee. Sure."

We walk down the block to the drug store on Main. It is getting late and there is almost no traffic on the street. The drug store is quiet when we go in and the soda jerk is talking to a couple of girls near the front of the soda bar. We sit down at one of the small tables at the very back and the soda jerk comes over to take our order. My dad knows I like to watch the jerk make ice cream sodas and tells me I can order one. This is a real treat, one I don't get very often, and I decide to go for chocolate. With my mother here, I would have to settle for vanilla this late in the day, but when it's just us guys, my dad cuts me a lot of slack.

My dad asks the jerk to bring their coffee first and I sit at the bar

104

to watch my soda being made. I know my dad is doing this because he wants to talk to the sheriff alone, but I don't mind. The drug store is very quiet and where I am sitting I can hear as clearly as if I was at the table. My mother has the nose in the family, but my dad and I have the ears and we can hear things other people can't. Even my grandpa can hear better than my mother or sister, though they are not hard of hearing like Miss Lampe, who runs the school library. I almost have to shout to get her attention sometimes. What I don't understand is how she knows when we're up to something. My mother is the same way, so maybe Miss Lampe smells trouble when it's brewing.

The funny thing is, I know my dad knows I can hear everything that's being said at the table. When I ask him about it later, he tells me he knows, but the sheriff doesn't. He tells me people talk more freely when they don't think someone else is listening and he wants the sheriff to open up as much as he will. Like a lot of things my dad says, I don't understand this until later on and I guess it's this way with kids. We're sort of like tape recorders soaking up everything up so we can play it back later. The thing is, we forget to play it back, or even that we took it in, and it's strange how memories come back out of the blue. When it does, it's always tied to something right now, though it's hard to see the connection until we think about it. It's strange how the mind works that way.

I watch the clerk take down a soda glass from a glass shelf on the wall behind the bar. He asks me if I want chocolate or vanilla ice cream, and I tell him one scoop of vanilla and one of strawberry, using chocolate sauce and peanuts on top. He nods and dips the ice cream, grinning at me when he makes the scoops extra large. Then he adds a generous dip of chocolate sauce and sets the glass below the soda spigot. This is the part I like best, watching the stream of soda water, thin as a pencil lead, shoot into the glass, cutting a tiny hole in the ice cream and making a frothy swill in the bottom of the glass. Then the clerk tops it all off with whipping cream out of a can, scatters peanuts on top, and crowns the whole works with a bing cherry. Just writing about it now after all these years makes me hungry for one. To a kid like me, a large soda made this way is heaven on earth. There is nothing better.

All this time I am listening to my dad and the sheriff talk. They get right to it as soon as their coffee comes. The sheriff is doing most of the talking, with my dad sticking in a question now and then.

"I will admit we probably do stop more cars with sixty-five plates," the sheriff is saying. Sixty-five is the license plate code for Todd County, which is the Rosebud Lakota reservation, though they call themselves the Sicangu. "I don't keep track but if you went back through our logs, it's probably true. But there is a reason for it, too. Most of the ones we stop are DUI, driving without a license or insurance, or all three. They are a clear and present public danger. To themselves as well as to you and me."

In the mirror behind the soda bar I see my dad nod. "Can you give me a ball park percentage?" he asks.

"I'd be willing to bet that if you went through the records you'd see something like eighty percent," the sheriff answers. "Of course, that's traffic stops where the officer calls in. Sometimes they don't, particularly if they know the people. They don't bust them, either. They just tell them to get the hell home and sleep it off."

"Why don't they arrest them?" my dad wants to know.

"Well, if they are DUI, we usually do," the sheriff says. "Sometimes if they are close to home and haven't hurt anything, we don't. I give my deputies lots of discretion whether to bring them in."

"Why wouldn't you bring them all in?"

The sheriff sighs. "It's mostly economics. It costs a hell of a lot of money to bust people and keep them in jail. More than the county superintendents have to spend. So we go for the worst cases."

"I take it, the worst cases are mostly Indians." The way my dad says this, I know it is not a question.

The sheriff nods. "White people aren't so...public about it. Or so violent, either, as a rule. At least, we don't hear about it. Not officially." He shrugs. "Then, too, you have to remember the rate of alcoholism is much greater on the reservation."

"I want to get back to what you said about violence in a minute," my dad says. "But I want to know about alcoholism first. Do you have any solid figures?"

The sheriff shakes his head. "No. The Public Health Service people estimate it at about fifty to eighty-five percent, depending on who you talk to. It's probably a matter of public record somewhere if you know where to look. The point is on the reservation it's more likely than not that whoever you see on the street is legally drunk or will be before the day is out. It wouldn't be a problem for us if they stayed on the reservation, but they don't. It's hard to buy liquor on the reservation, so they come to Winner or Valentine or White River or somewhere else to get more. And they don't wait to get home before they start drinking, either. Or even back over the county line."

My dad is quiet. I can see he is thinking, his pencil tapping on his pad. He makes a couple of notes and then says, "All right, I'll check it out. Go on."

"This is not just a white man talking, Junior," the sheriff says. "You ever read the New York Times Magazine?"

"About as often as I read the Wall Street Journal," my dad chuckles. "It doesn't have much news from South Dakota."

The sheriff laughs. "I don't read it either, but a cousin of mine in New York does and she sent me an article they ran not long back. It's about Pine Ridge. You see that?"

My dad shakes his head and the sheriff goes on. "I'll dig it out for you. Things are getting pretty tense there now, more than before. What I got my attention was what one of the tribal policemen had to say about the drinking problem. He said life on Pine Ridge is so hard people have to stay half drunk just to stand it. The point is, even Indians know there is a problem with alcoholism on the reservation."

"That's a problem we introduced them to," my dad points out.

"Yeah, I hear that all the time. 'I'm drunk and it's the white man's fault.' So I guess there must be a lot of white men around holding guns to the heads of lots of Indians forcing them to take a drink. Maybe that's a story that needs exposing."

My dad laughs. "Well, there is that. I see what you mean. But we are glad enough to sell it to them."

"We don't have much choice," the sheriff points out. "It is the law. Don't sell it to them because they are Indians and can't handle it and they call you a racist. Sell it and they tell you the result is your fault. I think things were better before 1938. We could at least bust people for selling it to them then. It's been an uphill fight ever since."

"That's when they legalized it? I remember hearing about it but not the date."

"I can't tell you the month, day and year. In my opinion, that's another date written in infamy for us around here. I talked to an old man over in Mission once. He told me that on the day it happened there were cars and trucks and wagons lined up for a mile waiting for the liquor store to open." The sheriff pauses and takes a sip of his coffee. "And what that tells me is that there was a market for it long before it became legal."

"You can't get around the fact we introduced alcohol to them," my dad says.

"No, but you can't get around the fact Columbus brought syphilis back from the West Indies, either. Does that mean the Lakota are to blame if I get a case of that? I don't think so, although I know a lot of people who wouldn't mind claiming that."

"So it boils down to individual choice?" my dad asks.

"That's the way the law works. I may incite you to riot, which means I am guilty of inciting you, but if you choose to riot, that's on your head."

"That's a white man's perspective," my dad says.

The sheriff studies his cup for a long time. Then he looks up at my dad and says, "Junior, I'm not some dumb assed hick sheriff, and I would appreciate it if you gave me credit for some smarts. I got my law degree from Harvard and was a Rhodes scholar after the War. Did you know that?"

My dad shakes his head. "No, I had no idea."

"Not many people do. I don't make too big a deal about it because with that and a half dollar I can usually buy a cup of coffee and a donut. I went to school to learn what they had to teach me, not to earn a living. The only reason I mention it is so you know I've been taught to think and I do think about things a good bit." He grins. "I suppose you've heard I've never pulled my gun except to clean it or put it away?"

"Now, that I did know," my dad says. I can tell he is surprised by what the sheriff has told him. I never thought about it before, but now I understand why. The thing is, over the years I have also found there are a lot of people like the sheriff living in remote areas of the country. They've been to the city and choose to live in the sticks, and like a lot of Midwestern country folk, they don't make a big deal about it. Prices change, but like the sheriff said, with that and a little money, they can buy a cup of coffee.

"Well, it's nothing to brag about, particularly," the sheriff laughs. "It's pure self interest. I like having that reputation so people don't get spooked and shoot when I have to arrest them. But I think you get my point. I work at rational response."

"They could have used more like you in Chicago a few summers back," my dad says.

"The way things were in Chicago a few summers back is why I am here in Winner," the sheriff says. "Now it looks like the same damned thing is going down in Pine Ridge."

"That's what I've been hearing. I don't understand what's going on there. The FBI is running the show and they're not the Chicago Police Department."

"The Fat Boy's Institute is way over rated," the sheriff tells him. "And they are the biggest part of the problem. Don't get me wrong. They have a lot of good people and you can't beat their police training. If they sent us their very best, things would be much different. The thing is, Pine Ridge is like Butte, Montana. That's where they send all the screw-ups with too much political connection to fire."

My dad talks to him about the Pine Ridge situation a long time, until the soda jerk reminds them he has to close up pretty soon. My dad pays the bill, giving me a look when he sees I've had two scoops of ice cream as well as the soda, but he doesn't say anything. I know he will later, but by then it will be all right. I know he won't say anything to my mother about it, either. Just having a soda before supper is bad enough in her eyes, but to her, two scoops of ice cream on top of that is almost as bad as stealing money from the collection plate.

The sheriff and my dad continue their talk as we walk back to the newspaper office and I sort of listen in. I can tell from how my dad is talking that things have changed with him and the sheriff. They started out the way my dad does when he interviews someone, but they are talking like my dad and grandpa talk now, and I like to listen. You learn lots of things you never learn at school if you listen while adults talk and you even learn a few things they wouldn't tell you by yourself, especially if they forget you're around. I am pretty good at that, helping them forget I'm around. Sometimes this makes my dad mad, and my mother, too, but he never yells at me for it. He tells me it's a useful life skill and I think sometimes he's proud of me, even though what I do makes him mad. Adults are sort of funny that way. They seem to like what they say they hate.

I'm walking behind my dad and the sheriff and by the time they get to the office, I know they have forgotten I'm around. When they stop at the sheriff's car, I sit down on the sidewalk with my back against the wall and they keep talking.

"You know, I never got back to asking you about violence," my dad says. "You were saying something about white people not being so violent when they drink."

The sheriff nods. "I think it's something genetic. Not good or bad, just genetic. I think some people are born with a metabolism to handle alcohol and some are not, and I'd be willing to bet fewer Indians have as high a tolerance as white people." He shrugs. "I don't know if it's genetics or culture, but Jews seem to have the highest tolerance and the Irish, one of the lowest." He grins. "I've seen a lot of Irish drunks in South Boston."

"I bet you have. But how does this tie into violence?"

"The same as it does with other people. Booze lowers inhibitions very efficiently, and I think most Europeans have some inhibition against losing control. So they drink just so much, and no more. They only allow themselves to go so far and the effect they drink for is different. You and I may have a beer to relax a little. With an Indian, I think life is so painful he drinks to forget it for a little while."

My dad nods. "I see. Anesthesia rather than sedation."

"Exactly. Only after a while the tolerance to the anesthesia builds up and it takes more to get the same effect. With heavier drinking, the inhibition threshold goes down."

"And the result is violence," my dad says. "What's so different about that and the way it is for white people? I've seen exactly the same thing you're talking about among white people. They get drunk, too, and they get just as violent."

"That's what I meant when I said Indians tend to be more public with it," the sheriff answers. "There are no secrets on the reservation. Everyone is related in some way to everyone else, so there aren't family secrets the same way there are among people around here, among white people. To put it another way, it's out in the open. It's not kept hidden like it is among Europeans."

"So you're saying being drunk and disorderly in public is not that different from being drunk and disorderly at home?"

"Yeah, something like that. I'm still trying to get my mind around it." The sheriff shrugs.

"Which tells me you still have an open mind," my dad points out.

"Don't say that so loud," the sheriff laughs. "I still have to win this election."

"What are you going to do if you lose?"

"I don't know. Maybe stay in town and become a public defender. I've kept up my license to practice law."

"Now that would be ironic, defending the same people you bust now."

The sheriff gives my dad a long look. Then he says, "This next comment is off the record. Agreed?"

My dad looks back at him, then nods. "Agreed."

"All I would be doing is the same job a different way," the sheriff tells him. "And I'd probably be better paid."

My dad thinks about this. "You're saying you defend Indians right now?" he asks.

"That's exactly what I'm saying," the sheriff answers and I can see he is dead serious. "I defend a hell of a lot more Indians than I bust. So do my deputies. And if you want to know why, it's very simple. Law enforcement is too important to be left to dumb assholes like certain state troopers."

My dad is silent and the sheriff adds, "You quote me on that and I'll call you a liar."

"Quote you on what?" my dad asks and the sheriff laughs. Then my dad remembers and turns to me. "This is just between us and the sheriff, Randy. This is a confidential news source. Understood?" I nod. Nothing is more sacred in our family than confidential news sources, and it is more than twenty years before I even remember this happened, much less mention it. Even now, I feel obligated to ask the sheriff if he cares before I take it to print.

Northern Lights

8 October 12, 1982. They gave back Jim Thorpe's gold medals today. Seventy years after he won them for the pentathlon and decathlon at the Summer Games in Stockholm, they finally gave them back, and it was not even his own country that did this. It was his native land who stripped him of his medals in January 1913, but it was the International Olympic Committee who finally restored them. The irony is that they did so four hundred and ninety years to the day that Christopher Columbus is credited with discovering the New World. I wonder if they knew, the members of the International Committee? It's no secret when Columbus Day is and there are Americans on the Committee.

A lot of people I talk to are very happy about this. They say justice has been done and an all American hero has been vindicated. They cannot understand why people like me say 'who-friggen-ray'. I guess no one who is not an athlete could understand what it would be like having prizes you have worked for years to earn stripped after the whole world has said you are the very best.

I guess no one who is not an outsider of some kind could understand the insult this adds to the injury you have suffered all your life. Not even the guys that raised a black power salute in Mexico City in 1968 understand. Their medals were stripped because they used the moment to make a political statement, and this was their choice. I believe they did the right thing, but at least it was for a personal action they chose to do. Jim Thorpe was nailed because he was a red nigger, and an honest one, at that. He didn't try to hide what he did. He didn't even know it was wrong and by today's standards he was more of an amateur than ninety-five per cent of the latest American team. No, his crime was being a Sac and Fox Indian, and leaving every white man on earth in his dust.

So now justice has been done and an all American hero is vindicated. I guess it may mean something to the people of Jim Thorpe's family, but Jim Thorpe is dead now almost thirty years. I think he might understand why someone like me says, "Who-friggen-ray!" What difference does it

113

make to him now? After all, he is the one who did it. He's the one they crucified for something he did not understand. He's the one who went on to become the greatest athlete of the twentieth century and I think if he were alive today and spoke from his heart, he would say the same thing I do. "It's about freaken time!"

Yet, for a while, Jim Thorpe had his medals. For two or three months, the whole world acclaimed him as the best athlete around. So what he would not understand is not being given the chance to win. I don't think he would understand how much it hurts to train for years and years and years, and to know in your heart you can win, and then to be denied the chance. I don't think he would understand losing his moment in the sun because his country decided to boycott the Olympic games for political reasons. I don't think he would understand not being able to compete because the Games were being held in the Soviet Union. I don't think he would understand being the fastest sprinter in the world and not getting to run for the gold. And I do not think he would understand why I did not even run in organized events after that.

Yet, the answer is very simple. The white men are just too powerful. There are too many of them and they are too well organized to beat them at their own game. This is what Crazy Horse learned, even though he beat them at Little Big Horn. They may not be the best, but there are too many of them and they are too well armed. With every victory like Little Big Horn, there is a slaughter like Wounded Knee. This is how they have taken the whole world, and this is what they did to Jim Thorpe for winning. Now they think by giving his medals back, they can rob us of the last thing we have, our anger and rage over what they have done to us since we first encountered them.

Well, it's not going to work, not with this Indian. Anger and contempt is all I have left. And this is something they can never take away. They can never make me love them or respect them. They can only make me hate them more. That may be possible.... (excerpt from John K's college journals)

I am there the day Johnny graduates from the University in Vermilion. It is May, 1985, six years after we graduate from high school. I go on to college back east, studying anthropology at Columbia, and Johnny goes to work on a horse ranch in Montana. This is not because he has to. His family may be poor but he is the fastest sprinter in the state, if not the world, and is offered several full ride scholarships around the country by major universities. He is also Indian and can probably get a full ride on that if he wants to go to a smaller school. I know he has the grades and test scores to get into Harvard. They came asking. I am not sure why he doesn't take any of these offers, but he just doesn't seem interested. What he is interested in is horses and there is a man in Montana he wants to learn from.

I lose track of Johnny over the first year, but the letters I get from time to time tell me he is still running. He still loves that and stays in shape, but he doesn't run in competition any more. He runs with the horses and runs long distance. The last sprint he ran would have broken the world record, but he slowed way down in the last few yards and came in two hundredths of a second under it. When I write to ask why he slowed down, he tells me he had the race won. He says that knowing he has the world record any time he wants it is enough. He says that's something they can't take away from him.

When I see him the second Christmas after we graduate, I ask him what the hell he is talking about. He asks if I know who Jim Thorpe is. I say isn't he the guy who said, "Hello, King," to the King of Sweden, and Johnny laughs. He tells me about Jim Thorpe. He tells me his original name was Wa-tho-huk, which means Bright Path in English. He tells me how Jim Thorpe got screwed out of his gold medals and says if they can do that to someone as famous as Thorpe, they can do the same to him. Why should he try for something that can be taken away? Besides that, he doesn't want to end up as an Apple like Thorpe.

I don't know what to say to this. He's right. Anything a human being has can be taken away, maybe even his soul. I ask why not do it for yourself, and Johnny tells me that is exactly what he is doing. Horses mean a lot to plains Indians and he has decided to learn everything he can about them. This is why he runs with them. He wants to become a trainer and someday own a ranch and raise good riding horses.

I tell him he's going to have to have money to do that and going to college is the quickest way to make some money. He laughs and tells me he's already figured that out. He tells me he is due to start school the very next month on a scholastic scholarship at the University of South Dakota. The Olympic experience last year left a bad taste in his mouth and he doesn't want to have anything to do with organized athletics. At least, he doesn't want to have anything to do with athletics organized by white men. I tell him just making the Olympic team last year is enough to get him a full ride track scholarship at just about any college in the country, even Harvard, but he tells me he doesn't want the pressure to win. He wants to become a veterinarian and raise horses.

Then Johnny tells me something I will never forget. He tells me what it is like to run with the horses, even the wild ones. He tells me what it is like to run a mustang down on foot, how it feels to gentle it to his presence in a single day and to ride it the next without it ever pitching. He ask me how many Olympic runners have ever done that. He says this is something not even Jim Thorpe did. Nor can anyone ever take it away.

So it is horses that finally get Johnny into college, and despite his scholarship, he works part time so he has money to send home to his family. Then, sometime in his first year he first meets Ellen and things change. She's about the only thing that can get his mind off horses for more than five minutes and when I meet her the next summer, I get scared. Ellen is as sweet as she can be, and sharp as a tack, but she is tall like a willow and very fair, with Nordic looks and long blonde hair that hangs half way down her back. There's no question she adores Johnny, but I see the looks they draw walking around town and I wonder if she is aware of them. I know Johnny must be. He's lived with this all his life, and when I ask him about it, he shrugs. He tells me she says it doesn't matter, even though her folks don't like her hanging out with an Indian. He also tells me he has never seen anyone with an easier way with horses, and I realize it is no use saying more. With Ellen he has what I found with Jenny, a soul mate, and if people don't like it, then they can damned well lump it.

As things work out, Jenny is with me today. She is finishing up her third year at the University of Minnesota and drove down to meet me yesterday. We are planning to get married the summer after she finishes her master's degree. She wants to teach a while before we have children, and for a librarian, it's better to have the master's. With that she can even land a pretty good job with the state as an archivist.

At the moment, I'm wondering what to do for the next three years until we marry. I graduated from Columbia two years ago with a second major in communications, and I've worked for the St. Paul Free Press ever since. I like the paper and I like living near Jenny even more. Yet I'd like to see a little more of the world. My dad will be retiring in a few years and I'll probably move home to take over the paper from him if Jenny agrees. I have seen enough of urban life to think Winner is a better place to raise kids. The Twin Cities are all right, except for the traffic, but they have their share of drugs and drive by shootings, too.

Nor are they a good place to be an Indian, either, and I want to raise our kids in a safe place. I also want them to learn both cultures, too.

So I'm at loose ends right now and I think that's a big part of why things turn out the way they do. Jenny and I will come out all right on the other side, but I don't know that going in. I jump in head first and I am damned lucky things turned out the way they did. One thing that does happen is that I get to see a hell of a lot more of the world than I will ever care to again.

I see I'm getting ahead of my story here. What's important is that today is my best friend's graduation and the love of my life is here with me. When I talk to Johnny by phone a couple of days ago to tell him we are both coming for graduation, he is on top of the world. He just bought his first horse, he tells me, an Appaloosa, and the way he talks, you'd think it was the only horse in the world. What more can he want, he asks. He's got true love and a good pony, and the rest will take care of itself.

What more can a man want? I don't have a good pony, just a battered old Subaru station wagon that has more miles than Methuselah's mule. I do have a good job I like and a good start on a career as a newsman, and God only knows I have true love. Yet, there is something missing. I am not sure what it is, but after a while in a place, I feel restless and want to move on.

That's strange for a guy who lived his whole life in one place and doesn't really want to leave when it's time, not even to go to school, but there it is. Then, living in New York I enter a whole other dimension, and nothing has been quite the same since. Compared to the Big Apple, St. Paul is as quiet as a graveyard and I'm always surprised to see how small Winner is those few times I go back to see my family. I love the quiet there, and there is something about the vast empty spaces that fills my soul in a way nothing else can. Yet, after a few days I am ready to head out again, and even St. Paul feels a little cramped to me when I get this way.

Johnny, on the other hand, would like nothing better than getting started with his ranch and giving Ellen babies to raise with the horses. I envy him that. It must be nice to know what you want so you can go after it, and Johnny has a plan. He's been accepted for veterinary school at Texas A&M, one of the best in the nation, and he says Ellen is trying to get a job there so they can be together. He says Texas is not like South Dakota. It's all right to be an Indian in Texas.

I wonder if Johnny knows what he's talking about when he tells me this, but I don't say anything. I know I wouldn't like being a Mexican in Texas and Johnny is dark enough to be mistaken for a Chicano. The few Texans I know seem to dislike anybody who is not white and from Texas. The only exception is John Wayne, and after making "The Alamo", he's considered an honorary Texan.

I feel Jenny nudge my arm and I look up to see Johnny coming towards us. I know something is wrong the minute I see him, and when he gets close, I smell cheap whiskey. I am surprised because for a long time Johnny quit drinking. The last time I saw him drunk was when we graduated from high school, and he looked a whole lot happier then than he does right now.

We greet Johnny and I ask him what's wrong. I think maybe someone died, and from the look on his face, it's someone very close, like Johnny's mother. I feel my throat tighten up, expecting bad news.

When I ask, Johnny doesn't give me a straight answer. Why do I think something is wrong, he asks me. This is his big day. He's graduating, summa cum freaken laud, from Hick State University. He says that should make anybody happy.

I ask him who died and he tells me no one. He tries to laugh it off but what comes out is a huge sob and he collapses in tears. He clings to me and sobs like a baby. I know he must be really drunk. He would never, ever show feelings this way if he was sober, not even if he was bleeding to death inside.

Jenny tries to comfort him but he pushes her away. He tells her something very rude in Lakota. Thinking of it later it makes me mad, but right now I am too shocked to be angry. This is not Johnny talking. This is the booze.

I can see Jenny is very angry. She snaps back in Lakota, saying something equally rude, and then storms off. I call out to her but she doesn't come back. She tells me I better get that drunk Indian off the street before the police bust him. I have never, ever seen her so angry.

I want to run after her, but I can't leave Johnny, not the way he is. So I help him get to my car. Once he sits down, he stops crying. He tells me he didn't really mean what he said to Jenny, to please tell her that.

I tell him he needs to tell her that himself and he nods. I ask him again what is the matter and he reaches in his jacket pocket and pulls out a square blue envelope. When he does I smell Wildwood Flower and know it is from Ellen. He tells me to open it and I do, dreading what I know she will say. Nor am I wrong. Ellen's letter is clear and to the point.

Dearest Johnny,

This is the hardest thing I have ever had to do. You are a sweet man and I love you with all my heart. This is what makes it so hard to say what I know I have to say, for your good and for mine.

I have known for a long time I cannot marry you. I did not want to admit this, not even in the secret places of my heart. I have never known anyone like you, and I don't think I ever will again. I wanted to spend the rest of my life with you, having your children and growing old together. But this cannot be. As much as I disagree with my father, he is my father and I cannot go against his wishes and marry you. That is not who I am.

No, that's not the truth, either. I mean, it is, but I know I could win him over with time. Despite his dislike of you, he is a fair man and would honor you if I insisted on making you my husband.

Johnny, I don't know how to say this any other way. I don't want to admit it, but I can't live with your anger. I thought I could love you enough to heal it but I can't, and as much as I love you, I also know I am one of those white people you despise so much. I could not bear to marry you only to have you come to hate me the way you do other white people.

There, I've said it. I know it will hurt you and I wish there were something else I could do, but there is not. I think it would hurt you more if I didn't honor you with the truth. The truth is that I will always love you the way I do now, but I cannot be your wife. I cannot be the mother of your children.

Please forgive me for not being strong enough.

Ellen

I read the letter through a second time, then put it away in the envelope. I look at Johnny, but his eyes are closed. Tears are streaming down his cheeks. I ask him if I can show this to Jenny and he nods. I tell him I will tell her he didn't mean what he said, but he has to tell her, too, the next time he sees her. Johnny nods and I tell him I'll be right back. I ask if he will be all right until I do, and he nods.

I am gone longer than I think. I find Jenny, but it takes a while to get her calmed down. She has never seen Johnny like this. She says he reminds her of their uncle who got drunk and beat his family all the time. I show her the letter and she reads it. When she is done she tells me it doesn't make any difference. Ellen did that to Johnny, not her. I tell her I need to go back to him. I am afraid of what he might do to himself if I don't. She tells me I can't keep him from hurting himself. Sooner or later if he is going to hurt himself, he's going to hurt himself.

I tell her I can't worry about later. I am afraid of what he may do right now. He needs me to help him get through today. I tell her he could use her help, too, and she gets very angry. She says he just told her what to do with her help.

I tell her that is the booze talking and she says that is exactly the point. He chose to get drunk. Now he wants us to rescue him and that's the worst thing we can do. We need to let him suffer the consequences of his choices.

Later I will understand that Jenny is right. I will come to understand tough love and what it means. At the moment, however, I don't know this and I get very angry. I tell Jenny I thought she loved Johnny. She tells me she loves him almost as much as she loves me. She says she wouldn't be so angry if she didn't love him. I can do what I want, she tells me, but she's not going to help him become an alcoholic. If I really love him I won't, either. I'll help him get sober.

I get so angry I can hardly see straight. I tell her I guess that's the way she will treat me if I'm ever down, too. I see people stopping to stare at us and realize I'm almost shouting. I tell her to just forget it and I'm sorry I asked. I storm off and I hear her calling after me to come back, but I am too angry. I shout over my shoulder that Johnny was right about her. I repeat what he said in Lakota and a lady passing by looks at me in shock. Then she looks away. She looks Lakota and Indians are good about that. They know when to mind their own business.

When I get back to my car, Johnny is passed out. I drive to the motel where I am staying and check out. Jenny has a room there, too, and I don't want her to be able to find us. I head east and then take the main road south. Johnny comes to for a minute and asks me where we are going. I tell him I'm going to get us a room in Sioux City. He asks where Jenny is and I realize he has completely forgotten what happened. Later I'll come to understand he was in an alcoholic blackout the whole time, but now I tell him to hell with Jenny. It's just him and me and screw the rest of the world. He says something I don't catch. Then he passes out again and I take us on into Sioux City.

Four days later, we make it back to Winner. I have trouble remembering what all we did, but I know we stayed drunk the whole time. When I come to the last morning I am hung over and broke, and we decide to head home. We luck out because I still have a full tank of gas. Johnny is passed out, but I settle our bill with a credit card that the clerk tells me is now over the limit and load Johnny into the Subaru.

We are still forty miles out of Winner when he comes to. I hear him patting his pockets for a smoke and I tell him we are all out. Then I hear him unfolding a sheaf of papers. He is quiet a minute and then asks me what the hell this is.

He hands me the papers but I already know what they are. I laugh and tell him we are now government property. He looks blank and I explain we enlisted in the Marines in Sioux City. I laugh at the look on his face. I tell him I'm not joking, we did it. We signed up for a buddy tour enlistment and we have two weeks to get our affairs in order. We are to report to the induction center in three weeks and from there we will go through basic training together at Camp Pendleton.

Johnny takes the news in without saying anything. Then he laughs. Why not, he asks. Why the hell not? Join the Marines and learn how to kill. Then he laughs again and tells me he understands. When I ask what he understands that's so funny, he tells me he understands why they say it is a good day for dying.

I look at Johnny and shake my head. He says stuff like this sometimes and it just about always makes sense when I think about it. Yet, I feel like pounded manure after the last four days so I tell him whatever, I'm too wrung out to get my mind around it at the moment. He laughs and tells me what I need a drink.

I say what I need is a new life and he gives me a strange look. I see he doesn't remember a thing and I tell him about the last five days. When I am done he is quiet a long time. "Jesus, Randy," he says after a while. "I sure screwed things up for you and Jenny, didn't I?"

I tell him I can't remember him putting a gun to my head and making me do it. I think it is better that I learned about Jenny now and not after we get married and have kids to worry about. Besides, what am I going to do for the next three years, anyway? I may as well play soldier. The pay ain't worth crap, but we could go for officer if we like it. We both have degrees.

"No," Johnny says. "Jenny's right. I didn't have to do what I did." He says he will talk to her and straighten things out when we get to town.

"I'm not sure I want you to," I tell him. "I've never seen her like that. Cold. Hard. Like a stranger."

"You don't know some of the stuff she's been through with family drunks," he tells me. "There's a very good reason she did that. I don't blame her."

"There's no reason to treat me that way," I tell him. "I've never treated her like that. Not ever."

Johnny gives me a look. "What was the last thing you said to her?"

I shrug. "I told her you were right about her," I say. Even as I say this, however, my very last words come to mind.

Hung over as he must be, Johnny catches the look on my face when this happens. He asks me what else I said and I repeat the words in Lakota. When I do I can see him getting angry. "What the hell?" I ask him. "All I said was the same thing you did. I don't even know what it means except something about her grandmother and a dog."

"I said that to her?" he asks me and I nod. I repeat the words exactly. He looks like I have just given him a hard punch in the belly.

I ask him what it means, but he shakes his head. He tells me it doesn't translate. He says it's one of the worst insults one Lakota can say to another.

"So tell her you were drunk," I say, but he shakes his head and tells me it doesn't matter. Even drunk he should not have said that to her, not ever. Some things can never be taken back, not once they've been said.

I tell him that's good because I don't want to take it back, anyway, not ever. Then he laughs and tells me I'm full of crap. He tells me my pride is hurt but when I get over it, I'll regret what I did. I try to argue, but my heart isn't in it. I know he's right. Because with the thought of Jenny gone forever, I feel very lost and very alone. At least, I will later when I let myself be honest about it. Right now I'm too hung over to think clearly and we're coming into the outskirts of town. So I tell him to let it be, I'll work it out with her myself.

I drop Johnny at his mother's house and head home. When I get there I see a car with Minnesota plates and I know it is Jenny. I almost drive on by, but there is no place else for me to go except Johnny's and I don't want to go there. Besides, this is my home and my parents, not hers. Although, by now Jenny is so much a part of my family I think they would kick me out first.

When I walk in the back door, I hear my dad say something and I hear Jenny and my mother laugh. I start to back out, but my dad has heard me and calls my name and I go on in. It gets quiet when I do, but then my dad chuckles. He tells me I look like the very wrath of God. My mother tries to keep a straight face, but she snickers and even Jenny brings a hand up to hide a smile. I don't see what's so funny until I go into the bathroom and see I have my shirt on inside out and fastened on a button off.

I take a quick shower to clear my head and when I get back to the kitchen there is just Jenny, sitting at the kitchen table. There is also a pitcher of what looks like tomato juice, but I know it is my dad's favorite hangover cure. I see he's left a bottle of aspirin, too, and I take three of these and drink down a full glass from the pitcher. Then I pour myself another one and sit down across the table from Jenny. I don't know what my dad puts in this. I don't get drunk often and I've never asked. Yet, I already find my head starting to clear.

Jenny is the first one to break the silence. She offers me an apology. She says she knows I didn't know what I was saying when I said what I did. I ask her what it means and she shakes her head. She asks me please, let it lie.

Seeing her like this, I find it hard to stay angry. I tell her I am sorry for acting the way I did and the next thing I know, Jenny is in my arms, crying. I tell her Johnny told me a little about their trouble with drunks in the family, and she nods. She tells me it was awful and when she saw Johnny drunk, it was like she was pulled back to a very bad time for her. She tells me that's why what he said shocked her so much. It wasn't the insult, so much, that bothered her. It was the idea that Johnny actually thought what he said might be true.

I tell her I understand, but I don't. Not really. How can I know without knowing what was said? I can see she does not want to talk about this any more, ever. Nor does Johnny. Still, I have the basic concept and I guess this will have to be enough for now. I think Jenny knows this and is grateful to me for not pushing. I am very aware pushing the issue will only push her further away. That's the last thing I want.

So I hold her a while until she stops crying. I apologize for running off and leaving her in Vermilion and she asks what Johnny and I did for the last four days. I tell her I'm not too sure, but at least we didn't end up in jail. She laughs, but I see she knows there is something I am not talking about. She also knows I know she knows, so she doesn't ask. We both know I will tell her sooner or later.

My dad looks in and starts to back out, but I tell him to come on in. I need to talk to him and my mother, and Jenny, too. He gives me a long look and then nods, and a couple of minutes my mother comes in with him and joins us at the kitchen table.

I don't know where to start, so I tell them Johnny and I enlisted a couple of days ago. I am not sure how they will react, but my dad nods. My mother gets very quiet and says if that's what I want to do, I need to do it, but I know she does not like it. Yet, it is Jenny who surprises me. At first, she looks very frightened. Then, after a moment, she smiles and looks very happy.

Later, when I talk with my dad alone, I ask him about this. He tells me that when I have children of my own, I will understand my mother's reaction. No mother wants her babies to go to war, and it doesn't matter that I am grown now. To mothers, their sons and daughters are always their babies. That biological connection is always there. While a father may not want his son to be killed or maimed by war, he also knows this is part of growing up for a man. To send a son off to war means he may get hurt, but to keep his son from taking the risks involved in becoming a warrior will likely maim him in a way that's even worse. It can kill his spirit. War can, too, he says, but it's less likely.

I know my dad is right about one thing. I really don't understand what he is talking about right now, and I guess it's because I don't have children. Thinking about this, I almost miss the next thing he says and I am glad I didn't. He says that what I'll discover, if I have not already done so, is that to a real warrior, his greatest adversary will always be himself. Knowing when to fight and when to talk may be the next hardest thing, but if a man has engaged with himself as the adversary, he will almost always be able to figure out what fights need to be fought.

At the time, I want to ask what he means, but I never get around to it. We move on to other things more pressing on my mind, and whenever I remember to ask him later on, it's never when he's around or when I can call. What I understand now is that it's one of those things we have to figure out for ourselves, mostly by making mistakes. Some lessons in the school of life are like this. With others, we can learn from the mistakes of others, and the pain we cause ourselves and the people around us is optional.

So while I want to know more about what my dad means, Jenny is more pressing on my mind. My dad always says there's no such thing as a foolish question. Yet, when I ask why he thinks Jenny responded the way she did, and not like my mother, he laughs like I have asked which way is up. "Randy, Jenny is a Lakota woman. Her people are warriors. I know it's deep in the culture and I think it may be genetic, too. You are her man and no Lakota woman wants a man who is not a warrior. She may be just as frightened as your mother, but she is also very proud of you. I'd never admit it to your grandpa, but Marines are the cream of the crop."

I think about this. Then I tell him about my phone call to the recruiter about our enlistment. The recruiter told me that since Johnny and I were drunk, we can get out of going if we want to. He said the military is strictly a volunteer service these days. They don't want anyone who doesn't want to be there. They can't afford to train people who are not willing to commit.

My dad thinks a long moment before he answers. "Randy, your signing up right now may have been a little rash. You may have acted on impulse and you may even have been drunk at the time. More than one guy has signed up because of woman problems. That's not the point. Can you honestly tell me, from your heart of hearts, that this is something wrong for you to do?"

My dad's question surprises me. What surprises me more is how I feel. I suddenly realize there is a part of me that's wanted to do this for a long time, just to see if I can make the grade. While it surprises me to hear the words come out of my mouth, I know as I tell him this that they are true. I never gave it much thought, but this is something I want to do. Maybe I'll like it and maybe I won't, but I need to see.

My dad nods and smiles, like any other answer would have surprised him, but he doesn't say anything. He just waits. Then I realize there is something else going on here, too. As screwed up as our way of life can get, I am part of it and it is part of me. This is like my family, for better or for worse. This is what I grow up knowing and what gives me all I have and all I am. A big part of being a man in any culture is doing the right thing, no matter what the personal cost, and, for me, this means being willing to put my life on the line for a system I do not always admire. I do not think in these terms, but I guess this makes me a patriot. The word is sadly out of favor now, but even as a young man I know it is time for me to serve. And it is right for me to serve this way.

I will not get my mind around this for many years. When I do I will realize the same can be said for those who are willing to go to prison or into exile to stand against a war they think is immoral. To my way of thinking, those who lost their citizenship or their personal freedom or even their health and lives protesting Vietnam, are as much casualties of war as those who go to fight and come home broken. They are every bit as patriotic and may be more so. There are many who disagree with me on this, but as Jenny says at times of me, they are simply wrong.

I will also come to realize that this is maybe even more true for Johnny than it is for me. As strange as it seems, those who we often treat worst seem to be our greatest patriots. One of the most haunting things I will ever see is passing the military cemetery north of Window Rock one Memorial Day weekend. The sign very clearly says that those whose remains lie there are Navajo veterans, and I am overwhelmed how many there are. Dozens upon dozens of white marble military grave markers stand in perfect formation, each marking a child of the Dinee who served this country, and each marked by a small American flag waving in the breeze.

As I pass by, I wonder, how can they do this? How can those so mistreated by the United States government be so proud to serve as its soldiers and sailors and marines and air corps? How can the living bear to see the ultimate symbol of their oppression flying over the graves of their brothers and sisters? To me the stars and stripes would be an abomination of desecration over the graves of my people, and if I were Navajo, I think I would like to burn every one I could find. Yet this is not true of the Dinee. They honor their children who serve in the military, and generation after generation sends its sons to fight the white man's war.

Even now I do not understand this fully. The closest I can come to understanding is seeing the way children from abusive families cling to the very people who cause them such pain. It is almost as if in giving up the abuse, they fear losing the very thing which makes them who they are. How are they to see themselves, if not as victims? How are they to live? What else is to become the central fact of their lives? Are the only choices they see being perpetrators or victims?

I think this may be true. I am not sure, but I am sure of this. As much as they may hate the white world for what it has done to them,

Indians do not avoid military service. This is as true for the Navajo and the Pueblos as it is for the Lakota. I suspect it is true for others, too. Indians seem to understand something we do not see or have forgotten, that becoming a warrior is part of becoming a man.

Right now, of course, I don't understand much of this at all. Who understands Jack Squat at twenty-four? I tell my dad I can't see that honoring my commitment is anything but the right thing to do. I need to go in.

"Then backing out now would be the worst thing you could do," he tells me. "Jenny would stay with you, but you would lose respect in her eyes. Yet, that's not the worst part of it. The worst part is that you would lose respect for yourself." He shakes his head. "I also think you'd lose your friendship with Johnny. I'm pretty sure he'd see your backing out as a personal betrayal."

I'm still in a fog from our binge, even though the shower woke me up a little. "Oh, I wouldn't try to get out unless we both did," I tell him. "I just don't want Johnny to think he has to stay in just because I signed up, too. I'd rather do the buddy tour, but I can go in by myself, too."

"Don't you understand yet, Randy?" my dad asks. "Johnny cannot stay home now. He's made a public commitment and backing out now would be seen as an act of cowardice. There's nothing Lakota despise more than a coward. He would rather die. Literally."

When my dad says this, I have one of those moments of clarity which come far too seldom. I remember what Johnny says when he hears the news we signed up and I come to understand something about my friend I never did. No matter how close we might be, or the fact we grow up in the same time and place, no matter what experiences we share, his world and mine lie in galaxies light years apart. I live in the world as a white man, and he walks into each day as a Lakota. The way we engage with life is very unlike because of this. What will take me years to understand about becoming a warrior and being a man, he already knows without knowing, growing up as he did. All this is summed up in one simple statement, "It is a good day for dying."

Queer Sights

9 November 14, 1985. "Cowboys and Indians." That's what Randy said. I was telling Willie Dill about the people in our part of South Dakota, how they've been at war with one another for a hundred and fifty years. I said it was almost like they don't know what else to do but fight each other. Dill laughed and said they sound like Southerners still talking about "the late war of Northern aggression." I said it's like a game we play, and maybe the only game we know how to play. Then Randy smiled and summed it up exactly, as he often does when we talk. He said, "Yeah. We play cowboys and Indians."

So it's still cowboys and Indians down home on the reservation, and one day on the road to Valentine I realized how hard it is to tell which is which. There was a car ahead of me, driven by someone wearing a western hat, but I couldn't see much else but the CB antenna on top of the car. The brim almost touched the side window and the driver had to slouch to keep the crown from bumping the roof. I wondered if this was a displaced cowboy or a local Indian. The plates were South Dakota, but not Todd County, so I couldn't be sure. Then I passed and saw the driver was definitely Lakota, but the way he was driving was pure cowboy, casual, relaxed, and not in much of a hurry.

I never thought about this before, but one of the odd things about our part of the world is how many of the Indians dress like cowboys and how many of Cowboys look like Indians, except for their skin. Indian men like to wear jeans and boots, with wide, tooled-leather belts held up with large buckles. They wear leather vests over bright western shirts, and they seem to prefer broad brimmed cowboy hats.

Yet the cowboys wear the same hats, and they use bright feathers to decorate the crown. They wear their hair long, pulled back in braids, like Willie Nelson, and they favor buckskin vests trimmed with fringe and beads. Like Indians, they drive beat-up pickup trucks and drink beer like prohibition is coming back tomorrow, and some of them seem to take better care of their dogs and horses than they do of their women and children.

Yet cowboys and Indians are a lot alike in a lot of other ways, too, like the way they drive. They have only two speeds and they act like they own the road. They tear around like bats out of hell or they poke along like they're being paid double time by the hour. It all depends on how the mood strikes them. The difference is that some of the cowboys have a little more money. Their trucks are a little newer and not many of them have Todd County plates.

I think the kinship goes much deeper than this and RD does, too. He says the thing he sees in common is the independent attitude which refuses to be tied down or fenced in. Or even crowded. He says another is self-sufficiency to make do or do without, and just behind this is a hunger for the empty land where a man is alone with his thoughts and his Creator, and maybe the company of a good friend.

I see this a little different. Or maybe not. From where I stand, it's a desire to live life on simple terms even a child understands. It's wanting a life where the other man is friend or enemy, where there is good or there is bad, and where agreement sealed with a man's word is better than a written contract. Decisions are easy to make living this way. Here and now is all there is and the past is dead and gone.

I know this is not how life is. That's not the point, not for us cowboys and Indians. To us, this is the way life should be. When it's not, we share a common despair. To ease our pain we share common cures and as many of us who are cowboys as are Indians become addicted to alcohol and tobacco. When the beer stops working, we draw into ourselves more and more, and we even strike out at those they love the most. When our guilt is too great to bear, we share a common end. Those of us too proud to take our own lives turn our faces to the wall and die.... (from John K's last journal)

Boot camp was the way boot camp always is. Too much has been said about this for me to add much, too many books and too many movies. I understand the military is a little different now, but I don't think much changes between World War I and when we go in. I think the movie, *Full Metal Jacket*, pretty much catches the spirit of things. Our DI is no crazy like the one in the movie, but the crazies are still around.

Johnny and I luck out and get a special weapons trainer on loan to the Marine Corps from the Army Special Forces. I'm not sure why he's on loan and he never mentions it. There are a lot of things that happen in the service that are never explained. There are also a lot of questions you learn to not ask. They tell you what you need to know when you need to know it. They consider everything else unnecessary.

Our DI's name is Willie Dill, and like I said, he is no crazy. He may be as tough as nails, but Dill is very clear about his mission and he makes it very clear to us. His job is to teach us how to stay alive while engaging a very dangerous enemy. There is nothing crazy about what Willie Dill ever does, despite momentary appearances, and there is a scientific efficiency to his approach which is scary. To tell the truth, I'd hate to find myself on the other side with him around.

I am in pretty good shape when we report for duty, but it is all I can do to keep up with the crowd. I'm built for strength, not speed, and Dill finds this out the first day. I come in ten minutes behind Johnny in our first long run, but I finish at a run, which most of the company doesn't. I also come in carrying not only my own pack, but another one for a guy who twisted his ankle.

Johnny, of course, is the first guy across the line and he's there so fast Dill doesn't believe it. The next day he tries running with Johnny to make sure he doesn't cut across, but Dill can't keep up. After that, Johnny leads the runs.

From the very first, Johnny takes to training like a duck to water. I am the only one who can handle him when it comes to hand-to-hand drill, and even the DI has trouble taking him down. He doesn't have to show Johnny something twice, either, like he does to some of the guys, and Johnny turns out to be the best shot in our company. The odd thing is that Johnny's never shot a rifle much until we get to boot camp. I am raised with guns and I've always been a competition shot. Yet, Johnny damned near beats my score when we shoot to qualify.

I can tell that even Willie Dill is impressed, but not everyone is. Take any group of people and there always seems to be one asshole who makes life hard for the rest. This time it's a couple of guys with an attitude from south Dallas. They think that because he is black, too, Willie Dill will let things slide when it comes to them. When they call him bro the first day, he makes them do fifty pushups on the spot. When a white guy snickers, he finds himself right beside the bros, doing seventy-five, and Dill asks if there's anyone else who needs to be reminded he is Sergeant Dill, there is dead silence.

What happens is that the guys from Big D call Dill a Tom behind his back, and when Johnny is made company lance, they do everything they can to screw him up. Dill knows what is going on, of course, but there's nothing he can do about it. The guys put out just enough effort to keep from getting tossed, and they never quite go over the line. At least, they don't when Dill or one of the other instructors is around.

I know there's going to be trouble with these guys. They have a point to prove and it's only a matter of when and where and how, so I keep my eyes open. I know Johnny is on them, too, although he seems to just ignore the bastards. What they don't know is that Indians are very good at this game of watching without letting the enemy know you are. They don't know much about reverse traps, either, or traps within traps. All they seem to understand is raw power, directly applied, and they make a big mistake thinking Johnny's restraint comes from fear. This almost turns out to be a fatal mistake, not for Johnny or me, but for them.

To give the devils their due, they wait for their best chance. They know Willie Dill is keeping an eye on them, and the other instructors are too. But the instructors are not always around and there is more than one way they can get at Johnny. It's no secret that we're friends, and Johnny warns me that if they can't get at him, they may come after me.

I ask Johnny why wait for them to make the first move, and he grins. He tells me he is thinking the same way and on a long night hike we work it out. The only question is how to set it up and that turns out easier than we expected. When we get back to camp a runner tells Johnny that Dill wants to see him right away. Johnny looks at me and I look at him and he nods. He tells the runner he will be there as soon as he secures his post and the guy takes off.

Johnny tells the company he's got to go see Dill. He wants them to clean up and be ready for reveille in two hours. When he says this, there are the usual groans. It's just past four in the morning and we're all dead tired. Johnny tells us to be ready and then heads out the door.

I strip off, grab a towel and some soap and head for the door, too. We're camped out and the shower tent is a hundred yards away through the woods. After I duck out of the big tent I look back. I see one of the bad ass brothers give the other a look and they grab towels and head after me.

I duck around another tent until they get by. I give them some time to get to the shower tent and find out I'm not there. Then I follow after.

When I get to the shower tent I start in. The two guys are just coming out of the stalls and when I see them, I duck back out the door. When they come charging out, I'm standing there waiting for them.

I am not sure exactly what happens next. The first guy goes down when I give him a bum's rush, but when I turn around, the second guy is coming after me with a knife. He expects me to try to get away, but I move in, trapping his knife in the towel and locking his arm in both of mine. I am a little rushed and I misjudge. I hear his arm snap and he screams. I feel the knife prick my foot as he drops it.

I don't have time to think, but part of me is wondering where the hell Johnny is. I turn around and see the blade of a razor coming at my chest. There is not much I can do but roll with the swing, hoping to reduce the cut, and I feel something like liquid fire go across my upper arm and chest. I duck and roll and come up ready to go, but I can't seem to get my left arm to work right.

What I see chills me to the bone. Johnny is in the middle of the razor man's back with both knees pinning the man down. He has the guy's razor and has a handful of the guy's hair in the other hand. I realize he is about to scalp him before he cuts his throat.

I holler at Johnny and he glances at me. I tell him not to do it, that I'm all right. He looks at me, then lays open the guy's scalp for six inches. Then he throws down the razor, and when the guy turns over, kicks him in the balls.

About this time, other people start to arrive. Willie Dill comes running up and picks up the knife, which is lying where the first guy dropped it. Johnny points to where he threw the razor and one of the other instructors picks that up. Dill hollers for a medic and when he comes, he sends him to me. I tell him the other guys need him worse and he asks me if that's makeup on my arm and chest. I look down and I am covered with blood. There is a foot long cut running from my left shoulder across my left breast. When he tells me I better sit down, I don't argue.

Dill asks if there was anyone who saw what happened and the guy Johnny almost scalped starts talking. Dill tells him to shut up and asks Johnny what happened. Johnny tells him he saw the two guys attack me with a knife. Then one of the other guys speaks up. He tells Dill he was following me to the shower and saw me run out just before they both came after me. He tells Dill that Johnny kept me from being cut again. Dill tells one of the other instructors to call the MP's.

That is not quite the end of it. We still have to tell our story again a few times and write a report. With the additional witness, the brass take our side of the story and the two guys from Dallas end up doing time in the brig. The only wrinkle happens when Dill comes to see me in sick bay two days after it happens. Johnny is there, too, and I am all wrapped up like a mummy. The cut was deeper than they thought and took some micro surgery to repair a couple of tendons.

When Dill sees Johnny and me he shakes his head. His face is as hard as a God of wrath. When he speaks, his voice is so quiet it sounds like the hiss of a snake. He tells us we are two of the very best troops he has ever trained, but if we pull anything like that again, he will dump us personally. I look at Johnny and he looks at me. It is useless to argue, so we say, "Yes, Sergeant Dill."

Dill glares at us a minute longer, then he grins. "Batman and Robin!" he says. "You two guys remind me of the McKee brothers."

We ask him who the McKee brothers are and he tells us to look in the mirror. Then he says, "That was really slick. I don't know how you did it, but it was very smooth. Don't ever do it again. Not on my watch. There are better ways."

I tell Dill we didn't know they had knives and he rolls his eyes. He asks if I am for real and Johnny says, "No, Randy's just a hick. Hicks don't carry knives."

This strikes Dill as funny. He laughs and says, "Yeah, but Indians do." Johnny nods. Then Dill holds out his hand and Johnny reaches under his fatigue shirt and comes up with a blade I've never seen. He hands it to Dill handle first.

Dill tries the knife in his hand. "Nice," he says. "Good balance." He hands it back to Johnny. "Why didn't you use your own knife?"

Johnny shrugs. "No time. His razor was handier."

Dill nods, then is all business. "All right, Lyle," he says to me. "You're going to miss most of the last week of training, but you already qualify. You can make up what you miss later." Then he turns to Johnny. "Lyons, do you think you can handle the last week as lance without screwing up?"

I can see Johnny is hiding a smile. Being made lance was one of the happiest days of his life and I can see he thought he was going to lose it. "Yes, Sergeant Dill!" Dill nods and tells him he better get back there when we're done planning the dismemberment of the Evil Empire. When he leaves, Johnny looks at me. "I'm glad he didn't kill you." Then he leaves and I don't see much of him until the day we graduate.

So Johnny finishes up the last week as our company lance and it's no surprise when he is asked to go on for airborne training. When he asks me what I think, I tell him to go for it. When he asks me if I am going to try for it, too, I tell him what Sergeant Dill told me when I asked if I could. My talents lie in other areas.

Johnny asks, "What talents? All you have to do is to be crazy enough to jump out of a moving airplane and lucky enough to survive it."

"I think Dill was referring to the second part of the equation," I tell him. "I will admit I am probably demented enough to jump out of the plane, but I'm not sure I'm sharp enough to survive it."

Johnny nods but doesn't say anything. We know coming in that the only guarantee we have for serving together is going through basic training, but now that's done. We go where the service needs us but it's hard to imagine being in the Corps without Johnny being with me. I know he is thinking the same thing. We get each other over the humps, and it's hard saying good-bye.

After he leaves I sit on my bunk wondering where I'll be assigned when a courier shows up and tells me to report to the commanding officer. On my way there I wonder how I've managed to screw up bad enough the Old Man wants to see me. I've been in sick bay most of the week.

When I get to the Colonel's office, he tells me to stand at ease. There is another man there, a naval Captain, but I never find out his name. The Colonel tells me they have been looking over my personnel file. He asks me why I've not applied for OCS since I have a college degree and I tell him the thought never crossed my mind. I simply wanted to be a good Marine.

When I say this, I see the Captain smile, but I stay focused on the Colonel. He frowns and asks me if I am aware of my psychological test scores, and I say no. He gives me a hard look when I do and tells me for a guy as smart as I am supposed to be I sure act dumb. I tell him I don't understand.

The Navy speaks up and tells the Colonel he thinks I am telling the truth. Then he asks me a few questions. Some of them are a little tricky but my answers seem to satisfy him and he nods. "I guess the examiner never told you your IQ, son, did he?"

I tell him the examiner told me it was none of my business when I asked and the Captain laughs. He asks me if I would believe him if he said I have an IQ of over one hundred and twenty. I tell him I would. One hundred is average and things have always come to me very easily. I also remember things pretty well, but that runs in the family. I am also pretty good with numbers and languages come easy.

The Colonel gives me a strange look when I say this and the Captain laughs again. He tells me I am damned good with numbers and asks me if I would believe him if he told me my IQ was over a hundred and fifty. I tell him I would not. I'm no rocket scientist. Then he hands me my file and points where he wants me to look. I see my score is one hundred and fifty-six. I tell them the examiner must have gotten me mixed up with someone else. The Captain assures me they checked this out already. I say maybe I got lucky and he shakes his head. People don't get lucky on standardized tests. He asks me what's wrong with being smart.

I don't have a good answer to this. I tell him in high school people kind of looked down on people who made too good grades, but in college it was just the opposite. He asks me how I would feel about working for the Navy and I don't know what to say. I tell him I did join the Marines and it's the Colonel's turn to laugh. He picks up some papers from his desk and hands them to me. These are my orders, he says. I will remain in the Marine Corps but I am being assigned to a special intelligence and language school. When I am done I will be assigned to a special inter-service cryptography unit. Even the fact I am being assigned to this school is to be kept secret. When anyone asks, I am to tell them I have been assigned to mass communications.

The Captain tells me he wants me to consider OCS, too. I tell him I will, but I don't really mean it. I like being in the Corps right now, but I don't want to make it a career. I have already seen enough of military service already to know this for sure. When my time is up I want to go back to civil life, to raise a family and report the news, and when my dad retires, maybe take over the paper. Or maybe not. Right now, intelligence school sounds interesting. With the right languages I might snag a job as a foreign correspondent later on and I damned sure don't want to spend the next three years polishing a rifle.

The strange thing about the way all this works out is that it throws Johnny and me together all over the world. When I see him next, six months after basic, he tells me he's been assigned to special operations. I've been around the spook shop long enough to know this most likely means black operations. Johnny was not only the next best shot in our basic class. He is also the one guy who never got caught on night patrol. He is a natural for the kind of jobs that never get talked about.

When I ask Johnny if he's changed his name to Hassan, he gives me a weird look, but when I tell him I am in mass communications, he laughs. Switching into Lakota he says, "So we both become hunters. Maybe we will hunt together." I don't know what he means, but I don't ask. Sometimes Johnny knows things he has no way of knowing, at least as far as I can see. Yet, it's not just a hunch. No, it's more like what the Celts call second sight, being fey, and with Johnny, it's tied to knowing where danger lies. I think this is why he never gets caught on night reconnaissance exercises and why he is such a good stalker. It is a handy thing to have, being a warrior.

This time is no different. Johnny is right and it isn't very long before I find out. On my first black operation out of intelligence school, my commanding officer gets taken out as we go in. I end up as field control for Johnny and another sniper whose name I never learn and I'm told I did all right. We accomplish the mission and we all get out alive. It doesn't get better than that in black ops. We even get the CO out, but I don't know if we do him any favor by it. The last I hear, he is still in a VA hospital.

Even as I write this, there is one of those strange coincidences which adds an odd post script to the incident at boot camp. A couple of days ago I have a visitor come to the office. He is a mild mannered man about my age, very well dressed in a very conservative suit. I have him pegged as a preacher right away and I wonder what he wants. Yet he also seems very familiar, too, like we've met before. I wonder what he would look like without the beard. We visit a while and he says, "You don't know me, do you?"

I tell him he seems to be someone I ought to know and he laughs. "How soon they forget. You saved my life, Mr. Lyons." He sees I still can't place him and he laughs again. "You saved my life by breaking my arm. I believe at the time I am coming at you with a knife, so I'm grateful it was my arm you broke and not my neck."

When he says this, I wonder if he is there to shoot me, but he raises his hands. "I am serious," he says. "I looked you up to thank you and to ask your forgiveness." Then he looks sad. "You remember Dechaun, the guy I ran with back then? He was the one who cut you. I doubt you heard about it, but he died in prison a few months back. Someone shanked him."

I can't help myself. I have been in the newspaper business too long not to smell a good story when I hear it. So I ask him what happens to turn him around and not Dechaun. It's a long story and he ends up coming to the house for dinner, but Jenny is used to this by now. It happens all the time and she gets to meet some interesting people.

To make the story short, Richard experienced a religious conversion while he was in the hospital waiting to go to trial for assaulting me. The arm required major surgery and he almost died on the table. What happened was a near death experience. Yet it was one of those NDE's which is scary and horrifying rather than peaceful, like most are. What he saw was not a peaceful valley, but a place of fire and pain. Yet even through the worst parts of this, he had a guide who kept showing him he had a choice. This is what turned him around. "I literally had the hell scared out of me," he tells me.

His conversion carried him through his brig time and when he got out he began to rebuild his life. "It was one miracle after another," he tells us, sitting at our dining room table. "Every time I really needed something it was there, tuition, money for books and even music lessons. It still works that way, and every time I get down and ready to give up, something happens to keep me going. God sends me a message or a messenger." He smiles and looks at Jenny. "Like your husband. Fortunately, they don't have to break my arm to get me to listen these days."

I ask him what he is doing now, and he says he spends his time trying to reach others like he was, brothers in white doing hard time. This is what brings him to South Dakota. He is working on a prison ministry to bring here and he remembered that Johnny and I were from this part of the world. Then he asks about Johnny and I tell him what's happened and what I'm doing, writing it up. He sighs and shakes his head sadly. "Then it's just you and me, RD. A man of God and his guardian angel."

"I don't know about that," I say. "I think Baalam's ass is a better comparison." I am not too familiar with the Bible, but that's one story I know. "I'm anything but an angel. Or a man of God."

"You fight it so hard, RD," he says to me. "You seek the truth and you fight it so hard, too. It's my prayer that you find peace." The strange thing is that when he says this I hear Father Alex telling me the same thing, and that night I sleep like I have not slept in months. I wake refreshed, but confused from a strange dream. In it, Richard and I are standing talking to someone whose face I cannot see and I am asking him a strange question. "Which of us is the angel?"

It's strange, how we come to be together in sunny Honduras, Johnny and me. The odd thing is how we come here by such different routes. Or maybe it's not so odd, either, if you think about the way our lives are so woven together at every point. Our karma brings us back together and our paths cross again and again.

From boot camp I am tapped for intelligence and am sent here and there for lots of special training. Johnny goes into special weapons and is trained in completely different places. Yet, the Corps is not that big an outfit, and we have complimentary specialties. So we run into each other fairly often after boot camp. I become a spook and he becomes an assassin. We work so well together on that first assignment the brass decide to make us a team and this is how we end up in Honduras. At this point, Ronnie Ray-gunz is Commander In Chief and we get sent in to help defend the western hemisphere from the minions of the Evil Empire.

Honduras means "depths" in English, and for me, this makes sense. Being there is the pits. There's nothing nice about it. The climate is hot and steamy, with all kinds of vicious critters that bite, chew, gnaw, and sting, and the two legged variety is even more nasty. This variety comes armed with everything from World War I vintage Mausers to the latest Klashnikov assault weapons, and from all I see down there, it's hard to tell the good guys from the bad guys.

As a matter of fact, the people we go in to help turn out as the real bad asses, but it takes a long time to figure this out. Until our very last mission there, we believe the stories we hear about the atrocities our allies commit is propaganda. Or maybe we want to believe it. Believing helps make the other stuff tolerable. Then Johnny and I see for ourselves first hand what the local regime we're supporting is really doing.

I think it's when we see a trooper bayonet a toddler that we know for sure. Johnny and I never talk about it later but it's the way the soldier does it that gets to me worst of all. Or maybe it's the attitude of the local captain. He acts almost bored, like he's seeing a fly swatted and the soldier acts like he is killing a rat the same way he's done a thousand times before. To them, it's obviously all in a day's work.

When this happens, Johnny goes ballistic and takes out the whole platoon. There is no time to think. I have a split second to make a choice. Yet, I'm so sick at what I see it takes me a second to realize what Johnny's doing. Then, just as I'm swinging my weapon to lay down cover fire for him, one of the locals gets off a burst that takes me out.

Everything after that is hazy, but even as I go down I think I hear something terrible and familiar. Through the haze, I see one of the local troops freeze, wide eyed with fear. Then his head disappears in a red mist and I hear the deep thunder of a fifty caliber machine gun Johnny's firing. When the red haze turns dark and the light fails, I still hear the pounding of the gun. It sounds like a war drum.

Johnny and I never talk about this later on. When I come to I still hear the sound of the gun, but Johnny is leaning over me. He can't still be firing. Then I realize what I hear is the pounding of the rotors of a chopper lifting us out and over this I can hear Johnny talking to me in Lakota. I hear him tell me what we have to say to the captain. Then I hear him pray to the four powers for me, and after that, I hear him sing the death song. When I hear this, I know he is singing for me and he is asking his grandfathers to meet me on the other side, in the spirit world, and to help me find my way there.

When he does this, something strange happens. I find myself looking into the eyes of the old man at Willie's funeral and I see Johnny and me above the earth high as eagles, riding shining white horses through the clouds. I hear him singing, only I am singing too, and the song is so beautiful it breaks my heart. I feel tears of joy washing my cheeks like warm spring rain.

I remember this now as I write. The memory brings great sadness, a deep longing for someplace I know but have never been. I do not know where this place is, but I do not think I will ever find it under the sun. The mountains are too high, too rugged. The air is too crystal clear and the sky is too cobalt blue. The light on the clouds is too intense, too mellow and still too bright, and the smell of the wildflowers is too deep and pungent. The way my body feels is too light, too strong, as if I could leap from one high peak to another or run through the high grass and flowers for days. The only name I have for this place is Home, and this is where we ride. So maybe Richard, the preacher, was onto something. I don't know. Maybe we are all three of us angels.

Later, when Johnny comes to visit the hospital, I tell him about this and I see tears come to his eyes. We are quiet a long while. Then he sighs and I know he wishes we were there now. When he asks me if I remember hearing him in the chopper, I switch over to Lakota and tell him I do, repeating everything he told me. After that, nothing is ever said about it, not ever again. We talk about other things and when the doctor comes to check on me later, I'm having a good time teaching Johnny how to cuss in Russian. What is so funny to me is Johnny's accent. The Lakota speak beautiful English, better than many of their white neighbors, but it is strange what he does to Russian.

When I get out of the hospital, the captain asks me to report on the incident and I tell him I don't remember much. What I do say confirms

Johnny's story and the captain takes it at face value. He may or may not believe me, but I know he is not going to push it. We are not even supposed to be in Honduras, and he knows it's easier to just keep quiet and let it lie. No one wants any stink on this one.

As it turns out, the burst from the local's weapon not only takes me out of the fire fight. It takes me out of Honduras and out of the Corps, too. One of the rounds grazes my spinal column, and for a while they didn't think I will ever walk again. Another round messes up a knee pretty bad, and that clinches a medical discharge with total disability. Vietnam veterans call this is a million dollar wound, but in Honduras, it's just another way to die. Without the chopper and fast medical treatment I would be dead from infection within days. Even with the best help, I am told it is touch and go for the first week and no one knows if I will make it or not.

These days I sometimes feel a little strange being on disability, as healthy as I am. Then the weather changes and the knee bothers so much it's sometimes hard to walk. The spine healed up well enough, though two vertebra had to be fused, but these are not the real wounds I carry from Honduras. The real wounds I suffer are the things I saw, for to this day I wake up in the middle of the night dreaming about it. I see the child killed. I feel the bullets hit my body. I hear Johnny's war cry and I see the soldier's head explode. Then I hear the sound of the chopper and Johnny singing the death song.

Then I wake up, sweating, with my scars burning and my knee a mass of pain. When I do, the first thing I want to do is call Johnny, just to make sure he's all right, but I never do. Not in all the years since he's back. We swear a vow of silence, a vow without words. And we do not break this vow, not ever. Now it's too late.

Yet I wish I did. Just once in all those years I wish I picked up the phone to call and tell him what I dream. It all seems so unreal now, like a nightmare we shared, and in the pale glow of morning light, with Jenny sound asleep by my side, I always wonder. Did it really happen, Johnny? Is it really true? Or is it all a bad dream? Will I wake from this bizarre dream within a dream we call life one morning? Will I find myself singing with joy as we ride through the high meadows of this place called Home?

The Desert Storm

10 July 5, 1993. I woke up in jail this morning. That's nothing new. Since I came back from the Marine Corps it seems to happen two or three times every year and I don't quite understand why. Most of the time it's from getting drunk and fighting, but I don't go out looking for a fight. I go out to have a good time with my friends. Sure, we drink, but why shouldn't we? It's our choice how to spend our money. So what if we even drink a bit too much? We don't hurt anyone but ourselves.

Yet, there always seems to be some fool around who just can't keep his mouth shut. There always seems to be some wise ass who thinks he can whip the whole world and all he wants to do is tell everyone about it. I don't care if he thinks that. I don't even care if he says it, but after eight or ten times, I get tired of hearing it. Who wouldn't? And why won't they just shut up when you ask them politely? What happens is they start hollering and shoving and the next thing I know, we all end up in jail.

Waking up in jail this morning was different. When I tried to remember what I did to get here, I couldn't and that was scary. I don't even remember going out to drink. All I do remember is going over to a friend's house to get a tire for my pickup. I remember him showing me some wild hemp he picked up on the reservation and asking if I'd like to try a little and I guess we did. I think I had a bottle of whiskey with me I bought earlier in the day, but I hadn't opened it yet. I wanted to get the tire fixed first.

When I asked the jailer why I was there, he just laughed and told me the usual. It wasn't until later in the day I found out it was public intoxication. The cop brought me in because I was passed out on the sidewalk and he was afraid I'd freeze if he left me there. The judge hit me with the usual fine and let me go. He didn't even give me a lecture about how I might not be so lucky next time. I guess he understood I know it by heart by now. Why waste his breath?

It wasn't almost freezing to death that scared me. That would be a painless way to go and I'm not scared of dying. What scared me about

143

not remembering is what happened to Lucy Eagle Wing. I went to school with her as kids in Corn Creek. After a drunk, she came to one morning in federal prison. They told her that she and her husband got into a fight and she killed him. She stabbed him with a kitchen knife, thirty-six times, so she must have been pretty angry. Yet, she couldn't remember it. She couldn't even remember getting drunk.

That's what bothers me. How can Lucy live with killing her husband? I know she loved him. We grew up together and she always did, even when she was mad at him. How can she live with what she did? I think in her shoes I would want to die, but she can't. They won't let her. They gave her life in prison and they watch her very closely. They won't even let her children come to see her until they're grown, but I'm not sure they'd want to. They were there that night. They are the ones who saw it happen.

This is what bothers me. What if I woke up in jail one morning and they told me I was there because I'd killed someone I love? What if it was someone like Randy or Jenny? How could I live with that?

(excerpt from John K's last journal)

I'm there the day Johnny comes home on leave from Panama and I'm there the day he gets back from the Persian Gulf. There's a world of difference in him in between. I'm sure the change begins a long time before I see it, but it's when he came back from Iraq I see the things that make me fear for him. Nothing's ever the same again, not even the way things are between him and me. He's changed, is almost a stranger when he gets back from the Gulf, and he will not let me in. I don't understand why. When I ask, he just shrugs it off. He tells me he has a lot on his mind.

What's different? That's hard to describe. When he comes back from Panama, he's still a Marine, and very proud of it. I am married a long time then and have children, but things are still the same between us. We are easy together, the way we have always been, and even the memory of Honduras does not cloud the time we have. It holds us even closer than before.

Johnny is a sergeant when he comes back from Panama. He has almost five years of service and he has moved up through the ranks as fast as anyone can in peace time. He has also managed to avoid OCS, mostly because he never officially graduates from college. There is some rule that you have to be there or excused from the graduation ceremony to officially graduate, and when Johnny and I enlist, he is not there.

We're somewhere in Sioux City.

A lawyer could clear this up with a couple of phone calls, but when my dad offers to help, Johnny tells him it doesn't matter. He is happy doing what he is doing and if he has a degree, the Corps might force him into OCS. My dad laughs when Johnny tells him he really doesn't want to mess with Official Chicken Shit, what we call Officer Candidate School. I can tell my dad doesn't like this. To him, there is something wrong with earning something and not claiming it. I agree with Johnny. Why bother if you don't need it? I'm not sure it makes any difference in the way things turn out, either.

When Johnny tells me about Panama, it's different from Honduras. This is very important to him and it is important for me to hear it. Honduras was shameful but Panama is righteous. Yes, we end up kidnapping a head of state and bringing him to the United States to stand trial for things he did in his own land. This bothers me, not because it happened to him, but because it takes our law into gray areas I think we would better avoid. There's the whole concept of national sovereignty at stake, and due process of law, but we have not honored sovereignty in our own back yard since James Monroe. Nor have we been too particular about safe-guarding civil liberties since the 'Seventies.

Yet, Panama is righteous. Sending Johnny and the rest of the troops in is one way of defending the Republic from a clear and present danger, and that is the bottom line. When a head of state starts poisoning the children of another sovereign state with drugs, he is declaring war on them, as surely as if he invades with troops. When this is done to an ally, it is betrayal, pure and simple. So I guess you can say Panama is righteous, if not legitimate, and when Johnny comes back, he seems healed of the hits we took in Honduras. He seems strong again, and I almost wish I was there with him.

The signs are still there, though, the signs of change. Looking back, I wonder how I miss them, but I do. Or maybe I don't want to see them. Maybe I want to think I am healed of Honduras, too, and so I don't look too closely at Johnny. Because I might see a reflection of my own pain, the pain that wakes me sweating in the middle of the night. So we shoot the breeze and get a little drunk and have to go to a sweat to get rid of the poison. When we do, it seems to be gone, and for a while we feel really good. It's like we're young studs again, bullet proof and holding the world by the ass.

Something happens, though. The night before Johnny leaves to go back we grab a hamburger and head for Valentine, just Johnny and me. There's a special rodeo I want to cover for the paper and Jenny doesn't want to go. I tell her not to wait up. We may spend the night there, depending on how late it is when we get done. I can see she doesn't like this, but she doesn't say a thing. She just nods and tells me to be careful.

It's been a long time since we are out together, just Johnny and me, and I am glad Jenny is not with us. We like to have her around, but it's good to be just him and me, too. We don't do anything we wouldn't do with her around, but it changes things. I don't know why, but it does and I think she knows this. My mother is always glad to take the kids when Jenny wants to come with me, so it's not that. She could come with us if she really wanted to and we would be glad to have her along. I think she knows Johnny and I need a night out, just him and me. We need to say goodbye the way men do.

We head out to Valentine. We don't even pick up a six pack of beer. We grab a burgers and shakes and head out in early afternoon. Jenny is one of the few Lakota women who cooks things the way I like and it's been a while since I've eaten a hamburger and curly fries. Or had a shake, for that matter. When I came back from Honduras I gained a lot of weight and had to change my eating habits, and shakes were not on the list. Neither are hamburgers, French fries or ice cream, the stuff I really like, so today seems like a real feast.

The strange thing is these things don't taste as good as they once did. The shake is so sweet I can hardly drink it and the burger and fries seem greasy, but I am not about to let this ruin my fun. I cut the shake with a pint of milk and smother the fries with lots of catsup. I learned that when I was in the Marines. Catsup and cheese spread and salsa cover a multitude of culinary sins.

Johnny wants to see Dog Ear Butte so we take the back way to Valentine. It's dirt roads a lot of the way, but it is shorter and we don't lose any time. Besides that, we're not in any hurry. The rodeo doesn't start until seven-thirty or eight and I have plenty of time to do my interviews. The main event I want to see is a cutting horse competition and that won't start until later on. So we go the back way and poke along, laughing and telling stories and remembering when this was our stomping ground.

We're quiet a lot, too, and after a long silence, Johnny smiles and nods. He begins to talk about how he misses seeing the way the cloud shadows play over the buttes the way they do out here. He also talks about how the air smells different, better. "This is country I understand," he tells me. "Not like the jungle."

I know he is talking about Honduras but I don't know what to say. All I want to do is forget Honduras, to put it as far behind me as I can. So I make a joke. I say isn't it just like the friggin' Marines to take two people like us, guys from the plains, and put us down in the middle of a friggin' jungle. Johnny laughs and begins to tell me about a platoon of recruits from New Jersey he ran into in Panama, and we move on. This is as close as we'll ever get to talking about Honduras. I know that is a mistake now, us never talking it out, but right then it is the best we can do. Honduras is just too painful to remember at the moment. At least, it is for me.

There is a thunderstorm building off to the southeast and we stop at the top of a tall hill to watch it a while. I guess it must be twenty-five or thirty miles away. While we watch, a big swirl of dust starts on the ground and then builds into a spout swirling up. At the same time, we see another swirl at the bottom of the cloud begin to twist down until a full funnel is formed. It's not a big one and there is nothing but cattle and grass over that way, so we just watch it go up and down, up and down across the prairie. What strikes me is how beautiful it is. I say something about it to Johnny and he laughs and says tell that to the people at ground zero. Yet, I know he sees the beauty of it, too. That's one of the differences between us. I'm a newspaper man. I talk about the things I see, one way or another. That's how I earn my living. Johnny does not, except in his journals, and by the time I get to read them, it's too late to tell him how good they are.

After a while we head out again. The day is getting warm and when we get to the turnoff to Smith Falls, Johnny asks if we have time to go by there. He would like to see them again. I tell him I'd like to see them, too, and we head south on the dirt road that leads down to the state park on the Niobrara.

Even though it's Friday night, there aren't many people at the park. The season is started but most of the tourists will get here in July and August, like they do most places. We have the trail up to the falls to ourselves and it's nice to be here without dozens of other people around.

Once we get in the shadow of the river bluff and out of direct sunlight, it gets cool again and when we get to the falls, it's almost cold. I set up my camera on a tripod while Johnny climbs down to the falls basin and stands with his face up, bathed by the mist. I think the best picture I have ever taken is Johnny standing there under the falls, his face and hands lifted and his eyes open, as if he is looking into Heaven. I don't know. Maybe he is, or maybe he's watching an eagle. What I do know is that the look on his face is one of utter peace. I keep a print on my office desk and it helps me when I am feeling down. It also tells me I am right. There is a change in Johnny between then and when he comes back from the Gulf war.

After Smith Falls, we drive on toward Valentine. Instead of going straight into town, I take the road down to the fish hatchery that comes into the city from the north. We still have plenty of time and those few miles of country along Minnechaduza Creek is some of the prettiest scenery in the state. Coming off the rolling plains, it's like going through a doorway into southern Colorado. Tall pines, some of them over a hundred feet, line the bluff canyon for miles and the coulees leading into the main drainage are covered with seedlings and mature growth stunted by lack of water. The closer to the creek, the taller the trees grow and the ground is covered with a generous duff of old needles.

I think Valentine, Nebraska, is one of the most beautiful small towns in the United States. The houses are neat and well kept, and the place is small enough to have a viable downtown business district. It is also very isolated. The nearest city of any size is Grand Island, almost two hundred miles to the south and east. Rapid City is that far to the north and west, and Sioux Falls is that far to the east. Traveling directly west, there are no major population areas between Valentine and Casper, Wyoming.

What makes it even more perfect for me is that it lies just north of the Niobrara River in a transition area between the Sand Hills of Nebraska and the Badlands farther north. The Badlands are awesome, almost breathtaking in their austerity, but the Sand Hills have a quiet beauty I find restful. There is a vast reservoir beneath the dunes that form the Hills and that makes for a shallow water table. It is not uncommon to find wetlands nestled among the desert hills. So even though they appear desolate, the Hills are full of life, wild flowers and grasses and many species of birds and native animals.

The thing about the Sand Hills is that for me, they are like a vast Zen garden. I can sit for long periods of time looking at the Hills with nothing on my mind except the movement of lines and shadows, seeing whatever is there. I can sit absorbed for half an hour in a yucca, or watching red ants harvest the new crop of seeds, feeling the constant wind wash over my body and through my soul. I can take my camera along, only to realize at the end of the day I have not shot a single picture. Nor does it seem to matter, for every time I go there and sit a while, I rise up refreshed in body and in spirit.

Johnny tells me this means I am an Indian, no matter who my parents are. We do not talk about this much now, but this is what the old man in Wood told me, too. He says a lot of Lakota don't know much about being an Indian, but I do, even though I don't know it. When he tells me this, I tell him I'll have to take his word for it. I can't see it. He laughs and says something in Lakota I don't understand, something about a squash.

I don't know about this. What I do know is that I am closer to Johnny than to any other man in this world, closer in some ways than I am to Jenny. At least I am until he comes back from the Gulf. Then it is like my brother has died and someone I do not know is wearing his skin.

When we get to Valentine, I stop for sodas at a drive-in and I head out for the rodeo grounds. Johnny has some things to do in town and we set up a time to meet for supper at the Bunkhouse. I drop in to see a friend who owns the paper there and we talk a while. I find out from him one of the fellows I want to interview broke his collar bone the night before and is in the hospital, so I drop by there. When I do, I hit the jackpot. All the guys I want to talk to are there in his room, laughing and cutting up, and they are glad to talk to me. I end up getting enough information for several articles, and they agree to talk to me when I phone later on to follow up.

I decide to put off going out to the rodeo grounds until later, so I run a couple of errands for Jenny. When I get to the Bunkhouse, I find Johnny in the bar drinking beer. I feel a little uneasy about this, but he seems fine and we order supper. The hamburger is reminding me of my catsup sins earlier in the day, so I order a roast beef dinner. I envy Johnny. He can eat anything that doesn't eat him first and he orders the chicken fried steak with lots of cream gravy and fries. Just looking at this is almost enough to give me heartburn on top of all the grease and onions and mustard. When I ask the waitress to bring me a seltzer, she gives me a strange look and he laughs. I fall in with the gag and tell her I heard they just changed cooks and want to be prepared.

Johnny seems to be in a good mood and we have a good time over supper. We're having coffee and pie when a rowdy group of five cowboys comes in. They are all in their early twenties and excited about the rodeo coming up. They sit down at a table across the room, but we have no trouble hearing what they're saying. Two of them are bull riders and are talking about the bulls they drew for the ride. The others are giving them a hard time and it's hard to hear ourselves think. Johnny looks at me and I nod toward the door. It's time to move on, anyway.

We head out to the rodeo grounds and look over the stock. Out of curiosity I walk over to the pens to look at the bulls the cowboys were talking about. I don't know them by name like the riders do, but they all look mean to me. The Brahmas are especially tough looking, with their dark brooding eyes and black on dark gray markings, and only one bull in the whole bunch looks like he doesn't belong. He is a big, beefy Hereford-Angus cross and the white and black markings on his face make him look like a clown. When I mention this to Johnny, he laughs and tells me I'm not a very good judge of bulls. He tells me he thinks that's the one the cowboys were talking about and he's the one worst of them all.

I tell him I may not be a good judge of bulls, but I'm damned good with bullshit, and the cowboys were slinging plenty of that. One of the cattle tenders overhears me and says Johnny is right. Old Harlequin has unseated more cowboys than any other bull in the lot and is still the toughest bull in the lot, even though he is getting pretty old. Yet, he's very gentle when nobody is trying to ride him.

I tell the cowboy I'll take his word for it and we end up talking a while. I take quite a few notes on what he says and a few good photo shots of him and Harlequin. I also get his address so I can send him a copy of the story when it goes to press and a release so I can use his picture. By the time we are done it's getting time for the grand entry and the cattle tender has to work the gates.

Rodeo is a slow moving sport, with long stretches of waiting followed by just a few seconds of action. A bull rider has to stay on only eight seconds and the longest event I can think of is barrel riding, or maybe wild cow milking. Most of the entertainment comes from the clowns. They fill in the time between riders with the things clowns do but their main job is to protect riders from pissed off bulls. Look at their outfits closely and you'll see many of them wear baseball shoes. This lets them swarm over the bull wire around most arenas like a monkey.

The thing about rodeo is that it allows a lot of time for visiting. It's like baseball this way. Other sports work the fans almost as hard as they work the players. Rodeo and baseball are very laid back and have a lot of time for other things like courtship and catching up with old friends. There's a lot of time for humor you don't find in football or tennis or any of the fast paced games. I think that's why people like it. The action is good and you can't beat western fashion if you like to dress up in a down home way, but it's the time it gives for the art of talkin' and spittin' I think people enjoy. That and looking at the horses. That's the other big thing. Rodeo is about horses.

Johnny and I find good seats in the stands straight across the arena from the judge's booth. The sun is down and the lights are on by the time things get rolling, so we have a lot of time to swap comments on horses and some of the more outrageous costumes the younger cowboys are wearing. Old time cow pokes wouldn't be caught dead in some of the things riders wear these days and we have a good time poking fun at this new crop of rodeo cowboys. What makes it even better is that no one else knows what we're saying because we're speaking in a personal cipher we've worked out over the years. It's a mix of Lakota and Spanish, with a few odd words we've picked up from around the world. It gets us some strange looks once in a while, but the white people think we're speaking Lakota and the Indians mind their own business. They listen, but they don't respond if it doesn't have anything to do with them. It's one of the things I like about Indians.

Sometime in the middle of the bull dogging, a couple of cowboys arrive and take a seat three rows behind us. The only reason I notice is that they are so loud. It is two of the guys from the bunch at the Bunkhouse and they've come to watch their buddies ride bulls. It's pretty obvious they have been drinking, too. It's one of those times I wish I had a video tape to show them once they got sober. I don't think they would act that way if they knew how silly they look. Or maybe they would. Some people just don't care.

Johnny gives me a look and I nod. We leave to find some other seats, but as we do, I glance back. Unfortunately, I make eye contact with one of the drunks. Maybe it's the way I'm looking at him, but he glares back at me and shoots me the bird. I ignore him and Johnny and I walk around to the other side of the arena. That's another good thing about rodeo. The action covers the whole arena, with gates located on each end in most places, so there's really not a bad section of seats.

Bull riding is usually one of the last events in most rodeos, and neither Johnny or I care that much for it. Since talking to the cattle tender, I'm curious about the bulls, and particularly about Harlequin, so we stay to watch. Sure enough, old Harley does things I never thought an animal his size could possibly do without falling down, and the rider lasts all of two seconds. Then, once he's shed his rider, Harley stops pitching and heads right to the gate, where the tender lets him in. His work for the day is done and he's ready to get back to his pen.

We decide to have a cup of coffee before heading home, but the only places open are the drive-in and the bars. The drive-in has a reputation of having the worst coffee in a four state area, so we head to one of the bars. I order coffee and Johnny has a beer, the first he's had since supper, and we talk about the cutting horses we watched.

We are only settled in our seats a couple of minutes before the rest of the rodeo crowd begins pouring in. Sure enough, the whole group from the Bunkhouse show up and the drunk from the stands spots us right away. He says something to his buddies and they look our way, but I can see they are really not interested in us. They are interested in ribbing the fellow who tried to ride Harlequin, and while they are loud, their teasing is good natured.

Even so, the rowdy who shot me the bird won't give it up. I see him trying to get his buddies interested, but they blow him off. I know he is going to stir up trouble so I tell Johnny maybe it's time we head on home. He is on his third beer now and I can tell he doesn't like it. He looks at the bunch of cowboys and I know what he is thinking. The two of us can take them all but he shrugs and drains his beer. I settle our tab at the bar and make a quick pit stop before I head out the door.

The pit stop is a mistake. When I cross the bar I see the bird man get up from his table and follow me out. A couple of his buddies come with him. Johnny is waiting for me on the street but before we can get into the truck, the rowdies come out of the bar and holler at us. I ignore them and start to get in the truck, but bird rowdy runs over and shoves the door shut. I am swinging my leg into the truck just then and the door slams to on my bad knee. Pain like white flame shoots up my leg and I almost faint.

Then the old reflexes kick in. I am as strong as I ever was and when I shove the door back at rowdy bird, I hear him scream as I smash the door back into him. He tries to stop it with his hands and the frame cracks a wrist. I know I can't put weight on my bad knee, so I use the truck door for a swing and when the heel of my good foot hits his jaw, the rowdy goes down for the count.

I glance around to see if Johnny needs help, but two cowboys are on the sidewalk, not moving fast, and a third one is almost jumping through his ass trying to get away. Two more come out of the bar just then and I hobble around to the front of the truck to face them. They see the guys on the ground and stop in a hurry. I can tell Johnny is about to go after them, anyway, but the fight is over and my knee is throbbing so bad I can hardly see. I tell Johnny to stop. I need to get to the emergency room.

Johnny helps me into the truck and drives me there. My knee is in no shape to push down the gas pedal, much less the brake, and I don't argue when they bring a wheel chair to carry me into the ER. We are still waiting for the doctor when the cops arrive.

I know most of the police and law officers around the area, but this is a new guy. I can see when he comes in he already has his mind made up about what happened. There is no doubt he comes here directly from the bar, so when he asks for some identification, I give him my press card and ask for the Valentine police chief by name.

This slows him down. He is expecting a couple of drunk Indians. He ignores what I ask and demands a statement. I tell him Jack Henson is a personal friend and I'll be happy to tell Jack all about it when he gets here. Otherwise, we'll wait to make any statements until we have an attorney present. I ask him if he understands these rights and I can tell Johnny is trying not to laugh.

I don't know what gets into me sometimes. Taunting cops is not wise and it's not something I normally do. I think if I were not hurting so bad, I would never make that last crack. I don't like people who hide behind badges and abuse their power, but what I have just done is no different. I flashed my press pass and claimed special treatment due to personal friendship with the Chief of Police.

On the other hand, we were the ones who were just assaulted, not the cowboys. I started to say we were the victims, but that's not quite right. We may have been the intended victims, but the rowdies got the worst end of it and maybe even a bit more than they deserved. I tend to over react a little when I am hurt and being shoved around, and maybe this is my part in all this. Yet, we tried to avoid trouble and there is no doubt in my mind the cop came here looking to bust us.

The cop's face turns beet red, but he doesn't react and I regret my words as soon as I see his face. I back off and ask him if we can't try it again and he has the grace to nod. This officer is going to be a very good cop some day.

I tell him our side of what happened beginning with the rowdy shooting me the bird in the rodeo stands. When I am done he asks Johnny his side of it and adds a couple of details I miss at the bar when I make my pit stop. The cop asks if there anyone who can vouch for our side of it and I mention a few people I know who were in the bar and in the stands. Lucky for us, one of them is the newspaper publisher here in town and another is the doctor we're waiting to see. When the doctor gets there a couple of minutes later, he sets things straight pretty quickly.

The doctor offers to check me into the hospital, but I tell him we really need to get home if I can. He tells me I am very lucky. The knee is badly bruised, but not broken, and it should be all right in a few weeks. Then he asks me what I did to the guy I took out and I tell him. He nods when I'm done and says he hopes I am never mad at him. I may have only touched the rowdy twice but his injuries look like he was hit by a truck. He will probably make it, but at the moment he is in critical condition.

When I stop to think about it later on, this bothers more than the knee ever will. I think of myself as a man of peace, but there is something inside me that is wild and will never be tamed. I'm not sure I would ever want to try to subdue it, but this side of me is a little scary. I never can tell what may happen when it gets on the loose, even though it never seems to come out except when I am pushed to the wall. I know it saved me from a bad beating by the rowdy and his friends, just as it saved me many times in the Marines.

Yet, it's been a long time now since I laid down my sword and shield took up pen and paper. I somehow thought this side of me was safely put away with the past. I guess this is foolish because I know it is still there in Johnny. I see it every time he comes home for a visit, but he is still a warrior. He is still a Marine and I expect it of them. I somehow don't expect to see it in myself, or in any married man with children and a mortgage who is headed into middle age. Yet I am a Marine, too and every once in a while there it is. It was only sleeping, and all it takes to wake it up is a rowdy drunk and a little pain. With a family to raise and maybe defend, I find this reassuring. What is scary is how close to everyday life this warrior lives.

Johnny is very quiet on the ride home. He is driving because my knee is in a brace and my head is in the clouds from Demerol. When I ask if he was hurt, he shows me the back of his hand and shakes his head. Not even his knuckles are bruised. Yet, even in my drugged state,

I can tell something is bothering him. When I ask what it is, he is quiet for a long time. When he speaks, it's been so long the sound of his voice startles me.

"This is what I hate about civilian life," he tells me. "What I like about the Corps is there is not as much of this bullshit." He glances over at me and I nod. I know what he means, but he tells me, anyway. "You know how it is. Corps life is not much different. You still have to put up with a lot of racism and other bullshit, but what matters is what you can do. Not yesterday or tomorrow, but right now. They don't care if you are black or white or purple or as green as a bonking bean so long as you accomplish the mission. That's the bottom line."

He shakes his head and I think he's done. Then I hear him talking quietly, almost as if he's talking to himself, and he is speaking Lakota now. "Here I'm just another crazy Indian, even to people in my family. Just another drunken Indian. I get into a fight and the law thinks it must be my fault and they want to shut me away. There I am a warrior. I am respected and honored for it." Then he turns and looks at me. "Do you hear what I am saying, my brother? You and Jenny are my only real family out here. When I am in the Corps, every man there will fight for my life, just as I will fight for theirs. They are my real family." Then he laughs. It is a bitter sound. "Doesn't that suck?" he says in English. "I am Lakota. I was raised on the reservation. Yet, the only place I belong in this stupid world is in the white man's Marine Corps!"

Going Home

11 November 15, 1995. Next week is Thanksgiving. I wish I had something to be thankful about. They tell me here that I need to work on my gratitude list, the things I am grateful for. They say what I need is an attitude of gratitude. They tell me that if I work on being grateful for what I have, I won't miss what I don't have.

I'm sure this means something to them, to the counselors here. They talk about being happy, joyous, and free, and I guess some of them are. They seem to speak from the heart and believe what they are saying.

I can relate to the stories they tell about their own lives, to the insanity of being drunk and strung out all the time. Some of them have done lots worse things that I have done, and for some of them it took more than one trip to treatment. One guy went seven times before he stayed sober more than six weeks and he says he has not had a drink now in eight years.

This is my third trip to recovery and I can't imagine living without drinking for six weeks after I get out. I can't imagine what it would be like having to go back through treatment four more times. Treatment only seems to make my drinking worse. The last time I went on a binge it was just before I came here. It almost killed me and the longest I have been without a drink in years is four days.

Except the time I was in treatment. I never drank then, though some of the people did. The first time I was in was two weeks but I stayed the whole thirty days the last time. This time they want me to stay a full three months and I don't see how I can do it. I am past the shakes, but the craving never goes away and I smoke like a chimney.

The guy who went out seven times is my counselor. He laughs at me and tells me I am full of bull. I tell him he is an apple Indian and he laughs some more. Then he tells me the Indian excuse won't work. All that will happen if I use that is I will end up drunk again and in even more pain. He tells me recovery is the easier, softer way, and if I follow his Twelve Steps I will get what he has. It is not magic, he tells me, but it will happen. Even to an Indian.

I don't know. What he says when I am with him makes sense. He has walked the road I have walked. He knows how I feel and what I am thinking, even when I do not. Yet, when I am not with him, I forget. I remember things I forget to ask when I am there and I can't remember what he told me that was so true. He tells me to write all this down and that is what I am doing. But after two weeks, I still feel like crap and I don't understand some of the things they tell us.

My counselor tells me not to worry about the things I don't understand. Accept them for now, he tells me. See if they work. I don't have to understand how a TV works to use it, do I? All I have to do is turn it on and tune it to the right station. That is what recovery is about. He says lots of stuff like this that makes sense when he says it, but I can't always remember what it.

One thing I remember is him telling me he doesn't understand all the concepts yet, but he has the rest of his life to work on it. He tells me some of the concepts don't make sense to Lakotas. We have to think about them our own way. Spiritual bankruptcy is one of these. We understand being broke. This happens a lot to most of us. We spend all our money and we are broke. We don't understand borrowing and paying interest, which is connected to white man's banks. We don't have banks. We never did. When someone is in need you give it to them if you have it. This is what families are for. Anyone who has relatives is never bankrupt the way white people are. To anyone who is not a relative, you owe nothing.

So we have to think of these things a different way, he says. Accept what you do understand and work with that. Lakotas understand being warriors. Work on gratitude. Work on understanding that. When we are busy being grateful, we don't have time to be hateful, to ourselves or others. Make war on resentment by being grateful.

So I guess I need to work on gratitude. All I can think of to be grateful for right now is if I were dead. Then I wouldn't have to worry about resentments or gratitude lists or fears or anything else. I would be asleep. At the worst I would feel nothing. At the best, I would be in the spirit world where they say there is no pain. I would be with my grandfather again, and with all the friends who have gone before me. The only ones I would miss are RD and Jenny, but they would be there before too long.

Maybe that's what I need to be grateful for. Maybe I need to give whoever is God thanks that there is a spirit world where there is no pain.

Maybe I need to be grateful I will be going there soon....

(from John K's last journal)

There is not a lot more to tell. I am not going to dishonor the memory of my friend with a chronicle of all he does in the last years of his life. He is insane then and I think it all stems back to the Gulf War. He is never quite the same after he comes home from the Marine Corps, and in my opinion, he is one of the casualties of Desert Storm, just as much as the few who died there.

Right after the Gulf War ends, he is all right. When he arrives in Winner on leave, he has been part of the ticker tape parade in New York and he is higher than a kite. He is sick, though, and I can tell he doesn't feel quite right. He tells me the military doctors do not know quite what is wrong with him. One of them thinks he may be showing symptoms of a non-lethal whiff of nerve gas, but others don't think so.

What Johnny tells me is that he is tired all the time. He has always kept in shape, but it is all he can do to run even a mile now. Tired as he is, he has trouble sleeping and his joints ache constantly. He is thirty pounds lighter than when he went to war and he is bothered by severe skin rashes and chronic indigestion.

We know now these are the symptoms of Gulf War Syndrome. We don't know if the cause is sarin or DEET or some of the biological weapons Sadam developed. We also know our guys breathed a lot of smoke from burning oil wells. What we do know is that about fifteen per cent of our troops who went to the Gulf reported strange symptoms which happened after they came back. At first the military denies these symptoms are related to combat or service in the Persian Gulf, but eventually the VA turns around and begins giving some treatment to veterans.

This does not help Johnny much. Within a year of his homecoming, he is back in Winner again. This time he is back for good. They give him a medical discharge and full base pay, but this is not helpful. What he needs is a place to be and something to do, and all his disability pay does is keep him in drinking money. It also acts like a magnet for all the wrong people. They use Johnny as a source of booze and he's generous with them. As long as he has money, he is good for a drink.

The first brush with the law happens three months after he gets back. I bail him out and he pays me back when the next check comes. He doesn't have to do this, but he does and I don't argue. Four months later I have to do it all over again. I don't say much about it, but he doesn't pay me back this time. After that Johnny doesn't call me when he needs bail. By the time I hear he's been arrested it's too late to intervene, even if I want to, and I'm not sure I do. I can be as pig headed as him, and I do. I wish now I had not, but this is what I do.

Yet, when I hear Johnny is in the hospital, I visit him. I know it won't do any good to get on his case, so I don't. We sort of patch things up after that and when he needs to go to recovery, he asks me to drive him there. The first time, I have to go get him after a week, and the second time is for a month. I try to be supportive in between, but there is a wall between us he will not let me through. Nor will he let Jenny, either, and this really grieves her. I try to stay in touch and she does, too, but Johnny doesn't call us back very often and he never comes to the house. This hurts us both a lot and after a while we stop trying so hard. I am sad to admit that, but we do.

Then he calls again and I find myself driving Johnny to the recovery center. This is the third time around for him and he says it won't work this time, either, but this time recovery is ordered by the court. The choice Johnny has is that he goes into recovery for ninety days or that he spends the same time in jail. I think the deciding factor is that he can smoke in recovery. A class action suit has made jails and prisons non-smoking places for guards and prisoners, too, and Johnny knows this. At the recovery center, he can go outside for a smoke in between sessions.

I know Johnny is not feeling well. He is more quiet than usual and falls asleep on the way to Rapid City. I take the back way to see the Badlands, through Wood and Corn Creek across to Wanblee. I am not in any hurry and Johnny has always loved the Badlands. He says things are very clear in the desert and the Badlands are a very spiritual place. I don't know about that, but I like them, too, and I can always take the Interstate home if I am in a hurry getting back.

I take the turn north on Highway 44. I am about to say something to wake Johnny when I realize he is looking at me. He has a strange expression on his face and I take a second look. I ask if there is something he needs but he doesn't answer. When I look at him again, there are tears in his eyes. I ask him what is the matter.

"Why are you doing this?" he asks me. I tell him it's because I'm his friend. That's what friends are for.

"Why do you even care?" he asks. "After all the crap I put you through?"

I tell him I don't consider it crap. He needs medical treatment and

I'm helping him get it. That's what friends do.

"You're taking me to jail," he says. "They may call it treatment, but it's not that much different from jail."

"I wouldn't know," I start to say, then realize how this sounds. I try to apologize, but Johnny laughs it off.

"No, man, you're right," he says. "You wouldn't know, but I would." He is quiet a long time. Then he says, "You think taking me there is being a friend." The way he says it, it's like he is talking to himself. "Well, if you think it's so good, why don't you go with me?"

I look directly at him. "If I thought that would do the trick, I would. If I thought a little ass kicking would help, I'd do that, too." I'm getting a little tired of his self-pity.

"You and whose army?" he says. When he does, for just a few moments, the old Johnny is back. I haven't seen this side of him in years.

"I wouldn't need an army," I say back. These days that's all too true. A five year old kid could kick Johnny's ass right now, but I don't tell him this. He knows this better than I do. "I always could kick your ass."

"Come on," he says, grinning. "Pull over. Let's see."

I laugh. "I stipulate it might take me a little trouble. I'm a little off my feed this morning. Not enough coffee yet."

Johnny laughs and tells me what to do with my stipulation. Then he turns serious again. "I mean it, man," he says. "Why do you put up with my bullshit?"

"Because you're my brother," I tell him. "I love you and Jenny does, too. That's why. Because we love you."

"After all the stuff I've done?" he asks. "Why do you love me? Why does she?"

"I don't know. We just do. I can't explain it but it's like what's happening to you is happening to me."

"Yeah," he said. "I know. Back in basic, when those guys jumped you, I knew you were cut before I ever saw it. I felt it across here." He traces a line with his finger across his chest. "I thought he killed you."

I don't know what to say, but he goes on. "Remember when those cowboys jumped us in Valentine? I felt it when he slammed the door on your knee. It felt like someone set my leg on fire."

"Jesus," I tell him. "I didn't know. That's how it was. It was awful." I look over at him. "You ever talk to anybody about this?"

Johnny shrugs. "No. What's there to talk about? That's just the way it's always been with you. Not all the time, but often enough." He looks at me. "Like right now. You have a tooth going bad. Third molar, upper left side."

I look at him so fast I almost drive off the road. The tooth only started bothering me the day before yesterday. Johnny laughs when I hit the shoulder.

I ask him if it's like that between him and other people, too. He shakes his head and says it's just that with me sometimes, and sometimes with Jenny, too. When I ask, he tells me it's like feeling your own pain, but different. It's more intense in a way.

I stop the truck and look at him a long time. "Is this why you drink the way you do, Johnny? To kill the pain?"

He nods his head. "Yeah, I guess so. I never set out to get drunk," he tells me. "I just end up that way. All I want is to feel a little better for a while, but I don't seem to know when to stop. Before I know it I'm drunk again." He looks at me. "Do you know what it's like having something like this you can't control?"

I think of the rage that sweeps over me sometimes. "Yeah, I do. Remember those offensive linemen? I was out of control and you saved my ass."

Johnny grins, remembering. "Just the way you saved my ass in boot camp," he says. "Did it ever occur to you it was my rage you were feeling?"

The truth of this hits me like a freight train. "Jesus!" is all I can say. I don't want to believe this.

"Think about it," he says. "Even when the cowboy slammed your knee with the door, you stopped. You could have stomped him to death, but you didn't. You could have killed the other guy, too, but you didn't. You broke his arm."

"No!" I tell him. "I was about to kill those two guys in the shower room. The rage was mine, not yours. You weren't in it."

"I wasn't?" Johnny says. "Why do you say that? I was coming down the hall. I saw the whole thing. I heard it all." Then he contorts his face and I hear the lineman's voice coming out of his mouth. "Why, hells bells! This looks like Jenny!"

I feel the rage sweep over me. Before I know it I am across the seat and have Johnny pinned against the door column. I have one hand around his throat and the other is bunched to drive his nose into his brain.

Then I see Johnny's eyes. There is no fear there, only a grief so deep it breaks my heart, and I let go, sit back in my own side of the seat. Suddenly, I find myself weeping in a way I have never cried before. "Jesus, Johnny!" I hear my voice saying. "Jesus!"

Then I feel the strong arms of my best friend holding me like a mother holds a frightened child. "It's all right, Randy. The devil is mine, now, not yours. I'll deal with it."

Like I said, there's not much left to tell. I never knew what my brother was facing until the year before his death. Nor did I know how to help him. After that, we never did talk again, although I tried. When he got out of treatment, I drove him home, but when I did, he was feeling good and we cut up the whole way. I thought he had it made and when he got drunk again, I was devastated. I was also angry, very angry with him for not letting me help fight this demon. Together we could have done it, the way we always have. Or we might have gone down together fighting, but that was just it. Johnny did not want me to go down with him at all. So he fought it alone. He avoided me and kept me away, and when it got too much for him, he took the honorable way. There is nothing cowardly in the choice he made, especially knowing why, and for whom, he made it. It was not for himself. It was for me and Jenny.

A writer from Sioux Falls picked up the story and tried to make a Pulitzer out of it. Johnny was one of the most decorated veterans to come out of the Gulf War, and I can't blame the reporter for trying. His slant even matches the facts on record. There was no question that Johnny took his own life and I am including the deputy's report for the record. The details are accurate:

```
Incident report (narrative): The undersigned
officer responded to a 911 emergency call at
12:04 AM on March 16, 1996. Radio log verifies
the call came in at 11:17 PM on March 15. Re-
sponse was delayed by distance & muddy roads.
The officer on crime scene first was the under-
signed & verifies no tracks were made by other
vehicles on the last half mile of road since
the last rain. Local weather records indicate
rain stopped at about 4:00 PM on March 15. At
the time of response, exact jurisdiction was
not clear. Todd County Sheriff department did
not respond because of lack of manpower & un-
certainty as to location of emergency.
```

The officer arrived at 12:04 AM (3/16/01) & dismounted to approach the house with caution. Lights were on but there was no response to three repeated loud knocks in which the Officer identified himself each time. At 12:06 AM Officer tried the door, which was locked, & went around the house to the back door. Officer knocked & identified himself twice, then tried the door, which was unlocked. Officer entered by back door directly into the kitchen. Subject was lying on the floor. Subject was identified as a male Indian approximately thirty-five years old. Officer checked for pulse at hand & throat, but could not find one. Officer called for ambulance & requested FBI notification since the subject appeared to be American Indian. Officer also indicated that jurisdiction might belong to Todd County but was instructed to do preliminary investigation & to remain on site.

The initial observation of the first Officer on the scene was as follows:

1. Subject was lying on the kitchen floor in front of the sink with his head in a pool of blood.

2. The left temple area of the subject's head appeared to have a gunshot wound. Powder burns on the temple area indicated possibility of self-inflicted wound. Officer noticed smell of burned gunpowder in kitchen.

3. What appeared to be a short nosed .38 pistol lay on floor about three feet left of subject. Strong smell of burnt gun powder noted in subsequent investigation indicates said pistol was fired recently.

4. An envelope addressed to one Randall Dale Lyle at the Thunder County Clarion was found on the kitchen table. Said envelope was sealed & was opened by the Sheriff in the presence of said Randall Dale Lyle when he arrived at the scene at approximately 1:45 AM.

5. Said envelope contained what appeared to be a suicide note written in the subject's

own hand. Handwriting was verified by lab ex-
amination as were latent fingerprints, which
belonged to subject only. Sheriff & Lyle wore
latex gloves & evidence was sealed in plastic
after reading.
6. Officer undersigned verifies content of suicide note & a photocopy is attached.
Subsequent FBI investigation confirmed initial
observations & indicates death by self inflicted gunshot. Undersigned Officer agrees.

The report was respectfully signed by Tom M. Smith, Deputy Sheriff,
Todd County, South Dakota.

I am not going to print Johnny's suicide note here. It is a matter of
public record for anyone to dig out if they wish. Even the reporter from
Sioux Falls had the decency to only print excerpts and avoid mention
of Jenny and me. The way it is written is ambiguous enough for the
reporter to read his own interpretation into it, and this is what he based
his story on. To sum it up quickly, he saw Johnny as a victim of racism
and the Gulf War. The Marines were where John K found a home, a
place he belonged and was respected for what he could do, not for who
his parents were. When he was given a medical discharge, this took
away everything he had and the only place he had to go was back to the
reservation. Because of depression from Gulf War Syndrome, he began
drinking and had several brushes with the law. This led into a downward
spiral which ended in suicide.

Of such material are Pulitzers made and the reporter's theory fits
the facts at his disposal. Yet, the reporter did not have all the relevant
information. What I have tried to set down here is the truth based on
what I know and have seen over a period of thirty years. I interpret
Johnny's suicide as an act of compassion and mercy toward others, not
as an act of desperation. There are those who might say I want to see it
this way because John K was my brother, but I know what he told me
that day on his last trip to rehab, and I believe him. I think the only way
Johnny knew to rid the world of his demon and mine was to take it to
the grave with him. Who am I to say it was not a good day for dying?
Or a good way to die.

Beyond The Stars

12 There is a lot of talk about existential hopelessness these days. This view of things has been around a long while, and the facts of the life of John K Lyle may give determined gloom mongers plenty of ammunition. Nor is there any doubt a case can be made for the hopelessness of the human condition. Yet, the facts do not reveal the whole truth, or even scratch the surface of the bottom line. They do not tell the full story and I am not sure the full truth can be told or understood this side of heaven.

The truth is that when I started this, I intended it to tell the story of John K in a very simple way. I did not imagine it would turn into a whole book, but over the months it has. There was simply too much to say for it to be any shorter and there is so much I have left out. To set it all down would take another year and at least another volume. Yet I think what I have written tells all I need to say to tell the truth of John K. Lyons, my friend and brother in spirit, if not blood. So I have given witness to the truth, the whole truth, and nothing but the truth.

Even so, as I look over all these pages I have written, I discover something else has happened. This story is not about John K alone. Nor is it just about the times and places where we grew to manhood, or the incidents which formed us. No, I think that in seeking the truth about Johnny and me I have stumbled on a deeper Truth, and even as I write these words, something strange and beautiful whispers in my ear. Nor am I sure just what I hear. Is it my imagination run riot or is it a whisper of love? Yet, how could I even think to imagine a celestial chuckle in the face of the tragedy I have told?

Yet it is there, and for the first time in many years I feel wrapped in a blanket of radiant light which warms the soul. I find strange tears of joy running down my cheeks, something else which has not happened in a long, long time, and I know I am standing on holy ground. I cannot remember when I felt this last, but I can when I felt it first. It was that day long ago at the funeral of Willie Lyons when I first received the sacred Bread of Heaven from the hands of Father Alex and drank the

Cup of Light Incarnate.

Like all great truths, the greater truth I have stumbled across, or been led into, is quite simple and very profound. There is a passage in the catechism in the very back of *The Book of Common Prayer* which tells us that "sacraments are outward and visible signs of inward and spiritual grace...." Father Alex reminded me of this not long before he died and I hope I never forget his words. "When we eat the bread and drink the wine, RD, they become part of us. They become part of our body. That's half of it. The other part is the real presence of God in the Sacrament. When we take it into ourselves it becomes part of us, too, and our spirits are somehow made one with God's spirit. To a true catholic, this means that whatever I do to you, I am doing to Christ Jesus, himself."

However, the catechism does not stop there. It goes on to tell us that sacraments are also "given by Christ as sure and certain means by which we receive that grace." It is here I begin to understand the greater truth that the story I have told about Johnny and me is about something much greater. The greater truth is that we are sacraments given by God to one another. We human beings are intended as the sure and certain means by which God's grace comes into the world, and others are the gift through which we are blessed. While I cannot say for sure how I was this for John K, I do know he was a living sacrament for me.

Will I see him again on the Other Side? I hope so, but I am not sure. Nor does it seem to matter that much. While everything I have seen in this life leads me to believe there is a much greater life after death, I have no way of knowing if this is more than my own hope for redemption of the grief we know on this side of the river Jordan. I would love to see my brother again, reborn in a body which will never die or grow old, and healed in his spirit so well that he will never weep again. I would like to roam the stars with him, to dance with him in the heavens to the Drumbeat of all creation, to lift our voices to sing with joy and delight as Warriors of a Light that darkness has never overcome.

Yes, I know this may only be my imagination. Yet, Father Alex once told me that imagination is the true language of God, and I suspect that if there really is a celestial realm, it will be something far beyond the limits of my own mind to conceive. The truth of the matter is that all this lies in the future, a future which may or may not be, and we need to leave it in the hands of a loving God. For our own sanity we need to let it go and commend the future to the loving care which gives us one another. Then we need to get on with the business of living our lives and learning to love ourselves and one another as much as we are loved.

The truth is that what is important to us is today, regardless of what is or is not to come. Knowing this, or believing it, I find it reassuring to find myself surrounded on all sides by grace upon grace. What is important to me today is that grace is always there when we need it most, incarnate in the flesh of those who bless our lives, and I find myself confronted with this miracle every day. This is what keeps me going when the way leads through the dark valley where the truth is hidden in shadows of doubt.

There is more I could say. There always is, but I keep coming back to two lines at the beginning of the Gospel of John which sum things up better than I ever will. While they were written about a cousin of the carpenter from Nazareth, they also tell me the truth of who John K was in my life and who I dare hope I may become in the lives of others. They are about who Jenny is to me, and about who my father and my mother were, and Father Alex, too. They are about every human being who has been there in my time of spiritual need, even those whose names I will never know. For it is by the gift of John K, and these countless others, that I have received, grace upon grace. As St. John says of himself,

There was a man sent from God, whose name was John… John himself was not the Light, but he came to bear witness to the Light, that all [whose lives he touched] might receive faith through him…

Now as I stand here at the grave of my friend John K, where I watched as our brothers filled in the deep hole where we buried him a year ago, I remember something I lost for a while in my grief. What I remember is that it was a rainy day, like the day we buried his brother Willie, and on both days the rain stopped as we lowered the casket into the grave. The rain stopped and the clouds began to break up, letting the last rays of the setting sun bathe the dirt mound covered with flowers. The wind was at our backs, from the east, gently caressing the high grass now turned gold with sunlight, and as we watched a marvelous golden light spread over the entire western sky. It was at that point the two children came forward to the grave, each holding bright colored balloons, and one by one they released them to the wind.

I remember how clear the air was, just as it is now, and I remember watching as the balloons grew smaller and smaller until they disappeared from sight high above us and coursing to the setting sun. I remember thinking that Johnny was free now, free to rise like an eagle, returning to the Beginning from where he came, and the memory brings joy. For as I stand here at the grave of my brother in Corn Creek and look to the badlands and peaks rising to the west, I can still hear the voice of Father Alex reading, not from his missal, but from *The Book of Common Prayer,* at the grave of Willie Lyons.

...all we are mortal, formed of the earth and unto the earth shall we return. For so you did ordain when you created me, saying "You are dust and to dust you shall return." All we go down to the dust; yet even at the grave we make our song, Alleluia! Alleluia! Alleluia!

Note from the Author

Someone once pointed out that nothing bad ever happens to a writer; it's all good material. As one might imagine from the dedication of this book, I once lived on the Rosebud Reservation. I served there as a parish priest, and the Sunday I began work, I baptized an infant I would bury six weeks later. Nor was that terribly unusual. For on the reservation, yesterday is tomorrow is today, and the dying never ends. *Lakota Spring* was written as an effort to come to terms with that experience and with the reality of reservation life.

Now I am surprised to see I am the author of twenty-five novels, six nonfiction books, and two collections of poetry. The titles in print are available directly from Amazon. My latest work is the twelfth book in the Jazz Phillips mystery series, *Jazz and the Last One Left*, a work in progress. Even so, *Lakota Spring* remains my favorite story, though *Ashes in the Outhouse* and *Murder in the Choir* are close seconds.

People often ask when I started writing. They are surprised to learn I was fifty-one when I completed my first novel, *Angels Fight Dirty*, even though I had been writing all my life. I was living in Hope Arkansas at the time and southwestern Arkansas later served as a wonderful setting for my first two Jazz Phillips novels.

Later on the experience of growing up in the Big Bend area of far western Texas served as the basis for my Texas Romance duo. These days I make my home with my wife and two furry 'kids' in the western reaches of Minnesota but I doubt I will ever write a novel about that. Garrison Keillor, whose work I admire, has pretty much covered the waterfront there. That's plenty good enough.

The following excerpt is from the first of Joel B Reed's
Texas Romances

Ashes in the Outhouse

Now available from Amazon!

Miss Milly

June, 1957. I saw the tall, thin woman smile the way she always did when she passed the old men sitting in the shade of the large live-oak trees in the courthouse square. They were always there, four or five of them, sometimes more, sitting around the square, not saying much. Most of them had a scrap of lumber they were reducing into thin shavings and they weren't in any hurry. Their cutting was sure and smooth from years of whittling and what they admired was the longest, thinnest piece they could shave. Later in the day they would head for the hardware store to sharpen the thin, worn blades of their pocket knives. Once in a while one of them would buy a square plug of hard black chewing tobacco and pass it around. Then they would return to the square to make more tightly curled shavings to stain with tobacco juice. Local folk called them the Spit and Whittle Club.

As the tall woman walked by, every one of the men would smile and tip his hat. "Good morning, Miss Milly," each of them would say and she would greet them all by name. They called her that because it was the polite thing to do in the South back then, even if she was married. Then, when she had passed out of earshot, the oldest man among them would say, "It just don't make no sense how the good Lord matched her up with Oliver Bates."

The others would all nod in agreement. And if the former mayor wasn't among them, the next to oldest would say "I guess He give her Oliver for her cross to bear." The other shavers would nod again and go back to their solemn ritual of making tobacco stained shavings.

That morning I was looking through the bars of my office window when Miss Milly came up the walk to the courthouse and I knew she was coming to see me. The courthouse was a big red building four stories high and the windows and portals were trimmed in light colored limestone. They left room for an elevator when they built the place. Years later they put one in, but when

I was first elected you had to walk up some broad, wide steps that led to the main floor. Then you had to go up a wide flight of marble steps to get to the court chambers, and on up another set behind a steel door to get to the jail on the top floor.

Yet, Miss Milly rarely had to climb to the forth story when Ollie was a guest of the county. Nor did she have to mount the outside steps to the main floor. Behind these steps was a cove with four steps down to the lowest floor. That's where my office took up a suite of four rooms behind a frosted glass partition. Next to that there was a large room used for public meetings and prisoner visits on Sunday afternoons.

"Good morning, Miss Milly," the clerk greeted her from behind the high counter that divided the foyer from the main office. I was standing next to the clerk and did the same.

"Good morning, Cheryl," Miss Milly said. "And to you, too, Sheriff. I haven't had a chance to congratulate you on your promotion." There seemed to be quite a bit of warmth in her response to me and I saw the clerk trying not to smile. It was none of her business, but I knew I better be careful or there would be talk.

"Thank you, Miss Milly," I told her. "I really do appreciate your support." Even so, I didn't extend a hand. My clerk was the county telegraph and there was no sense giving the gossip mongers more ammunition. I knew why Miss Milly was there but I asked, anyway. "Is there something we can do for you?"

Miss Milly nodded. I hated the way her smile faded just then. "I'm here for Oliver. I need to pay his fine."

I nodded. "May I have a word with you?" I asked, opening the swinging door at the end of the counter and holding it open for her. She passed close by and I liked the way she smelled. She didn't wear any cologne or perfume, but she smelled clean, like soap and water with a hint of wood smoke and something else.

I led her into one of the inner rooms and closed the door. "Please," I asked, pulling out a chair at the long table in the center of the room.

Once she was set, I took a chair at the nearest end of the table. "I hate to have to tell you this, Miss Milly, I said. "I'm afraid it's going to be more than a fine this time. Oliver's going to have serve time. The judge is going to see him this afternoon after we get him cleaned up, but he's really put out with Oliver after the stunt he pulled last night."

"What did Oliver do?" she asked. I hated the dread I saw in her cool gray eyes. They were the color of a mourning dove with small flecks of gold.

"There was a fight at Randall's and he broke up the place pretty good. He put Morris Acker in the hospital and then he took off and drove over the judge's yard. I'm afraid he tore up the rose bed. I'm sorry to have to tell you all this. The only thing in his favor is that witnesses say Morris started the fight. They were both pretty drunk."

"I'll be happy to pay the damages," Miss Milly answered. "It may take me a while, but I'm good for it."

I couldn't help but smile. "I know you are, Miss Milly. You're better than the bank, but it's not up to me. The judge is madder than a wet hen about his roses. Oliver's been up on charges too many times before this and I think the judge wants to teach him a lesson. I think he's looking at thirty days and maybe ninety."

Milly Bates nodded. "I understand," she said. "When can I see Oliver?" Her eyes didn't show much but I knew she'd sooner grab a rattlesnake. I think any love she may have had for Oliver was long dead by then.

"Not until tomorrow," I said. "Oliver's still passed out and he's pretty filthy, too. We're going to have to hose him down before he sees the judge."

Miss Milly reached in the sack she was carrying. She took out some well worn coveralls and a clean shirt, then clean socks and underwear. "He'll need this," she said. "I'll catch a ride in tomorrow afternoon."

"How are you going to get home?"

Milly Bates smiled. "It's not that far, Sheriff. It's a nice day to walk. It doesn't look like rain."

When she smiled, I saw a bruise on her jaw and I had to push the anger down. "Did Oliver do that to you?" I asked, pointing at the bruise.

"Oh, you know," she answered. "Clumsy me. I must have bumped into something. I'm always doing that. It's nothing."

"If he's mistreating you, Miss Milly...." It's good Oliver Bates wasn't in my gun sights just then. I don't abide raising a hand against a women. I know some folks think it's a husband's right, but they're dead wrong.

"No, Sheriff, please. It's all right. It's nothing. It will be gone tomorrow."

Right, I thought. I might not have noticed the bruise but I was looking for it. Someone had come to me to talk about it a couple of weeks before. She was a friend of Miss Milly who worked as a nurse at the hospital. She pointed out to me how Milly Bates never seemed to have any "accidents" when Ollie was incarcerated.

"All you have to do is file a complaint, Miss Milly." I told her. "We'll take care of the rest of it."

"No, Sheriff. That would just make things worse. It's all right. Oliver doesn't mean anything by it. It's the drink, you know. When he's not drinking he's a different man."

"We can keep him from hurting you, but not if you won't let us." There was no response but a shake of her head. I looked at her for a bit, then let it go. "All right. But I am going to give you a ride home."

Milly Bates tried to object, but I held up a hand and felt myself smile. "You're not the only one who can be stubborn, Miss Milly. I'm going to give you a ride home and I'm going to come and pick you up tomorrow. That's all there is to it. You need to pick up anything while you're in town?"

"You don't want to cause talk, Sheriff," she tried to argue but I could see her heart wasn't in it.

"There's always going to be talk," I said, grinning like a fool. When I did, Miss Milly blushed. "It's all right," I told her. "I need to see a couple of your neighbors, anyway."

Miss Milly looked at me intently. Her face was grave and it felt like those beautiful gray eyes could see right through me. Then she smiled and reached out her hand and put it on mine. I never felt anything that wonderful and I felt a little sad when she squeezed my hand and let go. "You're a good man, John Stone. Don't ever think that I don't appreciate what you do for me." I think she started to say more but changed her mind. "I accept the ride. Let me pick up a few things at the store and meet you back here in an hour."

"I could pick you up there."

That was the first time I ever heard her laugh, and I was surprised how soft and intimate it was. It sounded like sweet music and wasn't any louder than a gentle sneeze. "You really think that's wise?" she asked quietly, looking toward the door to the outer office. "Cheryl goes to fix lunch for Fred, doesn't she?" I nodded. "I'll be back here at ten minutes past twelve," she said.

I walked Miss Milly out and went into my office. I sat there a minute or two, then used the phone to call the jail. The jailer told me Oliver was still passed out and I called the judge. He agreed it would be better to see Oliver the next day and I called Cheryl into my office. I told her what was going on with Ollie. "I think I'll run out to Neville's this afternoon," I said. "I need to talk to him about some missing cattle. If anyone asks, just tell them I'm out on a call. I don't want Neville to know I'm coming."

"You want me to call Buzz to go with you?" she asked. Buzz Wilson was my part-time deputy. He earned most of his living as a parts manager at the local Ford house and probably got paid better than I did. I was lucky to have him. He had served as a military policeman and needed the extra income. He and his wife were saving to build a house and his father-in-law didn't pay that well.

"No, Charlie told me Buzz has missed too much work lately. I'll be all right. If I need help, I'll deputize Neville." I smiled when I said this but Cheryl didn't understand I was joking.

"Neville? That's like hiring the fox to guard the henhouse." Cheryl snorted. Neville Yates was the biggest crook in the county. Most of his income came from bootlegging, and I knew for a fact he was a receiver for stolen goods. He tried to sell me a hot pistol once before I became a deputy. Even his kinfolk didn't trust him.

No, I thought. It would be like using a thief to catch a thief. While it couldn't hurt for Neville to think I'm a fool, I had no intention of deputizing him. "You're absolutely right, Cheryl," I told her, keeping my voice and face serious. "I was only teasing but I want to talk to him today. I don't think it will come to needing a deputy." It crossed my mind yet again that my clerk didn't have much sense of humor. On the other hand, I knew it wasn't her fault. She was raised that way.

I told Cheryl I needed to finish up some paperwork and not to disturb me unless it was urgent and went into my office and closed the door. Yet, when I sat down at my desk and got out the file I needed, I didn't get started right away. I sat there for a while thinking about when I first met Milly Bates and what I knew about her.

Oddly enough, we met in church. Back then you needed to be

something in Texas if you wanted to be accepted in the community and Dan Jenkins, the sheriff who hired me, told me it would be good to find a church. "I don't give a damn which one you choose, Johnny," he told me. "Folks won't trust you until they can hang a label on you, so pick one and join up. It's a damned good source of information about what's going on in the county."

"Which one do you belong to?" I asked. I've always been a free thinker and it really didn't matter to me what the preacher said or what anyone else believed.

"I go to the First Baptist," Dan told me. "It's the biggest church around and a lot of the upper crust go there. They don't believe in drinking, but a lot of them do it, anyway. But God help you if you're caught dancing!"

The sheriff laughed. "You know why Baptists don't make babies standing up?" I shook my head and he said, "Someone might see them and think they're dancing!"

I laughed. It was an old one I hadn't heard in a while. "Then that's where I'll go," I told him. "What do I have to do to join?"

"It might be better if you went to a different church, John. It would give us a wider base of support."

"All right, then, which one is the second biggest?"

The sheriff grinned at that. "You're going to do all right around here, Johnny. The First Methodist is almost as big and the rest of the upper crust go there. One word of advice."

"What's that, sir?"

"When you go fishing, never take just one Baptist with you. Always take two."

I had heard this before but I asked, anyway, "Why's that?"

"One will drink all the beer."

The next Sunday I wound up at the Methodist Church. It was the church where I grew up and I liked it. The people were friendly and the preacher was a young man not long out of seminary. His sermon was well thought out and he didn't read it. He delivered it without notes but with conviction, like he was speaking from the heart about his own spiritual journey. He was also concise and to the point and he only talked for about twelve minutes. As my daddy used to say, the mind can only absorb what the butt can endure.

I also enjoyed the music. They were having a special event that day and the church had a very good choir. One of the ladies caught my attention and it didn't take me long to learn her name. Nor did I have to ask. After the service I heard a couple of ladies talking about a woman in the nursing home that needed something, and one of them said, "Let's ask Miss Milly. She'd know."

Sure enough, she pointed to the lovely tall lady I'd noticed in the choir. For a while I thought she was single or a widow. She didn't wear a wedding band and I was thinking about asking her out. Then I overheard someone talking about something her husband had done. When I asked the sheriff about him, he told me Oliver Bates was the worst drunk in the county.

"Some of the things he's done, I don't know why someone hasn't shot him. Yet," he added. "I think it's mostly because he ain't worth the price of a bullet."

One of the things I noticed early in life is how human beings always seem to want what they can't have. It took me by surprise just how much this applied to me when it came to Milly Bates. When I went back to church the following Sunday and watched the choir sing, I was struck by how beautiful she looked. She was tall and slender, almost my height, with her dark hair pulled back in a French braid, and when she sang a solo, it was like she was pouring out her soul. Her face was radiant, almost like a bride, and I don't think she was singing for the congregation. She was singing like a mockingbird sings, because she had all this wonderful music inside her she needed to let out.

Still, when she sang, I felt a well of sadness building up inside me, even though she sang with obvious joy. It was a terrible sadness that reminded me how empty my life was without someone like her to grace it. I thought what a waste it was for a woman this wonderful to be coupled with a man like Oliver Bates.

I was listening and thinking so deep I wasn't aware of the tears that ran down my cheek. Then the elderly lady next to me handed me a tissue when Miss Milly was done. "It's beautiful, ain't it, Deputy? She sings like an angel. It's such a shame."

I couldn't have agreed more. I left the church feeling both uplifted and terribly sad. Oddly enough, Miss Milly saw me walking out. Years later she told me I looked like I'd lost my very best friend. I told her it was for a best friend I never had. It was a stupid thing to say, but she seemed to understand.

※

I must have sat there fifteen minutes before I shook myself

away from my sad thoughts and plunged into my paperwork. I finished it off and was waiting for Miss Milly when she showed up promptly at nine minutes past twelve. She was carrying a small paper sack. "I'm ready," she told me. "Are you sure about this? We will probably be seen. I don't want to start any talk."

"I guess I could cuff you," I answered. "That would really give them something to talk about."

Miss Milly laughed nervously, as if she thought I was serious. Seeing me unlock the gun rack and take down a shotgun, she asked, "Are you expecting trouble, Sheriff?"

"No, I'm just being a good Scout," I told her. Seeing her confusion, I added, "That's the Boy Scout motto," I explained. "'Be Prepared.'"

"Of course," she answered, laughing. "How silly of me. And giving me a ride home is your good deed for the day."

"No," I said lightly. "It's an honor." Seeing her flush, I wanted to bite my tongue. What was the matter with me? "I beg your pardon," I told her. "That didn't come out right."

Once again, her wonderful grey eyes searched mine. "You must never apologize for being a gentleman, John Stone," she assured me. "Thank you for the compliment. I'm just not used to it. Are we ready to go?"

Neither of us said a word until we were out of town. Once we were over the bridge, Miss Milly turned toward me. "Tell me about yourself, Sheriff. I know you grew up here but you haven't lived here all your life. What did you do before you were a deputy?"

"After graduation, I spent the summer following the grain harvest and spent the next four years at the University. I had to work my way through, so I didn't have much time for anything else. Then I joined the Coast Guard and found out I liked law enforcement more than I did boats. I was lucky they let me serve most of my time on shore. Sea duty always made me sick as a dog. That's about it."

Miss Milly looked at me. "It's a long way from the Coast Guard to Rutherford County, John," she pointed out. "How did you get from there to here?"

I shrugged, wondering what prompted her to use my given name. Yet, I liked it. "Well, I made high grades in college, Miss Milly. I studied anthropology with a minor in Spanish, and that, along with my record in the Coast Guard, got me in the West

Virginia State Police Academy. They had a reputation for being the best in the country."

I slowed for a stray cow in the road. "Then I worked with them – West Virginia – for a few years until I got tired of the East Coast. It was way too crowded and things were a little too organized. Then I heard about a deputy's job opening up here and I applied. Dan Jenkins almost didn't hire me. He told me I was too qualified. Said I wouldn't last a year. Someone else would hire me away. I told him that wouldn't happen. I also pointed out I grew up here and knew all the players, and hiring someone as well trained as me at the pay they offered would score him points with the county commissioners. I think you probably know the rest. How about you?"

"Oh, I'm not that interesting," she answered.

"You are to me," I told her. The way she looked at me told me I just stepped in a fresh cow pie. "I apologize, Miss Milly," I told her. "I didn't mean that in any improper way."

She laughed then, the first time I'd ever seen her laugh like that. "You just surprised me, John. Why don't you call me Milly, at least when we're not around other people?" She thought for a minute. "Well, I didn't grow up here. I grew up in Callahan County and you must have been gone by the time we moved here. My mother owned a house in town and my daddy worked road construction. He was a heavy machine operator and sometimes in the summer we'd go to where he was working and stay a while. He did a lot of road work in Colorado and Wyoming, and I just loved it up there."

She smiled when she told me this, but it faded as she went on. "Then my mama died when I was sixteen, and my daddy kind of fell to pieces. I was the oldest so I had to take care of the younger ones. Poor daddy started drinking heavily and we went through some hard times. I stayed on until the youngest was out of school. After that, I got married and ended up here in Rutherford County." As she spoke, she became more and more sad, and when she was done, she sat quietly. Her eyes turned inward on her grief.

I wanted to ask how she got tangled up with Oliver Bates but held my peace. The last thing I wanted to do was bring up painful memory. Then she looked at me and it was like she was read my mind. "I know you want to ask how I met Oliver, John. I don't mind your knowing but that needs to wait for another time."

"Of course, Miss...," I started to say but caught myself. "Of course, Milly. I didn't mean to pry."

"You didn't, John," she smiled. "I started it and turn about is fair play." I really liked the way she said my name. It was very intimate but not improper.

We talked about other things, but I can't remember what. What I do remember is enjoying the conversation. When we arrived at their place, I walked around the car and opened the door for her. "You're such a gentleman, John," she said, offering her hand. I reached out and she took my hand in both of hers, pulling herself out of the car. "Thank you 'til you're better paid," she said, smiling. She seemed reluctant to let go of my hand and I wasn't in any hurry for her to do so. "I enjoyed the company."

"You're more than welcome," I answered. "It was my pleasure. I'll be here to get you about noon tomorrow."

"I'll be waiting," she said, smiling. "I'll have us a nice lunch ready." She reached up and touched my cheek. Her touch was wonderfully soft and it was all I could do not to take her in my arms.

I know she saw this in my eyes, the desire, the struggle, the sad resolve. "You're an honorable man, John Stone. Thank you for your restraint."

"That's by choice, Milly," I answered. "Not by inclination. I beg your pardon if I'm speaking too plainly."

She was still holding my hand and ignored my apology. "Well, how can there be virtue without temptation? Don't put me on a pedestal, John. I'm a sinner just like everyone else. It's good that one of us is strong, isn't it?"

She released my hand, reluctantly, I thought. I tipped my hat and she smiled. Then I got out of there before I did something rash. She was still standing there looking after me when the road curved and I lost sight of her in the dust.

www.ingramcontent.com/pod-product-compliance
Lightning Source LLC
Chambersburg PA
CBHW060745180626

46818CB00002B/447